WITHDRAWN

FIC
ENGSTROM   Engstrom, Elizabeth.

The northwoods
chronicles

THE NORTHWOODS CHRONICLES

THE NORTHWOODS CHRONICLES

A NOVEL IN STORIES

ELIZABETH ENGSTROM

FIVE STAR

A part of Gale, Cengage Learning

GALE
CENGAGE Learning™

Detroit • New York • San Francisco • New Haven, Conn • Waterville, Maine • London

GALE
CENGAGE Learning

Set in 11 pt. Plantin.
Printed on permanent paper.

LIBRARY OF CONGRESS CATALOGING-IN-PUBLICATION DATA

Engstrom, Elizabeth.
   The northwoods chronicles : a novel in stories / Elizabeth Engstrom. — 1st ed.
      p. cm.
   ISBN-13: 978-1-59414-705-0 (alk. paper)
   ISBN-10: 1-59414-705-1 (alk. paper)
   1. Missing children—Fiction. 2. Middle West—Fiction. 3. Supernatural—Fiction. I. Title.
PS3555.N48N67 2008
813'.54—dc22   2008016373

First Edition. First Printing: August 2008.
Published in 2008 in conjunction with Tekno Books and Ed Gorman.

Printed in the United States of America
1 2 3 4 5 6 7 12 11 10 09 08

CONTENTS

Contents

INTRODUCTION:
VARGAS COUNTY

Children disappear in Vargas County. There's no soft or kind way to put it. In days long past, I lost a sister and then my Weesie and I lost our son. Some live in peace with the specter, some rise up and make accusations, but all of us breathe a sigh of relief when our young'uns reach puberty and we don't have to worry about them no more.

Newcomers to this area of the northwoods have someone arrested every decade or so, usually a husband making the police report at the behest of his hysterical woman. Recon John was the last to have been so poorly treated, but of course there was no evidence. John just leads what they call an alternative lifestyle is all. He didn't steal no kids. And us older citizens, we know it ain't no transient doing the deed.

No, the disappearing has been going on regular since long before I was born, and I'll be seventy-three this year about the time the ciscos spawn.

It's a curious thing, this. Children just vanish. One moment they're there, the next they're not. Curious, too, that people continue to live and raise their young'uns in Vargas County with this cloud hanging over them.

It happens regular, and too often for comfort, but not often enough to bring the UFO guys up here to investigate. Some people, like that egghead weirdo Kevin Leppens, says there's a pattern to it all according to some high-falutin' space theory. Says it has to do with the stars, or the stock market or the price

7

of rice or some idiot thing. He told me one time that the universe is orderly, and that there is a pattern to all things, but I never bought that. This always seemed to be too *human* a thing to be predicted mathematically.

And, of course, nobody ever believes it could happen to them. Just like polio in the fifties. Some people didn't believe in it, but that didn't keep it from striking down lots of youngsters.

And just like people in the fifties, the people in Vargas County tend to have lots of children. A survival compensation, I say, like rabbits, whose best self-defense mechanism is in their numbers.

I was a baby when my sister was took, and away at war when my little son disappeared, so I didn't grieve too much over their losses. But I was at the Benson place last Friday night and watched it happen with my own eyes.

Like me, both Margie and Jimbo Benson grew up in Vargas County and they had a touch of the holier-than-thou. Some people in these parts take themselves a little too serious when tragedy skirts their doorway. Their Jesus-speak gets loud when a young'un goes missing, something that doesn't comfort the grieving parents none at all. Some of those folks way out in the weedier sections of the county even cut a goat now and then, I'm told, to appease some angry gods.

Mostly I believe that if you live the good life in Vargas County, you take the bad with the good. It isn't that I have a hard heart, it's just that life is hard sometimes, and if that particular hardship doesn't agree with you, then you ought to be spending your days elsewhere. I think living with the prospect of losing a sibling or a kid or a grandkid grinds the sharpness off our emotions. Folks who live elsewhere are likely to have that cutting-edge type of fear and love, but those of us in Vargas County, well, we have other things, I guess. And those elsewhere folks, they have their own crosses to bear. Guess we opt for Vargas

County, and I don't know as we make that choice very consciously.

Anyway, I'm kind of the local grandpa to everybody, though they all call me Uncle, and they all been taking care of me since my Weesie died four years ago. Last Friday night, I was looking for something to look forward to, and told Margie and Jimbo I'd sit their babies while they went out for a romantic dinner on their anniversary.

Jimbo writes for the weekly and Margie runs the diner in White Pines Junction. They're hard workers and nice straight-up people. I was in Margie's place when I overheard her say to Jennifer that it was their fifteenth anniversary on Friday, and when she came around to fill my coffee cup, I volunteered my services.

"Oh Uncle Bun," she said. "Think you can handle those rascals?"

"Think they can handle me?" I asked, and gave the pretty girl a wink.

Margie went right to the phone to call Jimbo, and came back to give me the particulars. They decided to drive all the way into the city for a fancy dinner and some dancing. I said that would be fine, I'd bring my pillow and put myself on the couch—just be sure there was plenty of breakfast in the cabinet. Margie smiled and went right back to the kitchen and her Triple-A book to make hotel reservations.

The following Friday morning dawned with something unfamiliar in the air. Overcast skies held the summer temperature down with an occasional gray drizzle. Birds didn't come to my feeders and I even stayed in bed an extra hour. The whole town seemed subdued. People went about their business, but in a hushed, quiet way. I didn't hear anybody laugh all day long.

The second time I cut myself, I put my whittling knife away and declared that the whole county was having a bad hair day and we all needed to just ride it out. Things would be back to normal in the morning.

If I'd only known.

The only other thing I had on my calendar that day was to tell the sheriff that I'd serve as Santa again at the Christmas street festival. I drew that RSVP out as long as I was welcome down at the police station. Then I stopped by Doc's to talk with him about the fall fishing situation, but he was not feeling much like talking, either. I popped in to smile at pretty Kimberly in her dress shop, but she was deep into doing her bookwork, so having nothing else to do, I went home to my little trailer behind the marina, sat on my front porch and rocked, while things got darker in White Pines Junction.

At six o'clock, I got my hat and a slicker and walked the two blocks to Margie and Jimbo's place. Margie looked as pretty as a bride in a little pink dress and I hardly recognized Jimbo out of his fishing waders. They had overnight bags already in the car, and, giggling like newlyweds, they kissed the boys, thanked me and were off for a romantic interlude.

I heard the car pull out and a minute later, it pulled in again, and Margie came in for another round of hugs and kisses. She shrugged at me as if she didn't understand herownself and, in retrospect, that memory gives me the chills.

Jason was on the computer. Jason was always on the computer. A state science project champ with an oversized brain, Jason kept himself busy and out of trouble.

Micah was the lively one. At five, he knew he was trouble and, from what I could tell, he admired that in himself. Micah was the one who'd bring home strays, get lost in the woods, would likely blow hisself up someday.

But Friday night, Micah cried when his parents left, but they wouldn't change their minds about going. They gave him a little scripture to comfort him, but he sat on the couch wide-eyed and looked scared.

I checked on Jason, to make sure he wasn't looking at any of those dirty pictures on the Internet, but Jason was a good boy, eleven at the time, doing a research paper on muscle fiber. I popped popcorn, and he came down for some, but what Micah and I had on the television didn't interest him, so soon he was back upstairs again.

Micah couldn't be settled down. I tried everything: books, television, pulling a quarter out of his ear, but he wasn't having any of it. About seven o'clock, he went upstairs, got his quilt and his teddy, came back down and climbed into my lap.

I put in a Disney video, and I held him and his little boy heartbeat in my lap all evening.

At ten, I went up to tell Jason it was bedtime, but Micah clung to me all the way up the stairs and back down. We went outside for a breath, but the night was still and silent and made the boy whimper. So we came back in, I made a bed on the couch, and Micah cuddled down with me for the night.

Weesie and me raised three daughters, and I don't ever remember a time when I cuddled them to sleep. In those days, the wife did those things. And then there was always the prospect of losing them that made me shy of it. Maybe getting older has changed me, but lying there with that sweet little boy breathing hot child-breath and trusting me the way he did moved my heart around.

I didn't sleep. I was wide awake with the wonder of it all, wishing I could turn the clock back to hold my little girls, to hold my Weesie, or even to have Weesie see me holding this little Micah the way I would have held my little Henry, had I ever got the chance.

Which means I was wide-awake when Micah got taken from me. Right out of my arms.

There have always been lots of theories about the disappearings, and I suppose I've subscribed to them all at one time or another, but the reality of it shot all those theories to hell.

One minute he was there, the next instant he was not, and his quilt, still warm with the scent of him, settled to the couch with a vacant place inside it. Micah had been snatched.

I rose up with a roar, which seems odd, as I knew immediately what had happened and it stole my heart right out of my chest. I came off that couch and threw open the door and what I saw stunned me more than the snatching.

More than saw. Felt. Smelled.

The air was an unusual color—sort of a thin blue in the cool foggy starless night, and there was a dimension to it that I'd never seen before. It felt hollow. And there was the faint stench of an electrical crackle.

I heard music, like nursery rhymes, and I heard laughing. Children's laughing. But it was a hollow laugh, vacant like the air.

"Micah," I called, and they taunted me, "Micah," they said in a sing-song voice, "Miii-kaaah."

And then I thought of my own son and Weesie's grief and I whispered, "Henry?" and I heard, or thought I heard, or imagined I heard, or hoped I heard, "Papa?" And the air thickened up and the rain began and the strangeness of it all disappeared.

The police located Margie and Jimbo, who have never stopped blaming themselves. I was taken in for questioning, of course, though I was never a suspect.

And while I was at the station, Kevin Leppens waltzed in with his laptop under his arm, put it down in front of Sheriff Withens and said, "Watch this."

Kevin had charted every disappearance ever recorded in Vargas County, and right in front of the sheriff's eyes, he hit "enter."

The computer ground its gears for a moment, then spit out a date.

That Friday just passed.

"See?" Kevin said. "Rhythm. They can be predicted."

"When's the next one?" Sheriff Withens said, his eyes narrowing as if fey little Kevin had just become a suspect.

"I won't do that," Kevin said. "It would ruin this place. I just wanted you to know, Sheriff, that it isn't some *body*, it's some *thing*. It's natural, like spring. Like the tides."

The sheriff looked at me, the only witness to this exchange, and said, "You keep this under your hat, Bun."

I knew what he was talkin' about, because my first reaction was to throttle that kid, and choke the information out of him. Others might not have my kind of restraint.

Margie and Jimbo have stayed in their house. Their hearts've solidified a bit, but they still keep banging away at that church as if they mean it. They think if they'd went to church twenty-four hours a day before Micah got took, whoever took him would've opted for some other kid. They could still lose Jason as he's not yet twelve, but they stay because of hope. They hope to get Micah back, though none of the kids have ever come back. Wouldn't you think they'd take that boy and be off outta here at next light?

But they haven't. And everyone else stays, too. Life is good in Vargas County. We have a strong tourist-based economy, harsh winters and magical summers. Nobody wants for much of anything, except those of us, maybe, who've had kin snatched. But Vargas County offers other things to speculate on besides fishing, where the kids have gone, and the hope that they'll come back.

I'm going to give Kevin Leppens and that computer of his some time to cool off, and then I think I'll go try to persuade some information from him. Gentle persuasion. I don't want to cause a riot, I don't even want the county to know his secret. We've lived with this situation for hundreds of years, and there ain't no reason to change it now just because Kevin Leppens got himself Intel inside.

But maybe I could find out enough just so's I could be in the right place at the right time and get to hold my little Henry in my arms and feel his soft cheek. Just once. Just for a moment. For Weesie, because I believe that wherever she is, she'll know.

Life is good in Vargas County, and everybody has his or her reason for staying or leaving. I've stayed because I'm old and have nowhere else to go, or so I tell myself. But I think it's because there's no other place anywhere like here, and we feel privileged to be a part of it in spite of our collective grief over the kids.

Maybe after reading some of the tales of this northland, you'll see the magic and come visit. Maybe you'll spend a few tourist dollars, and maybe you'll put down roots. It's been known to happen before.

Pearce and Regina

Pearce Porter took a look around the tackle shop and wondered where to begin. With poles, he guessed. He needed a fishing pole if he was going to be in White Pines Junction for the year.

His life travels told him that locals were naturally suspicious of outsiders, so he had to become one of them as quickly as he could. These people, locals and tourists and seasonal residents all, fished. So if he was to minister to their souls the way God and his church agreed he was to do, he had to become one of them.

So he'd start with a fishing pole.

He picked one out of the rack and admired it, then quickly put it back when he saw the price tag.

"Muskie rod," someone behind him said, and Pearce turned to find a barrel-chested, gray-haired man in khakis and a blue polo shirt. "They're expensive, but they're sturdy. You fishing for muskie?"

Pearce held out his hand and introduced himself, then admitted he didn't know what a muskie was.

The man with the big face, twinkly eyes and glossy teeth picked out a much smaller pole. "Game fish," he said. "Predator. Chances are, you're looking for something more like panfish," he said. "Crappie, perch, maybe a small walleye or two."

"Fine," Pearce said as he looked at the price tag on the smaller pole. That was far more reasonable, especially since it already had a reel attached.

"Need more?"

"Everything, I'm afraid."

The man picked up a tackle box, opened it and started plucking things off their pegs and dropping them into the box.

The bell on the door dinged, but neither man looked up.

"And finally," Doc said, for Pearce had learned that this gentle, man in his late fifties owned the tackle shop and went by the name of Doc, "line." He dropped a spool in. "Got a fishing license?"

"Nope."

"Come on, then, we'll fix you up."

Pearce followed Doc to the checkout counter, between the rows of mysterious things hanging on hooks, past the live wells of minnows and leeches and suckers, to the front of the store where a giant toothed fish grinned down on them from the wall overhead.

"My wife, Sadie Katherine, takes people out as a panfish guide," Doc said as he copied information from Pearce's driver's license onto the fishing license form. "She can teach you how to use all that gear to bring dinner home to your family."

Somebody dropped a whole box of something noisy in the back of the store. Pearce looked around, but couldn't see anyone.

Doc tallied the bill and Pearce pulled out his wallet. As he did, the front door opened again, and four bearded men wearing baseball caps came in, laughing with the camaraderie Pearce hoped to be sharing with them soon. Doc greeted each, then made change for Pearce.

He wanted to stay to meet the men, his new neighbors. He wanted to talk and joke, but he didn't know the lingo, didn't know the area, and until he knew what questions to ask, he felt like too much of an outsider.

He made an appointment to meet up with Sadie Katherine,

and then left, brand-new gear in hand, as the other guys took his place at the counter, leaning with elbows, hips and familiarity, and envy gripped Pearce's heart.

Maybe it was time he insisted on his own church, settled down in one community and made it home. This was too hard every couple of years, moving to a whole new culture. Hard on him, hard on Regina.

He threw his purchases into the trunk then, unwilling to leave town with the taste of envy in his mouth, slammed the trunk and eyed the small dress shop across the street. He could go over and introduce himself as the new pastor, something he hadn't been able to do at the tackle shop for some reason, though Doc gave no indication that he was anything but a fine Christian man.

White Pines Junction was as pretty a little town as he'd ever seen, Pearce thought as he looked up and down the small street. Tidy little storefronts, just like he imagined a little Bavarian ski resort would look like. Or something. He didn't really know. It had a little grocery, the tackle shop, a real-estate office and a couple of other shops. The diner, at the end of the block, seemed to anchor the place. Across the street was the little dress shop, the boat dealer, a gas station, the post office, and a couple of little shops, with the lake at the other end of it. All around were tidy little houses with tidy little yards. He and Regina had been given a nice little parsonage on the grounds of the church, and it all looked like something out of a fairy tale.

He started across the street when he heard the tinkle of the tackle shop bell, but didn't turn around. He didn't want to see those four men pile into one truck together, laughter on their tongues, tackle shop bags in their hands.

A lovely young woman greeted him in the dress shop, introducing herself, and when Pearce told her who he was, her smile slipped a fraction and her hand slid from his handshake.

She looked out to the front window and said, "Is that your wife?"

"No," Pearce started to say, because he left Regina at home with her monthly migraine, but sure enough, she was standing by the car, hands on hips, looking at the dress shop. "Why yes, I see that it is," he said. "Has she been in to meet you?"

"Sort of," the young woman said.

"Well, I'll be taking over the Sunday services beginning this Sunday at ten o'clock, and I would be delighted to see you and your family in church."

"No family," the girl said, peering out the window. "She's gone now."

Pearce looked outside and could see no evidence of his wife. Rats, he thought to himself, it's starting again.

"Sometimes," he said, "people get attached to a pastor and have a difficult time with his replacement, but I hope you'll give me a chance."

"Might as well," the girl said.

They shook hands again, Pearce reluctant to ask her name again. Was it Kimberly? He should have remembered it when she told him the first time.

He left the dress shop feeling like he did a pretty poor job of salesmanship, and was resentful that selling had to be part of his job.

Maybe White Pines Junction had a hospital. He could go there and meet a few people who would then feel obligated to come on Sunday. He wanted to give a good sermon, and he was always better in front of a full house.

But there was plenty of time for that. This was only Tuesday. Now he had to go home, find Regina and nip this behavior in the bud before it got out of hand like last time. If she didn't start acting like a pastor's wife, he'd never get a permanent church.

She was home in bed by the time he got there, telltale redness in her cheeks and perspiration on her forehead, her yellow dress tossed over the arm of the chair.

"How are you feeling?" he asked.

"I think I better go to the doctor in the morning," she said weakly.

So she'd been in the tackle shop and heard his fishing arrangements with Sadie Katherine.

"I'm going fishing in the morning," he said, "as if you didn't know."

She turned on her side away from him.

"You have to stop following me, Regina. Already the folks in town have noticed."

"I'm not," she said petulantly.

"I saw you," he said. "You're stalking me."

Her silence made him want to slap her, but of course he never would. She was sick, and he needed to get her some help. He sighed. They'd been down that road a few times before, too.

He stood up and went into the kitchen to fix dinner, worry heavy in his heart. Regina usually didn't start this jealousy thing or whatever it was for a good six to eight months into a new assignment. He'd put up with it for four to six months and the church would move them to a fresh location.

But this time. . . . They'd not been here a whole month yet and already it had started.

A bad omen for certain.

Pearce got the hang of fishing fast under the private tutelage of Sadie Katherine, a wily, gray-haired woman with a peculiar face and a quick smile. They met at five a.m. and had a full bucket of fish by eight. Pearce learned enough about his gear to rig it himself and catch his own from then on out, as long as the ice stayed off the lake.

He caught a glimpse of pink in the forest along the bank of the lake as Sadie Katherine motored them back to the dock.

And another flash of pink behind a tree as she showed him how to clean his catch in the little hut built for exactly that purpose.

Pearce paid her, thanked her, invited her and Doc to church on Sunday, then took his catch home.

He was rebagging it for the freezer when Regina came in, legs scratched and bleeding, twigs in her hair, frost on the ends of her hair. She'd been crying.

"I saw you kissing her," she said.

"Don't be silly."

"I told her husband."

"No, you didn't."

"Yes, I did and he's coming to kill you. With a big gun."

Pearce finished what he was doing, washed and dried his hands and then went to her and held her.

She clung to him, sobbing.

He didn't know what to do. "C'mon, let's see to these scratches," he said, and she followed dutifully to the bathroom where he washed off all the blood, kissed each scratch and put ointment on it. "If you do this in the summer, you'll be sick with poison ivy," he said.

She nodded like she understood, but he knew she didn't.

When she was all cleaned up, he washed her face and then took off her torn and stained pink dress and put her to bed. He took off his clothes, got in next to her and held her close.

Her hands began to rub him in a most pleasant manner, and he let her do that for a while, as he puzzled yet again over her situation and what to do about it.

And then it came to him. She wasn't cut out to be a pastor's wife. She didn't like doing all those pastor's-wife social things. Regina had a style of her own and he'd been trying to stuff her

20

into a mold that didn't fit. The answer was obvious.

"Honey?" he said.

She stopped what she was doing. "What?"

"I think you should get a job."

"No," she said, "a baby."

"No baby," Pearce said.

"Please? I'll be a good mommy, Pearce, you don't know what a good mommy I can be. Please? Pretty please?"

It wasn't as if this was a brand-new topic of conversation, but this time Pearce thought he ought to consider it. If she had a baby to obsess over, maybe she'd leave him alone. "Okay," he said, but cringed as he did so, as if he were sentencing his poor, unborn and as-yet unconceived child to a dreadful life.

Regina caught her breath in disbelief. "Really?"

"Really."

"Right *now*," she said, and climbed on top of him. As demanding as she was, he found that strangely stimulating and he responded in spite of himself. When he cried out, "Oh God," at the critical moment, he meant it.

The next moment, to his surprise, she got up, showered, fixed herself up a little bit, then sat, prim and proper at the breakfast table. She took small bites of the omelet he made, ate her toast dry, drank a big glass of water, and wiped her mouth daintily on a paper napkin, which she then folded and laid next to her plate.

"Are you all right?"

"I'm going to have a baby," she said. "I need to go shopping."

Pearce extracted a twenty from his wallet and gave it to her, and she jumped up and hugged him with childlike enthusiasm. Then she smoothed her dress, tucked the twenty into her little purse, and sat down to wait for the stores to open. Strangely pleased, Pearce went into his study and began to prepare

Sunday's sermon.

He heard her leave, and he enjoyed the silence. Regina was accustomed to leaving him to himself when he was in his study, but it had taken him many years to train her to leave him alone, and, while she finally agreed, she never understood. He always felt her hurt feelings seeping through the cracks around the door. But when she was out of the house, he felt truly free. In fact, he resented having to spend this time working. He could watch television, or read a book in the living room, or just be alone in the house, without her jumping into his lap or trying to attract his attention in a million different ways.

She was a joy, she was his joy, but she was also a burden.

He worked in peace, and about the time he stretched and was beginning to consider making a pot of coffee, he heard the front door slam. A moment later, she threw open the door to his den and stood at the threshold, staring at him with an accusatory glare made up of pain and hurt and wildfire.

"Honey?"

"I hate you," she said, turned on her heel and a moment later, he heard the bedroom door slam.

Oh lord.

He counted to one hundred very slowly, then got up and went to the bedroom. Instead of the soggy, sopping, sobbing mess he expected to find on the bed, she was sitting on the edge, her knees together, her hands folded in her lap. Her face was tear stained, but composed.

"Hi," he said.

"I can't hate you," she said. "It's not good for the baby."

"Why would you hate me?"

"For bringing me here. For letting me think I could have a baby."

"I don't understand."

"You know what goes on here. You know about the babies

disappearing. You never wanted to have any kids, and your way of getting around that was by bringing me here so I could have babies and they'd disappear so that you wouldn't have to have them around. It wouldn't be your fault." She hiccupped, but kept her actions under control.

"Honey, I don't have any idea what you're talking about. We're going to have a baby, I said so. If it didn't work last night, we'll try again tonight. Don't worry."

"They disappear, Pearce, the babies in this place disappear."

"Disappear?"

"Magic. Evil magic. Witch stuff. That's why the church sent us here, don't you know? They want us to kill the evil here."

"Did you have lunch?" he asked. "Let's go wash your face, have a little something to eat, then we'll investigate this thing about the babies." He sat down on the bed next to her. "Nothing's going to happen to our baby, Regina. I love you and I love that baby, and we're going to be a nice little family, the three of us."

She looked up at him with trusting, childlike eyes, and he nodded. A big tear tripped over the lower lid, skidded down her cheek and fell on the back of his hand. "C'mon now," he said. "Let me cook a nice dinner for you and that baby in there."

"Okay," she said, and sniffed.

"If you're going to have a baby, you've got to let me take care of you," he said.

"Okay," she said.

"I'll take good care," he said, and opened his arms. She fell into them and began to sob all over again. He just held her tight.

"I want to be a good mom," she choked out.

"You will be," Pearce said and rocked her back and forth. "You will be."

★ ★ ★ ★ ★

The next day, when Pearce came home from his daily search for people to minister to, he found the kitchen filled with empty grocery bags, the hallway full of aluminum foil boxes and the spare room covered in foil—walls, ceiling, windows. Regina started when she heard him at the door, and looked up from where she was affixing the last bit of foil to the wall with a strip of duct tape and said, "What do we do about the floor?"

"What are you doing?"

"We're going to sleep in here from now on. And the baby will have to stay in here until he's twelve."

Pearce looked at the room, which gave him a headache, and his wife kneeling on the floor, which gave him indigestion, and turned away. He went to the kitchen and began folding up the paper sacks. They came, he noted, from all three of the stores in White Pines Junction. She must have bought them all out of foil.

Bags stowed, he put water on to boil and began to mix up a tuna casserole. Why couldn't she fixate on prenatal nutrition, or learning nursery rhymes, or finding the best school in the neighborhood? Instead, she'll be going to UFO conventions before long. She'd be speaking at them. She'd dedicate their child to them. She'd be marshalling the U.S. Army against them, for god's sake.

The whole thing gave Pearce a headache. And a heartache. And it made him nervous about his career. Eventually, he'd like to settle down with a church and a congregation of his own, live in the parsonage and raise a whole bagful of kids, but how was that to be done if Regina wasn't going to let their firstborn out of his mirrored room until he was twelve?

She was troubled, and it was becoming time for him to take some action. They could move from Vargas County, but he didn't think that would solve the problem. It would take care of the current paranoia, but something else would surface.

No, it was up to Pearce to take the situation in hand and deal with his wife. Firmly, but gently. The way Jesus would.

"Honey?" he called. "Do you want garlic cheesebread with your tuna noodle casserole?"

She was by his side in an instant. "Yes, yes, yes," she said.

"Okay. I'll slice the bread and you sprinkle the cheese."

She got the canister down from the shelf and stood next to him, waiting for him to make the first slice so she could sprinkle.

"Regina, have you taken a pregnancy test yet?"

"Why?"

"I was just wondering. If we're going to have a baby, we ought to know when, so we can prepare."

"Nine months," she said.

"I think we should take a test."

"No tests. The aliens could go through the garbage and see it. Then they'd know where to come." She buttered the bread, then sprinkled the garlic cheese, careful to get both even, all the way to the edges. "Let's name him Spartacus."

"Who?"

"Our baby."

"What if it's a girl?"

Regina silently buttered and sprinkled. "Let's eat these now," she said, and looked up at him with the trusting eyes of a child. "And then let's have ice cream."

Pearce looked into those eyes and remembered why he'd married her. She had been so youthful, so fun, so sweet, and she looked to be the model of a perfect clergy wife-in-making. But this disease, or whatever it was that had sprouted in her mind, was growing more prevalent and turning her maturity clock backwards. He was afraid for her. "Okay," he said, and put the bread in with the casserole. When it came out, they sat down and ate all the toasted bread and let the casserole bake.

Tomorrow, he thought. Tomorrow we'll eat that casserole and then we'll go to a doctor.

But the next morning, she threw up. Pearce sat on the floor and held her head while she puked into the toilet, and his spirits took a serious tumble, along with the realization that with the morning sickness would surely come a baby. She still needed some kind of help, although Prozac or something of its ilk was clearly out of the question now that she was carrying a child.

Regina grew ever more beautiful in the following days, while Pearce's sleep was disturbed by visions of childproofing their home, and not only for the baby.

He knew she was sick, and would need some type of treatment, but, for the time being, he could handle it. He just had to monitor her progress, make sure she ate properly, saw to her personal hygiene, kept her safe and made certain that she wasn't left alone.

As he was fairly new in the community, he wasn't much missed. He still found time to prepare sermons, and preached them to a thin audience on Sunday mornings, Regina prettied up and sitting in the front pew. Eventually, her condition became obvious, and she was the first one to poke her belly around at people so they'd notice. They began to get congratulatory handshakes and a few invitations to dinner and such, which he discreetly declined.

Things work out somehow, he thought, and was glad that they were new enough in the community to be fairly invisible. They'd be moving on, according to the church, not long after the baby was born, and that too, was good. They didn't need to make any lasting impressions or relationships here. The fewer questions about the new pastor and his strange wife the better. One day at a time, he coped increasingly competently as what amounted to being the single parent of his pregnant wife.

By the time Month Nine rolled around, Regina was wearing

aluminum foil helmets around the house and Pearce had to keep her inside. She had her moments of lucidity, but they were fleeting. He worried about the fact that he hadn't taken her for prenatal medical help, but she was young and healthy—in body if not in mind—and he made sure she ate well and got enough sleep. But what he really worried about was the genetic significance of what was happening to her, and the chemical imbalance it surely caused in her system and how it would affect the baby.

Oh well. Nothing to be done about it yet.

But when the pains of childbirth began, Regina was not to be controlled.

She had spent the day singing at the top of her lungs, and marching around the house with a wooden spoon, the tinfoil hat tattered and bent, but securely on her head, while Pearce was trying his hardest to concentrate on the sermon he was writing.

"Ow," Regina said.

Pearce jumped up to see what she'd done to hurt herself, but what he saw chilled him. She was standing in the middle of the living room, wooden spoon at her feet, and she had her hands around the swollen lump of a belly. Her time had come and he was unprepared. In fact, he had worried over the course of action, knowing that this day would come, but having never made a decision about anything, he was totally and completely unprepared. Now he had to consciously calm himself before he panicked and scared Regina.

"What's happening, pumpkin?"

"It hurts me."

"The baby's coming," he said, his mind racing. If they got in the car right now, he could get her to a hospital in the next town where nobody knew them. He could make up a doctor's name, and say they were just passing through, and the baby was early. . . .

"Ow!" She hit her stomach with her fists. "Make it stop."

Oh man, Pearce thought, she hasn't seen anything yet. She'll need drugs. "C'mon, let's go to the hospital."

"Hospital?"

"Yep. That's where they get the baby out of your tummy without it hurting."

"Then we'll bring it home?"

"Yes." He moved to hug her, but she dodged him.

"No. The baby belongs in here." She opened the door to the tinfoiled room, where every possible surface, including the crib mattress, had been covered with foil.

"Why?"

A puzzled look came across her face, and Pearce was happy that whatever had happened to her brain had progressed to the point where she forgot all about the UFO stuff. "C'mon, Regina, let's go get that baby out of your tummy, and then we'll bring him home."

"Okay," she said, but then a pain gripped her and like a little wild animal, she started to scream, then slammed out the front door and ran through the snow, screaming, toward town.

Pearce chased her, and caught her a block away, her tinfoil hat askew and caught in her hair. She was out of breath and pain and fear showed feral in her eyes. "Honey? Honey, settle down, now listen to me. I can make the pain stop, but we've got to get into the car to do it."

"No!" she started to yell and beat her fists against him.

He held her tighter, trying to control her, but her legs buckled the same time as she bit his arm, and he let go.

Pearce looked at her on the ground, in the snow, her little yellow cotton dress up over her skinny knees, tears running down the sides of her face as she looked up at him, and he didn't know what to do.

Then Jimbo's truck pulled over, and he jumped out with his cell phone to his ear. He said, "Are you all right, Pastor?"

It was all Pearce could do to keep from crying. "She's in labor."

"Can you come over here, honey?" Jimbo said into the phone, then he folded it and put it in his pocket. He squatted down next to Regina, who shrank from him and turned to hug her husband's legs. "Hi, Mrs. Porter," Jimbo said. "So you're about to have that baby, are you? Bet you're excited."

Regina sat up and started to bawl.

"Margie's on her way over. You know she's had two sons, and she'll help you, because she knows what to do."

A contraction gripped Regina, and her face went red. When it was over, she just said, "Get it out of me. Get it away from me!"

"We need to go to the hospital, honey," Pearce said, and gave Jimbo a look he hoped would translate into taking his side.

"That's right, Mrs. Porter," Jimbo said. "Babies come out in hospitals."

Margie came running across the street, shrugging into her parka, and gasped when she saw Regina in her little cotton dress on the ground in the freezing snow. "What's going on?"

"Mrs. Porter's going to have her baby," Jimbo said, "and she's not quite up to it."

"Give her your coat," Margie demanded, then sat down on the ground with Regina while Jimbo put his sheepskin Levi's jacket around her shoulders.

"Time for the hospital?" she asked.

"Don't want to go," Regina whined.

"They'll stop it from hurting," Margie said, and Pearce was amazed at how easily everyone fell into communicating at Regina's level. Apparently he wasn't as secretive with her condition as he thought he'd been.

"Okay," Regina said, then began to stand up. Margie put one arm around her, and Pearce got on the other side of her, and Regina began to shiver with the cold as they walked slowly back to the house, toward the car. Pearce was just about to ask Margie to go along for the ride, when Regina stopped, dead in her tracks.

"Oh, no," she said softly, and liquid trickled out from between her legs into the snow.

"It's okay," Margie said, but Regina wasn't hearing her.

"Something's happening," she said, and, for a moment, Pearce looked into her eyes and saw the woman he had married.

"Let's hurry," he said to her, and she nodded. They picked up the pace, and while Margie got Regina settled in the front seat, Pearce grabbed the keys and his wallet.

"Can you go with us?" he asked her under his breath.

"Can't," she said apologetically. "Diner. But it's not far. Take County Road M east four miles, turn north. There's a sign. It's another ten miles. You'll be there in no time."

"Thanks," he said, then got in the car with his silent wife, who was disentangling the foil from her hair. He started the car and sprayed gravel as he fishtailed around and out onto the county road, not even using his turn signal.

Four miles. He punched the trip meter so he'd know, although he was certain he'd seen the blue marker sign. "You okay?"

She didn't answer. Pearce took a deep breath and looked at her. She was calmly sitting, her backrest reclined a little bit.

"Honey?"

"They're coming for us," she said, her voice rising with hysteria.

There it was, the blue sign with the H for Hospital. He

turned, and stepped on the accelerator. The air seemed to thin out and he took deep breaths to compensate.

"Oh, no," she said. "No, *no!* Oh Pearce, do you hear them? Oh my god, it's so sad."

Pearce slammed on the brakes and the car slid to a stop on the shoulder of the road, just in time to watch Regina's belly deflate like a punctured basketball. "Honey?"

"Oh," she said as if she were as mystified and amazed as he at the sinking of her abdomen. It was the sighing "oh" of an epiphany, of a disappointment, of an acceptance.

"Honey?"

She turned to look at him with eyes that were as old as his, and no longer held childlike merriment. She took a great, heaving breath, almost a sob, and let it out slowly.

"Are you okay?"

She caught another ragged breath, then said, "Perhaps."

"Do you need anything? I mean, what happened?" He put his hand lightly on her stomach and felt only soft, giving flesh whereas only a moment ago, it was hard and ripe. He felt panic rising, but tempered it in the face of her unearthly calm. Was the baby on the floor of the car? "Should we go to the hospital?"

"That might be prudent," she said, "although I doubt that there is a real need." She picked up the battered piece of a tinfoil hat and began to unfold it and flatten it out on her knee.

"Honey?" Pearce turned off the engine.

"Yes?"

"The baby?"

"Gone." Another sobbing sigh, and this time a few tears came with it. "Gone to be with the rest of them. And they took something of me with it."

No kidding, Pearce thought. What happened to the child-woman he'd been dealing with for the past year?

Kidnapped, he thought. *Snatched. Mother and child together.*

Exactly what Regina had been afraid would happen.

"Let's go home," she said.

Or not, he thought. The disappointment Pearce felt surpassed anything he had ever encountered. He wanted that baby, he looked forward to having that baby in the house. We could just start this car and keep on driving, he thought, because we don't have anything here, we don't have any roots, we don't have any furniture, we don't have any friends. We have Jimbo's jacket, but we can send that to him. Or keep it. We could just keep going away from this damned place, and find ourselves a decent place, a place where children don't disappear and take their child-like mothers with them. Let's just keep going, he wanted to say to her, let's just be irresponsible for once and get out of here. To hell with the church, to hell with White Pines Junction, to hell with the dreams of home and family and a parish of our own. Let's just run and keep running until we fall down.

Or until we can find a place where we can realize our dreams.

But instead, he started the car and turned it back toward home. "We'll have explaining to do," he said.

"There is nothing to explain," Regina said. "There is no explanation." She folded the aluminum foil into a tiny square and set it on the dashboard. "I'm sure I ought to take a day or two to rest, but then I'll have to make a casserole for Sunday's potluck."

Pearce had no answer for that. He not only missed his baby, but he missed his wife. This sensible creature next to him reminded him of the woman he had married, but not the woman he had come to love. He pulled back into the driveway, ran around the car to open the door and help her out. She took off the soiled cotton dress and put on a sensible flannel nightie that had languished in the bottom drawer of her dresser for over a year. Then she got into bed and asked for a cup of hot tea.

When Pearce brought it to her, she took his hand and kissed

it. "Perhaps you ought to go fishing one of these days," she said. "Make a few friends in this community."

With those few words, Pearce's shattered dreams began to reassemble. He remembered what it was like to have friends, buddies, a congregation, the hope for his own church. A proper clergy wife. Solid standing in the community. The family part could wait for the next assignment. One of these days the church would give them their own parish. Maybe the next one would be the permanent one.

Whatever had just happened was not necessarily a tragedy, he decided. Life is long enough for each of us to achieve our dreams in time, isn't it?

"Good idea," he said. "Now you rest, and I'll check in on you a little later." He kissed her cheek, then closed the door quietly behind him. As he passed the tinfoiled room, he wondered if she had been right about that, too.

Well, he'd get his parish now that he had a normal wife. And life would be simpler, and much more normal.

But that didn't exactly mean better, did it?

A good topic for next Sunday's sermon.

THE FISHERMAN

The old man parked his decrepit old Pinto nose-in to the weeds. With stiff joints and arthritic fingers, he gingerly but persistently unloaded the gear—pole, bait bucket, lunch box, thermos, tackle—then slipped thin shoulders into a flotation vest and zipped it up the front. Sadie Katherine knew almost everybody who lived in Vargas County, but she didn't know this gent.

A chill wind blew across the lake. Sadie Katherine organized her tackle and kept a worried eye on him as he took small, shuffling, old-man steps down toward the dock, and she wondered what the missus would do if he failed to return at sunset with dinner in his creel.

Would they go hungry?

Or did they live in that beautiful new home on the bluff? Maybe he kept that rusted Ford out of sentimentality, its upholstery stained with fish odor, its sun-rotted visor poked full of lures and flies, the bumper tied on with thirty-pound-test line. Maybe the wife drove a nice, new Eldorado, white, with climate control and no fish smell allowed, thank you very much. Maybe instead of fishing for survival, their freezer was stocked with salmon and lamb and their meals were expertly cooked by a woman who came every day to do the heavy cleaning.

Or did they live *behind* that big new house on the bluff, in the shack with the bright blue tarp for a roof and frozen mud for a floor in the winter?

The half-horsepower motor started, and he putted gently

away in his rowboat, still the master of his ship, the captain of his fate, his wool hat firmly pulled down, earflaps sensibly warding off his death of a cold.

Sly fox, Sadie Katherine thought. She bet he knew all the secret holes in the big lake. She was tempted to turn around, jump back into her boat and follow for a distance, but if he were as sly as she gave him credit for, he'd never lead anyone to his secrets. He'd rather putter around the lake, trying to throw the interloper off his trail until the sun set and the fish lost their appetites and then he and his wife would have no dinner. He would come in, stand his pole in the corner of the shack and shrug apologetically, the provider defeated. She would put away the frying pan, desperately trying not to show her disappointment. With nothing else to do, they would get into their small, hard bed and hold each other, stomachs growling, and wonder at the whim of fate.

Or would they dress up in nice, comfortable, retired-folks clothes and order trout almandine with a fine white wine at a restaurant in the city? Maybe they would then spend the rest of the evening calling long-distance grandchildren and laughing.

Sadie Katherine turned to watch him, and did so just in time to see him and his boat slip into a sound-muffling shroud of mist that she hadn't noticed a minute ago.

The chill wind grew to gale warnings as evening approached. The red ball of a sun set behind a horizon crusted thick with mist, and the temperature dropped.

All night Sadie Katherine lay in bed next to Doc, listening to the wind try to pry open her house and she thought of a lonely rowboat with a half-horsepower outboard, bobbing on a white-capped lake in a raging spring storm.

At dawn, the wind drove rain, leaves, branches, garbage and other debris horizontally as she drove back to the lake. The Pinto was still there, its hatchback covered with wet leaves and pine needles blown about by the wind.

Did he live alone? Was there no one else to raise the alarm?

She drove to the big new house on the bluff, but even as she went up there, she knew that was not where he lived. She kept driving, around behind, to the shack.

The rain took a breather as she jumped out of her car and ran to the door.

A tired young woman opened the door. She'd been mopping up rainwater. A big-eyed toddler clung to her dress with one hand, the thumb of his other solidly in his mouth.

A baby whimpered from a crib across the single room.

They looked like something from the thirties, something from Tobacco Road. Sadie Katherine didn't know people lived like this in White Pines Junction, and she wondered about their circumstances.

"The old man . . . ," Sadie Katherine said.

Her face flushed with what appeared to be hope. "Is he dead?"

"I don't know," Sadie Katherine said. "He went out in his boat last night and didn't come back. I'm worried."

"Oh," she said, looking back at the water dripping through the patchwork roof. "That don't mean nothin'."

"Your . . . father? Grandfather?"

"Looney old fart," she said. "Don't know who he is. Calls me Myra. My name's Cindy."

"Hi, Cindy," she said. "I'm Sadie Katherine."

"Want coffee?" she asked, and Sadie Katherine was touched that this woman who had nothing was still willing to share.

"Sure," she said, and sat down on an unstable chair. The little boy detached himself from her and went to the crib. The baby stopped crying and they both stared at their visitor with big eyes while their mom poured coffee. "So he doesn't live here?" Sadie Katherine asked casually, curious but trying not to pry.

"Don't know that he lives at all," Cindy said as she put a steaming mug on the plywood table. "Can't seem to get rid of him." She swept crumbs from one end of the table and sat down. "Don't know if I want to."

The rain started up again, spraying cold mist right through the cracks in the wall, and beyond the wind, beyond the creaking of the cabin, came the sputtering of a car. An old Ford. Cindy met Sadie Katherine's eyes and raised an eyebrow. The toddler took a step back into the shadow behind the crib.

"Myra?" a voice called from outside. The door opened and he came in, impossibly dry, a lilt to his frail step, one earflap cocked up on his hat, a plastic grocery bag in his hand. "Hi, Myra!" He looked at Sadie Katherine. "Charlie! Long time, buddy."

Sadie Katherine looked at Cindy, who just shrugged.

"Amazing catch last night." He held up the bag with proud enthusiasm. "Fish couldn't wait to jump into the boat." He set the bag down in the sink. "I think it was the calm moon."

He looked at the place on his skinny, freckled wrist where a watch could be but wasn't, and said, "I'm late for Rotary." He kissed Cindy on the head, shook Sadie Katherine's hand and shuffled out the door, letting it bang behind him. The rattletrap Pinto sputtered off into the distance.

He came and went so fast, Sadie Katherine barely had time to register all of his idiosyncrasies, but it seemed as if one of them was a gentle transparency.

The two women just looked at each other. Then they both jumped up and Cindy led the way to the sink.

She upended the bag and out fell a rock, a hunk of seaweed, a flattened juice bottle, an empty motor oil can, a rusted fishing reel, and a fine, firm, fresh rainbow trout.

"Stay for breakfast?" she asked.

THE BOG POLE

Kimberly paced her little living room, biting the flesh around her thumbnail. Every once in a while she'd pause and look down at the body of her husband, prison-thin, in new jeans and white T-shirt, with her brand-new Gingher sewing shears protruding primly from his right eye. She wanted to kick him, he made her so mad, but that would be useless. She didn't want to touch him. Ever again.

So she paced, and waited for Natasha. This was the second time today she'd paced, waiting for someone to show up, and she was damn tired of it. First, it was waiting for Cousins to arrive on the Greyhound. She must have burned up a million calories pacing that one off. She didn't want him back. It had been ten years, she'd carved out a nice little life for herself in White Pines Junction and if there were going to be any changes in the way she lived, it wasn't going to be with a drunken, ex-con idiot at her side. But she didn't know how to tell him that. He'd been gone ten years, and had written her faithfully every month, long letters, pining for her and his life in the north-woods.

And he finally did arrive, swinging down from that bus with a light step, and a much older face. He grabbed her up like they do in the movies, and swung her around and said, "You and me babe," then gave her a hard kiss on the mouth that bruised her lips. He had only a little carry-on, like a vinyl gym bag, which he threw in the backseat of the car. He took the keys from her hand, and jumped into the driver's seat. "Point me the way."

Against her will, she directed him to her little lakeside cottage, the one she had worked hard to buy and pay for, no thanks to him. On the way home he declared his intentions: A thick steak, a cold beer and a good fuck. In that order. Well, he could get the first two at Margie's if he brought his own beer, but the rest of it would be over her dead body.

Or his, as it turned out.

As it turned out, he didn't want just one cold beer, he wanted a whole bottle of Jack Daniel's. And then he didn't want anything to eat, he just wanted her. She dodged him until he grabbed her, boozy prison breath in her face, and with desperate strength she never knew she had, she fought her way over to her sewing table, pulled on the fabric that was draped over it, until those gleaming silver plated Ginghers fell right into her hand. The next few minutes were blurred in her memory, but she remembered not being able to breathe, and him saying something about "this is the way it's done around here, and if you don't fight, you won't get hurt." She swung her arm just as he turned her over and leaned back, and instead of getting him in the back, like she thought she would, those scissors went right into his eye.

God.

She kicked him off of her, stood up, hiccuped a few times, quietly shrieked a few times, stomped and paced and freaked out for a moment, had a deep swig of that Jack herself, took a deep breath, straightened her clothes, and then sat down to contemplate her next move.

All her options were ugly. She could see nothing but going to prison herself for the rest of her life, writing long letters back to Natasha every month, pining for her little lakefront cottage. So she called Natasha, asked her to come over, "It's *very* important," she said, and then began to pace again, waiting.

"Jesus god!" Natasha's hand covered her mouth, her eyes wide. "What the fuck?"

"I know, I know," Kimberly said, and she wanted nothing more than to put her arms around Natasha and comfort her, which in itself would be comforting. But that was not to be. No arms around Natasha, not after all these years, and not for all the years to come. "Can you help me? I don't know what to do."

Natasha surveyed the scene, then went directly for the bottle on the coffee table. She took a swig, passed the bottle back to Kimberly, then sat down on the sofa. "Jesus," she said. "You've got to call Sheriff Withens."

"I'll go to prison."

"Self defense. You got bruises?"

Kimberly shrugged. "Isn't there another way?"

"Like what? Bury him in the garden? Make fertilizer for your bamboo plants? Listen, Kim, nobody is going to have a hard time believing this was self-defense. Nobody liked Cousins, especially not Sheriff Withens."

"You're the only one who knew he was coming home."

Natasha raised an eyebrow and took another sip of Jack.

Kimberly took that as a good sign, and enthusiasm lit a fire in her. "We can do this, Nat. We'll haul him out to the boat and row him out to that bog on the island. You know the one? We can push him down under. The turtles will eat him in a week, and nobody will ever know."

"I've got to admit it has a touch of poetic justice."

"Me rotting in prison does not."

"I will not be an accomplice, Kimberly. If we do this, you have done it by yourself. You must respect me enough to never bring my name into this."

"Okay."

"We will never discuss it again. I'll tell Mort we played cards."

"Okay."

"All right." Natasha took a deep breath and another swig. "Jesus, I can't believe we're going to do this. Go get a sturdy bamboo pole and something to bind his wrists and heels."

Kimberly ran out the kitchen door, and into the greenhouse, its moist, earthy smell like a perfume. She grew bamboo in this greenhouse; was up to two hundred and four varieties of the fascinating stuff. Alongside one edge was a drying rack, and she picked out a piece of timber bamboo that was about three inches in diameter and eight feet long. It should work perfectly.

She brought the pole into the living room, and saw that Natasha had pulled all the draperies and turned out the porch light. She'd salvaged the shears and was in the process of cutting Cousins' pants off. Kimberly got a length of bulky-spun yarn from her basket and worked at tying his wrists together, and then his ankles. They threaded the pole between and hoisted him onto their shoulders like a hunted-down pig. Which he was. He was a pathetic figure, hanging naked between them, skinny ass and all.

They marched him through the kitchen door and down the path to the pier and swung him into the little boat Kimberly kept tied up there. She ran back up to the house, grabbed jackets for the two of them, then pulled the blanket out of the dog's house and threw it over Cousins' gleaming whiteness.

Kimberly started the little outboard, Natasha cast off the bowline and they headed across the lake.

Now that action was being taken, Kimberly felt calmer, although she was shivering inside her down coat. It was cool on the lake in the night, but not cold enough to make her shiver. Delayed nerves, she told herself, but it didn't help. The trusty little outboard putted its way across the dark and silent lake and just as they reached the island, a big moon came up over the trees, and the world went black and silver.

The island was marshy, with no beach. Kimberly nosed the boat into the weeds, and Natasha jumped out with the bowline into water up to her knees. She tied the line to a tree stump. The boat wasn't going anywhere. They ended up dumping Cousins out into the water and dragging him across the marsh, because the weight of him on their shoulders made them sink too deeply into the marsh to walk.

Kimberly and Natasha had discovered the bog on the island last summer when they were looking for a private place to sunbathe nude. They'd taken Kim's boat out to this island, sure to be vacant, since all it really was, was marsh. Not likely any families water-skiing from it, and no fishermen would come ashore there. The marsh solidified about fifty feet in, and there they put their towels and opened the wine and had themselves a fun day and an allover tan. Not that Natasha needed a tan, but she seemed to enjoy being naked as much as Kimberly enjoyed Natasha being naked. Anyway, as they were exploring the small island, they found a hole in the middle of it, and inside was a deep well of blackish-green slime. Stagnant bog. Natasha, who owned the motel with her husband, and heard all the fishing stories, said that the bog was thick and mucky. And when Kimberly thought of a place to stash Cousins' body, she thought immediately of thick and mucky. It was perfect.

Once they were again on solid footing, they threaded the pole through Cousins' bound ankles and wrists, and hoisted him back up on their shoulders.

"Tell me again why he went to jail?" Natasha asked.

"Robbed the mini mart and made his getaway on his snowmobile. Left tracks right to our apartment."

"Too stupid to live."

Kimberly agreed. She slowed down as they neared the bog. She could sense it. She could smell it. She did not want to fall into it. Natasha said it was like quicksand; the more you moved, the deeper it sucked you down. They lowered Cousins to the ground, then Natasha picked up the bamboo pole and probed the ground in front of them. But when they got to the bog, they could see it. It was dark black in the night, as if it sucked the struggling moonlight right down to be eaten by turtles, too.

They went back and dragged Cousins as near to the edge as either one of them wanted to step, and then Kimberly picked up the pole and began shoving his body closer.

"Want to say a few words?"

Count on Natasha to sense gravity in the absurd situation.

"We could have been a family, Cousins, if you'd have been a little smarter," Kimberly said. "And it's mostly my fault for making a bad choice. I wish you well on your journey through the afterlife, and God have mercy on all our souls."

Natasha nodded. "Amen," she said.

Kimberly pushed until Cousins began to disappear into the muck. The back of his head and his shoulders floated like polished ivory in the moonlight.

"Push him under the edge," Natasha said. "His body has to go under the island."

Together they maneuvered Cousins' remains to the far side of the bog, and then poked at him until he completely disappeared under the grass.

When he was gone and didn't come back up, Kimberly's knees gave out and she sat down hard and began to cry.

"Do that at home," Natasha said. "I've got to wash my clothes and get cleaned up before I go home to Mort. I smell like bog."

Kimberly put her fears and broken heart and emotional exhaustion on hold for one last trip across the lake. She promised herself that once she got home, she could break down and it could last a while.

But, in the morning, she realized she had to act completely normal, so she got up, showered and dressed, and opened up the dress shop like she always did. Nothing could look out of the ordinary.

She figured two weeks with the turtles and crayfish and she'd be home free. If Cousins didn't emerge within two weeks, if some fisherman needing an emergency field toilet didn't come upon him within two weeks, she would be fine.

It was going to be a long two weeks.

By the end of the day, she hardly believed it had happened. She had decent receipts with all the tourist ladies in town, keeping themselves busy spending money while their husbands spent their days on the water. She was dog tired by the time she locked the front door and turned the *Open* sign to *Closed* and went about straightening the shop and doing the cash report. Just as she was ready to leave, there came a knock on the front door.

Sheriff Withens.

Panic welled up in her, but she smiled and waved, and gave him the "just a minute" hand sign. Then she made herself look busy for ten seconds while she got her breathing under control.

Relax. Relax.

She unlocked the front door and let the sheriff in, an old, rugged man with a face she had grown to love over the years. She didn't like the fact that he was suddenly the enemy. "Hi, Sheriff."

"Kimberly," he said gravely, and closed the door behind him. "How you doing?"

"Fine."

"Had a good day?"

"Not bad. Why? What's up?"

"You know Cousins has been paroled?"

Kimberly felt the blood drain from her face. She felt the sheriff's warm hand on her arm. She felt the floor rock gently beneath her feet.

"Come on, now, let's sit down." He led her to the chair

designated for bored husbands.

"I guess I knew it was coming up," Kimberly said. "Is he here?"

"The prison notified me that he was released yesterday. You haven't heard from him?"

"No. But I suppose I shall."

"You two haven't been in communication?"

"He writes to me, but I don't write back. I don't want to have anything to do with him."

"Is it his intention to come back here?"

"I think it is."

"Well, I'll be looking out after you, Kimberly. Don't you worry about that. If you see him, you let me know, so I can keep an eye on him, okay?"

"I'm so sorry, Sheriff. I feel like I've brought bad blood to White Pines Junction."

"Things happen, Kimberly. You were young then, very young. You were what, nineteen?"

Kimberly nodded.

"Nobody begrudges you a bad decision in your youth. Especially since you've turned out so good. Just keep in touch with me, okay?"

Kimberly nodded, feeling herself back on somewhat solid ground. "Thanks for coming by."

She saw the sheriff out, locked the door, and decided to put the cash report off for another day. She went out the back way, locked it up and went home to the last of the Jack Daniel's and a hard, dreamless sleep.

The morning dawned with a low dark ceiling of clouds and the scent of storm on the air. Kimberly had to turn extra lights on at the shop to make it look pleasant, but business was brisk, as it always was on a stormy day. Thoughts of Cousins were far away, as if it were all a dark fantasy. Life returned almost to normal, with few thoughts of him, and those that came were benign, like when he had been safely locked away.

The rain that had threatened all day began just as she totaled the day's receipts. By the time she locked the door, she had to run to her car. The sky darkened to midnight prematurely, with a strange greenish cast to the horizon where the sun ought to be setting. Big storm. She went home, laid out the candles, made a fire in the wood stove and put the teakettle on it, then put on a sweatshirt and sweatpants and waited for the maelstrom. She wished she still had the dog. Someone to cuddle with on the couch.

Natasha.

Nope. Don't even think about it.

She sipped her tea and listened to the wind beginning. The rain was blasting the north side of the house, and the wind was coming up hard.

The truth was, she would have left the northwoods years ago, right after Cousins went to prison, if it hadn't been for Natasha, and the friendship she offered. Kimberly was in love with Natasha, enough so that she would never declare her feelings. Natasha would be horrified. And besides, Natasha was a married woman. Kimberly tried to like men, but they just weren't her passion. Natasha was her passion, and if she couldn't have her, then she would be content to be near her. Nothing thrilled Kimberly more than Natasha stopping in at the store, buying some outrageously New York item that Kimberly had ordered, knowing it would achieve perfection on Natasha's tall, lean, ebony body.

But Kim had to be careful. She didn't want to lose the friendship by taking an inappropriate step.

And Natasha had gone to the mat for her, too. Participated in Cousins' removal. They were sealed together for eternity by that act, one that could never be mentioned ever again.

Two weeks. Two weeks, less two days, and she would be home free.

The wind picked up and started throwing stuff around outside. Kimberly went to the window and checked on the greenhouse, but it was fine.

She grabbed a pillow and blanket and decided to sleep on the couch in front of the fire.

Bright morning sun shining through the living room windows woke Kimberly. Storm was over. She got up, stretched, put the kettle back on the stove, noted that the power had never gone off, strangely enough, then looked out the back door to check the greenhouse. What she saw made her knees go wobbly again.

The island. The bog island, the island with Cousins' body buried deep within it, was outside. Her pier and the little boat tied to it had been pushed aside and washed up on the lawn, and the island had been blown up alongside of it.

This happens, she tried to tell herself. It was not Cousins coming back to haunt her. It was not. She had heard of these islands blowing about in windstorms. One time, an island blew across a channel inlet and fishermen had to be rescued by helicopter. That had been a big island; nobody knew it was a free-floating thing until that storm. This was a smaller island, maybe fifty yards across, but big enough to house pine trees and bushes. Big enough to walk on. To tether one's boat to, to sunbathe nude on, to bury one's husband in. It had every right to be blown around the lake.

Cousins was not driving it; Cousins was dead.

Kimberly stuck her feet into gum boots and went outside. The earth had been turned in the storm and it still smelled a little wild.

The island had beached itself right at the edge of her lawn. She stepped onto it from the yard, gushed around a few steps,

47

and then found firm footing. She walked, with trepidation, toward the middle of the island, toward the bog.

And there he was, floating in the middle of the small, green-black pool of slime. The bamboo pole was still there, so with heaving gasps and sobs, Kimberly picked up the pole and shoved Cousins back under the grass. It took a long time to get him entirely underneath the island, as things were surely churned up under there, but, eventually, it was done, and she was sweating and boggy and crying and a mess.

She didn't even know if there were any turtles under there to do away with him anymore. She ran, as fast as she could under the circumstances, back to the house, and against her will, dialed Natasha's number.

"Kimberly, hi! Some storm, eh?"

"Natasha, the storm blew the island into my pier. It's in my backyard!"

"You're kidding."

"No, and he was out! I had to push him back under with the pole."

"We're not talking about that, Kim." Natasha's voice was muffled as if she had turned away from Mort and held her hand over the phone. "Deal with it."

"He's in my backyard!" Kimberly heard a shred of hysteria in her voice and she didn't want to let it get a handhold on her. She stopped and took a deep breath. "I'm sorry."

"We'll talk later, okay?" Natasha said.

"Yeah, okay."

"Bye now."

Kimberly hung up and looked out the window. She felt as though a demon had started to stalk her and she didn't know what to do. Sheriff Withens? No. Pastor Porter? No. Margie? Definitely not. She'd just deal with it. Like Natasha said. Deal with it.

And deal with it she did. Every morning she had to poke him back under the bog. Every morning when she went out there, the island, like a huge white elephant, was there, and every morning, she found Cousins floating in the black goo. Every morning, like a mantra, she would pick up the bamboo pole and push him under. It was a chore she added to her daily routine, like watering the growing bamboo and ordering new stock for the shop.

But it took its toll.

Every day she was surprised, all over again, to see the island outside, nudging her broken pier. Each day she walked down the lawn, stepped onto the reedy mass and walked through the swampy undergrowth, and each day she saw Cousins' stark white shoulders floating still, like bleached bones on black macadam. Each day she picked up the bamboo pole and shoved him, each day with more and more vehemence, until his sorry carcass was out of sight. Then she'd slog home, crying more often than not, to her little cottage and her other life.

Why weren't the turtles eating him? Or the crawfish? Why wasn't he decomposing? Too ornery, she supposed. He probably tastes bad.

And then one day, at least three weeks after the storm, long after Cousins should have been completely recycled, Sheriff Withens paid another call on her at the store.

At closing, like before.

"See you've got yourself a permanent resident," he said.

Kimberly, nerves strung to the shrieking point, reacted too fast. *"Resident?"*

"The island," Sheriff Withens said. "You've got yourself some additional real estate there, free of charge." He smiled, and Kimberly wasn't sure if he was being nice or toying with her like a cat with a mouse.

"Wrecked my pier," she said.

"Know what we call that island? Dead Man's Float. It's been around for a hundred years, probably. Broke off Castle Point long before my daddy used to take me fishing out on that lake. Sometimes it floats free, sometimes it takes up residence for a time, until another wind storm blows it off to a new locale."

"Dead Man's Float?" Kimberly divided store receipts into nonsensical piles and kept clipping them together with paper clips in nonsensical order.

"Don't know how it got that name. Funny, how things are named around here. Anyway, you okay? Heard from Cousins?"

"*Cousins?* Is this a joke?" She'd had enough of the sheriff's games. If he had something to say, he needed to come right out and say it.

"No, darlin', not at all. I just figured he'd be coming up here to see you, is all. I'm wondering if it isn't a little strange that he hasn't showed."

"He's got no business with me. We've got nothing to do with each other. I never want to see him again and I think I made that quite clear to him, and to you. I'm not expecting to see him up here. I don't want to see him up here, and if he comes up here, I will not see him."

The sheriff cocked his head and looked at her.

"Is that clear?"

"Yes indeedy, Miss Kimberly. You're doing okay, living out there by yourself?"

"Yes."

"And the store?"

"Fine."

"Keeping up with your, you know, your chores?"

"Okay." She threw down her receipts in angry exasperation. "*Okay!* Come and look. I'm sick of it. I'm sick of it all. I'm sick of the work, I'm sick of the worry, I'm sick of . . . I'm just fucking sick and tired of *it all!*" She grabbed her jacket and headed out the back door. "C'mon, then," she said to him, impatient, suddenly, to have the whole thing done with, get her butt in jail, and begin the rotting process. One of them was going to rot in jail. If it wasn't going to be Cousins, then it might as well be her.

The sheriff followed her out, then got into his own car and they proceeded the half mile to her little house. She left the car door open when she got out, and kicked off her high-heeled pumps halfway down the back lawn. She didn't even stop to take off her panty hose or worry about her expensive dress. She didn't look behind her to see if the sheriff was following. She just stomped down the lawn, stepped onto the island, and sloshed her way across it to the bog.

The sheriff was behind her, she could hear him.

The bog was empty. No body floating. No Cousins. No nothing, but the nice, long, straight piece of timber bamboo that had served her in this strange capacity since that first night.

"Almost forgot about this bog," Sheriff Withens said behind her. "It moved here with the island intact, eh? Odd stuff, that."

"He comes out of there every morning," Kimberly said.

"He? He who?"

"Cousins."

"Comes out of the bog?"

Kimberly nodded and then started to cry. "I poke him back under with that pole," she said, and then collapsed against his ample chest and began to sob.

The sheriff put big arms around her and held her for a long moment. "What if I took over that chore for the next week or so?"

"Huh?" She swiped at her runny nose.

"Let's you go into the house and get a nice cup of tea, Kimberly. I think I'll call Doctor Sanborn and see if he can come by to see you. Meanwhile, don't you come out here on this island until I tell you it's okay. I'll take care of poking Cousins back down under the bog."

She nodded. It didn't make any sense to her that the sheriff would help her hide the evidence of her murder, but what the hell. If he wanted to come out here and poke Cousins back down under every morning, it would be a big load off her shoulders.

She let the sheriff take her back home, and he put the teakettle on while she sat on the sofa and listened to him talk on the telephone to Dr. Sanborn's wife who agreed to have the doctor phone in a prescription. She felt such relief she could barely believe it. And she hadn't said a word about Natasha. She'd go to jail by herself for this crime. When the sheriff left, she'd call Natasha and tell her that she was going to prison. Taking Cousins' place.

But Natasha's line was busy, so Kimberly just went to bed.

In the morning, the sheriff's car pulled deep into the drive. He got out, wearing gum boots, opened the trunk and hauled a long bundle out, hoisted it on his shoulder, where it bent in a very convenient way, and then made his way down the lawn and onto the island. It was heavy, she could tell by the way he staggered under its weight.

She began to iron a blouse to wear to jail.

A half hour later, she heard the patrol car start up, and sure enough, Sheriff Withens drove off. She went to the shop and acted as if nothing was wrong.

The next morning was a repeat performance. And the next. And the next.

After about a week, the sheriff began to bring her a donut and coffee in the morning at the shop. She'd drink the coffee, and he'd eventually say, "You going to eat that?" eyeing the donut. She'd shake her head, and he'd take it off her hands.

They wouldn't say much, just stand around conspiratorially.

Another week went by, and every day the sheriff took a long wrapped bundle of something over his shoulder to the bog. And Kimberly began to relax.

And then there was another week of the sheriff's early morning visits to the bog, empty-handed. And then no more visits by the sheriff.

Until one evening, when the sun set late and the fireflies came winking around. Kimberly was sitting on the back porch enjoying a late cup of coffee when the patrol car pulled into the drive. He waved to her, then went on down the lawn and onto the island.

She waited.

Twenty minutes later, he was back, the bamboo pole in his hand.

"Coffee, Sheriff?" she asked once he got within range.

"Thanks, no, Miss Kimberly," he said. "It's too late. I'd be up all night." He leaned the pole next to the porch, then climbed the stairs and sat next to her. "Storm coming," he said. "Make sure you've got firewood and candles and fresh water."

She nodded.

"Fine pole," he said. "Where'd you get such a thing?"

She pointed at the tall greenhouse with her chin.

"I'll be damned," he said. "Well, it did the trick, that's for sure. I was running out of places to store them, if you know what I mean."

She didn't know, and she didn't ask.

"Guess I'll be going on home now. I'll bring you a donut now and then."

"That'd be nice, Sheriff."

The wind woke Kimberly at three-forty-six a.m. It was a strange wind out of the southeast. It rattled things in her house and greenhouse the way normal winds didn't, and when a dark dawn came and she finally got out of bed, Dead Man's Float was where it ought to be, out in the middle of the lake.

SKYTOUCH FEVER

Margie was just topping off Sadie Katherine's coffee cup when the bells on the diner door jangled and Margie whispered "uh-oh," softly so only Sadie Katherine could hear.

"Hmm?" she responded, not quite registering. It was the first of June, and Sadie Katherine always spent the first morning of the month in the diner, drinking Margie's strong coffee, eating something fresh-baked and reading the *Almanac* for the month. Sunspots were due, she discovered, and that might play havoc with the cisco spawn. Fish were superstitious by nature, and therefore easily frightened by irregular forces of nature they could feel but not see.

"Here he comes," Margie said, then tapped Sadie Katherine on the wrist.

"What?" But by the time she looked up, she knew just exactly what.

Kenneth Cale.

Their eyes locked and he came walking toward her, wearing his brand-new Eddie Bauer trendsetter outdoor clothes, looking like the million bucks he had in petty cash. His silvering hair was neatly trimmed, and his blue eyes sparkled under the brim of a pink Kitty Hawk ball cap. Kenneth could pull off wearing a pink ball cap, probably the only man Sadie Katherine knew who could. Or would.

"There you are," he said, and breathed mint across the table as he slid into the booth.

"Coffee?" Margie asked.

"Please," he said, without taking his eyes off Sadie Katherine's.

She felt her stomach tighten. She wanted Doc to be here with her while she talked with him.

"Doc told me I'd find you here."

"Oh?" Good. At least Doc knew Kenneth Cale was in town.

"You look better every year, Sadie Katherine."

"Thanks. You're looking mighty fit your ownself." She was amazed her tongue worked. Why did she get so dry-mouthed when she was around him? She was at least ten years older than he, not to mention literally rough around the edges with more calluses than he had domestic employees. Yet she resisted the impulse to pat her hair, check the corners of her eyes, look at her teeth in the reflection of the napkin holder. Good lord, she thought, aren't I old enough to be able to handle the likes of Kenneth Cale?

"I'm here to do some fishing," he said.

"Found yourself a guide yet?" Sadie Katherine almost bit her tongue as those traitorous words fell out of her mouth. This was the same game they'd played every year since the first time they laid eyes on each other, what . . . seven, eight years ago? And every year he hired her exclusively, and took all her time for two weeks. For which, of course, he paid well enough for her and Doc to go to Florida for a little bonefishing every year. But after last year, she swore she'd not guide him again. He was dangerous to her. Dangerous to her and Doc, and she had talked with Doc about it, and hoped that Kenneth wouldn't come back again this year. But here he was, and she was as helpless under his charms as she had been last year and the year before that. It was his eyes. The blue of his eyes. The deep, fathomless, sky blue that made Sadie Katherine crazy. Nobody else had eyes like that.

"There's only one guide for me."

Margie interrupted the strange intimacy he wove between them by slamming a coffee cup on the table and sloshing hot coffee into it, spilling some on the table and not bothering to clean it up.

Margie was Sadie Katherine's closest friend, and so of course she knew. And her contempt for the hopeful homewrecker spilled over into her professional duties.

Kenneth didn't even seem to notice.

Sadie Katherine gave Margie a thin-lipped smile of gratitude, then he sucked her attention back to his tanned face and those sky-blue eyes with the snowflakes that floated in them. They whispered promises to her. Promises of a different life of wealth and city lights, of society and manicured nails, of facials and gold jewelry. No, not really. Those were the promises that Margie and Doc thought she saw, and they were there all right, but Sadie Katherine thought she could have all that junk if she wanted it, and she wouldn't need Kenneth Cale to find it.

No, Kenneth Cale illustrated something far more insidious. Something blue, like his eyes. Something deep and precious, something longed for yet unrecognized. He activated a yearning in Sadie Katherine's soul that she didn't have when he wasn't around. Or if she did, she didn't know about it.

"Let's go fishing," he whispered, and, like an automaton, she slid out of the booth, stuck her *Almanac* into her black nylon backpack and followed him out of the diner, not daring to look back at Margie, whose intense and disapproving brown eyes stared holes in the small of her back.

Outside, the spell lessened, and Sadie Katherine was all business. She readied the tackle while he readied his gear. They walked down to the dock together, Kenneth with bundles, Sadie Katherine with buckets and poles, and they arranged them in the bottom of the boat in a dance they had done dozens of times before. "Fish won't be biting until late this afternoon," Sadie Katherine said, looking at the morning sun sparkling on the lake. She tested the pressure in her sinuses, looked at the way the birds flew over the water, looked at the ripples. "If at all. This isn't the type of weather that makes them bite. Tomorrow will be a better day."

"That's all right. I'm ready to get on the water," Kenneth said.

They got in the boat, Kenneth untied the line, Sadie Katherine started her little outboard and they motored out onto the lake. She knew exactly where the fish were this time of day, this time of year, and she'd be damned if she'd take him to them, even if they wouldn't take a second look at his stupid designer fishing line.

The summer heat would burn right through their clothes with no shade, but even though the heat came on with a vengeance, goose bumps kept rippling over Sadie Katherine's arms. She hunched in her shoulders, steering the boat by bumping the handle with her knee. She hit the kill switch as they reached the spot, and the boat settled into the silent water with a soft surge from its own wake.

Kenneth chose a pole and picked carefully through the tangle of barbed hooks in a white bucket. He held up a purple plastic worm and Sadie Katherine nodded at him, although she knew that no self-respecting fish would ever want to eat that. For some reason, she wanted to punish Kenneth. She wanted to hurt him, because she was afraid he was going to hurt her. She was afraid of him, and that made her angry. Her anger made her want to bite him.

Baits in the water, Sadie Katherine tried not to look at him, and they fished in what she hoped was companionable silence, but, inside, she was churning. She didn't want to be out here with him, didn't want to be alone with him, was mentally kicking herself for being so stupid to just come out here with him at the crook of his little finger.

At least Margie saw them leave the diner together. Boats were everywhere on the lake, people enjoying the summer by fishing, waterskiing, swimming. They were in public. And Doc knew they were together. Maybe Doc would close up the tackle shop, jump in his boat and motor on out to check on her. If he did, she might just tell Kenneth to find his own way home, step over into Doc's boat and go home with him, cook him a nice dinner, get naked, wrap herself around him and hold him tightly to her all night long.

"I've missed you," Kenneth said.

"I'm married."

"I'm sorry, I know you are, but I can't help my feelings."

She looked over at him, and he was tending his line, not looking at her. She knew the feeling. He was confessing his soul to the water, something she had done daily for years, only, in this instance, he made sure she was there to listen to him. It was easier to talk to someone if you didn't have to look at them. She let him talk, and vowed not to interrupt.

He continued. "I get home and look at my calendar and it's a whole blasted year before I can get back to see you and it makes me want to blow out my brains. I have a photograph of us on my desk, and every day I have to will my hand to not dial your phone number. Every day of my life is torture, just going through the motions until I can get back up here and be next to you in your little boat, fishing. Talking. Laughing. You understand me, Sadie Katherine, in a way that nobody ever has before."

There was a long pause, and Sadie Katherine squirmed in the silence like a worm in her bait can. "I'm married," she said again.

"The last thing I want to do is ruin your life. I can see you've got a life here, fishing, guiding, making a living with Doc in the shop. I don't know why I have to tell you all of this, but I just have to get it out in the open. It's blowing me apart."

"Once said, then, it doesn't need to be brought up again, is that right?" Sadie Katherine felt like he had transferred his explosive feelings to her gut, and she resented it.

The boat dipped under his weight shift, and then he touched her shoulder. Reflexively, she looked at him and there were those eyes. Blue like the depths of the sky.

"I look at you and I see you in silks and pearls. Gold jewelry and diamonds on your fingers." He picked up her left hand and they both looked at it. Weathered and slightly spotted, it was the hand of a rugged, sixty-year-old outdoorswoman, not the pampered hand of a society lady. The nails were trimmed close, but they were ridged and unpolished, and there were scars and scabs from fish teeth, fishhooks, fish knives and recalcitrant boat gear.

She looked at that hand and envisioned it with long, painted nails and diamonds instead of Doc's plain gold band. Instead of the threadbare denim at her wrist that partially covered her steel Swiss Army watch, she thought of a sky-blue silk sleeve that gently caressed a slim gold watch. She'd have her hair professionally colored, instead of letting it grow gray and cropped short at her ears. She'd wear earrings, and makeup, and slacks and drive a Mercedes instead of Doc's old truck. She'd have facials and massages.

But where? New York. Ugh. No fish, no trees, no country. No friendly dogs running loose, no cats and raccoons hanging around the fish-cleaning shed. No steady seasonal customers, no Margie, no Uncle Bun, none of the community she had enjoyed here for so many years. Sixty was too old to make another new start—she didn't even know what language they spoke in New York.

And what about Doc?

"What about Doc?" She couldn't believe those words came out into the open.

Kenneth took those words as a finger hold and began to work them. "I don't know about Doc," he said. "It would be a terrible thing to hurt him, but everybody has to follow their bliss, Sadie Katherine. You are mine, and my world is a good one. It lacks only one thing, and that's you."

She turned from him and reeled in her line. "I have a good life right here."

"I know you do, and that's one of the most attractive things about you. You're not running from anything. You have the ability to be satisfied wherever you are."

That's a laugh, she thought. "Don't assume that. You don't know my history."

"And I don't care. You're the woman for me. I knew it the moment I laid eyes on you and there isn't anything anyone can do or say to make me change my mind."

He touched her again, and, despite her will, she turned to look at him. The shadow from the brim of his ball cap took the power from his eyes.

"I can go away. Say the word and I will never darken your threshold again. But before you do, please give me the courtesy of thinking about it overnight."

Sadie Katherine brought in her lure, hooked it to an eye on the pole and reached for the small motor. Kenneth went back to his rig, slowly reeled in the line, and, just as the bait was at the side of the boat, a small crappie grabbed it.

"Hey, look at this," he said as he held it up, dangling and wiggling on the end of his line.

Sadie Katherine smiled at him, but there was no joy for either of them in a harmless, previously happy creature falling for a temptation. Not today. She knew it and he knew it. He unhooked it and threw it back, then sat down.

She started the motor and headed back for shore.

Doc had the barbecue fired up and steaks on when she pulled in to the driveway. Aluminum foiled potatoes were in a three-roll pyramid on a plate and a tossed salad with butchered tomatoes were in her favorite salad bowl on the picnic table. "Hey!" he said, barbecue fork in his hand.

"Hey," she said, and went in to wash her hands. He knew. Doc knew Kenneth was in town, and he was afraid. That she had the power to make Doc afraid made her mad, or sad, or something, but she had nothing to say to him that would put his mind at ease. She had to think about it overnight. And the more she thought about it, the more she didn't like what she was thinking.

She looked at her face in the mirror. Her eyes were too big, her lips and mouth were too big, her narrow face had too many spots and scars and wrinkles. She had no idea what Kenneth saw in her. She looked like an old fish. She looked like she belonged with Doc, an old fisherman, a rustic soul who knew water and knew himself and just wanted to live a clean, clear life with his tackle shop and his woman.

But now he lived with fear, and she couldn't help him. She wished she could. She wished she could walk out there and put her arms around him and say, "Don't worry, Doc. I'm yours and you're mine and that's all there is to that." But she couldn't.

"Damn you," she said to her reflection, then went out, with a fist twisting her gut, to pretend to eat the meal he had prepared.

"Have a good day?" he said, then speared a nice, perfectly seared porterhouse and put it on a plate.

"Sunspots coming on the eighteenth," she said, and shook the bottle of A.1. A gust of wind came up and blew leaves across the yard. She shivered.

"Let's go inside," he said. "I thought we could get a meal in out here before the wind came up, but I guess it was just wishful thinking."

They each grabbed plates and dishes, and recreated the table setting in the little dining room that looked out through sliding glass doors to the picnic table, the smoking grill and the Leppens' backyard. Doc went back out for his steak while Sadie Katherine poured them both ice water and put on the coffeepot. When he came back in, she ripped a couple of paper towels from the roll, handed him one, and they sat down to eat. "How was your day?"

"Good. Lots of fishermen in town. Heard tell of a forty-four-inch muskie caught on Dupont."

Sadie Katherine nodded and sliced open her baked potato. She had no appetite. She wanted to leave the table and go for a walk or something, but she knew that would scare Doc even more, so she stayed put and tried to eat.

"Do some guiding today?" he asked.

She nodded, chewing salad, then salted her potato.

"I was thinking come Thanksgiving, if the lake's froze up, we could go somewhere warm this year. Florida maybe, or the Bahamas."

"That'd be nice," she said, and felt tears pushing against her eyes and a hot ball of emotion stuck in the back of her throat that wouldn't let her swallow the food in her mouth. She gulped it down with some water, then cut out the bone from her steak. "I'm going to give this to Cane," she said, and got up from the table. She knew her attitude, actions and talk seared Doc just as good as if she'd laid him on the grill, but she couldn't help it. She couldn't sit across and make small talk while so much was going on in her mind, and it wasn't all about Kenneth.

Yes it was, it was all about Kenneth, about the things he made her think about. Long for. Remember. Oh god, she wished he had never come up to White Pines Junction looking for some fishing action. She'd give about anything to go back to the peaceful life she and Doc had before he butted in.

She stood on the front porch and whistled for Cane. Little gusts blew leaves in swirls across the lawn and around the front end of the truck. The fluffy white Samoyed didn't take long to come from wherever he was and run up to her, all bright-eyed smiles and happy curly tail. He took the bone from her hand as gentle as possible and ran off to chew it in private. "Life's so simple for you, isn't it?" she asked as she watched him plop on the grass and begin to gnaw.

Sadie Katherine remembered when life had been simple for her, too.

The door behind her opened and closed and then Doc's hands were on her shoulders. She loved the feel of them, big square fingers that knew their way around delicate little knots in two-pound-test line as well as a hardworking chainsaw, as well as all her body's pleasure points. "Stay with me, Sadie Katherine. Please," he whispered in her ear and one tear found release from the burning emotion, skipped down her cheek and fell to the porch. She didn't speak, her silence thunderous, and soon she felt a kiss on the top of her head, then the hands were gone and the door behind her opened and closed again.

Oh god, it hurt so much. Life hurt, it hurt so badly she didn't know if she could endure it. She wished she had known about the cramping pain in the gut that could come from just living.

She gripped the weathered railing and felt the rough wood dig into her hands. What if she had known about this traitorous human emotion? Would she have made a different decision? Would she have forfeited this feeling of wood in her hands because decisions might hurt her? Would she deny herself the warmth of Doc in their bed, his big arm around her, holding her close as he snored? Would she give up, even once, the happiness in her heart when he smiled at her across the breakfast table as the sunrise pinked the sky?

No, she had made those choices, and they had been good ones. Perfect ones. Happy ones. Satisfying, fulfilling, normal choices.

Could she trust herself to continue to make reasonable choices?

She had to. She had no one else to trust, given her history.

Doc was clearing the table when she came back in. "Think I'll go on to bed," she said.

"I've got some bookwork to do, and then I'll join you," he said without looking at her.

Sadie Katherine wondered if she had already made her decision. Otherwise, she'd be comforting him. The fact that he wasn't pressing her made her love him even more. Made her ache for him even more.

She slid out of her clothes that felt too big, and stepped into the shower, turning the water on hot and full force. She liked how it started out startlingly frigid, and then gradually warmed up to the point where she had to add cold to mix in. She liked the extreme in temperatures. She soaped up, loving the slippery feeling of the soap on her skin, taking particular care to notice every motion of her hands, her fingers, as they manipulated the washcloth, and she was alive to the sensations of the water and the soap and the air. And afterward, the cold breeze when she opened the shower door to get the towel. And then the towel on her skin, and the comb through her hair, and the look in her eyes that didn't look like the eyes of any human she had ever encountered.

Doc was downstairs a long time, and when he came in, he wore a T-shirt and boxers to bed.

"Make love to me," Sadie Katherine said, and tugged gently on his T-shirt.

"I don't know that I can," he said.

She kissed him gently. "Please?"

He snorted a sigh that sounded part frustration, part resignation, part inadequacy of words, but she ran her fingers up his strong, hairy arm and lightly skidded them over the tough beard on his jawline. "I know you're—"

"Shhh," she said, and lifted up on an elbow to kiss him.

One of those big hands, those marvelous hands, slid around her waist and pulled her to him as he turned over on his side. He kissed the hollow of her throat, and she closed her eyes and luxuriated in every sensation.

Pay attention, she thought to herself. Be present every moment and listen to the music.

And as symphonies have moved people to tears for as long as there have been symphonies, Sadie Katherine was crying by the time Doc entered her and she felt that completing fullness only a woman can experience. She let the tears flow, and they moved together in rhythm and harmony. When it was over, she mourned for the loss of it, but all good things eventually come to an end.

All good things eventually come to an end.

She would have talked with Doc about it then, when they had disengaged and disentangled, but he cupped one of her breasts in his big hand and began to softly snore.

Remember this, she thought, not only the physical sensation, but the feeling of warmth, and safety, and love.

But then, all good things eventually come to an end.

When the gibbous moon shone through the bedroom window, Doc turned away from her, snoring the deep sleep of the unencumbered.

Sadie Katherine slipped out of bed and into jeans and a sweater. She carried her shoes to the front porch, where Cane thumped his big tail in greeting. She tangled her fingers in his thick fur and smelled deeply of the salty scent of him, then put on her shoes. "C'mon, boy, let's go for a walk," she whispered.

They walked together through the silent town, shrouded in a light low fog and overseen by millions of stars. They walked past the diner, and Sadie Katherine felt a twinge for Margie. They walked past the motel, and she felt a sadness for Mort and Natasha, and for Kenneth Cale, their guest.

This was a community filled to the brim with longing and grief.

Was that a fact of the human condition?

She and Cane got to the boat launch, and Sadie Katherine swept mayflies from the picnic table in front of the fish-cleaning shed, sat down on it and looked out over the water, silvery in the moonlight. Cane jumped up and sat next to her. She stroked his soft foot.

"The longing is back," she whispered to him. "I thought I had escaped it. I yearned for so many years to touch the blue of the sky that I actually did it. I've been doing it, Cane, for years now, and it has been wonderful, but now it's not enough. It's back, that horrible longing. It's the blue in his eyes. They're the same color as the sky, and I can't stand that."

Cane lay down and put his head on her knee as if he understood. She scratched the top of his head and fingered the soft fur of his thick, standup ears.

"I can't live with this longing and I can't hurt Doc." With the words came the emotion, full-bodied and forceful. Sobs shuddered through her, and in the middle of the horrible pain, she managed to remember to feel it completely.

She even heard the echoes of her pain as it flew across the water and back again.

"I don't even know what I'm longing for," she cried, and buried her face in the dog's fur. He stayed still and calm as if he understood her need. When the sobbing subsided, she wiped the tears from her face with the back of her hand, wiped them across her lips and tasted the saltiness. Remember that, she thought. "I just know that when the longing starts, it doesn't stop. If I have to live with it, I'll have to do it where I won't hurt anybody else. I certainly can't make Doc live with it." She took a deep, ragged breath.

Doc. The feel of his lovemaking was still fresh on her skin, and her heart turned over and lay on its side when she thought of him waking up in the morning alone. "I wonder if I'll remember him the same way he'll remember me," she said.

She stood up and walked down the boat ramp to the water's edge, then lifted the sweater up over her head. She took off her shoes, and then her jeans, folded everything neatly and placed it in the middle of the rough concrete ramp.

"Good-bye, boy," she said to Cane. "Tell Doc to catch and release."

Then she walked into the water, fighting the panic as the cold liquid closed over her head.

She looked up through the greenish haze and saw the moon, then felt her kin swarm around her in curiosity. Her memories faded as her gills opened and she breathed deeply, gasping. Then she darted deep down into the seaweed where she had been spawned. She waited quietly for the daylight and the clear, ringing blue that she both loved and feared.

And longed to touch.

THE NORTHERN AIRE
MOTEL

Cook took care of the business of registering them while Missie examined the lobby. It was a big log lodge, just like in the movies.

She, of course, thought immediately of cobwebs on those log beams twenty feet in the air, and wondered how they were dusted, but she couldn't see anything from the lobby floor, so she stopped looking for flaws. The place was neat and clean, and well tended, though the woman that Cook was talking to looked as though she were well into her eighties.

The pine front desk had a deer in a forest carved into its front and was topped by a dark green Formica countertop. Next to it was a card stand with picture postcards of the north woods. Missie picked up a nice one of a lake at sunset, and on the back was red-stamped, *Northern Aire Motel, White Pines Junction.* They were all stamped like that. The carpeting was a fairly new forest green with a dark viney theme running through it that matched the countertop and was pleasing to the eye. Nice antique furniture in the lobby, with exquisitely shaded lamps. A pair of old leaded-glass French doors led to a small dining room. She wandered in.

A sign on the wall said, "Continental Breakfast 6-9am - Dream Report 8-9am - Coffee pot on all day - Box lunches available with 24 hr notice."

Inside the dining room were eight or ten tables with chairs, a tall coffee pot that did indeed have its indicator light on and a stack of Styrofoam cups.

Missie poured two cups full and wandered back to see how Cook was faring with the old lady.

"This is my wife, Missie," Cook said, and put his arm around her.

"Marjorie Atkisson," the woman said, and extended a frail hand over the counter. Missie set the coffee down and reached for her hand. Just before making contact, the old woman said, "Now don't squeeze." Missie thought that she could probably break every bone in the frail woman's hand with a good handshake. So they touched skin and it felt nice, that light handshake. She smiled into the woman's sharp blue eyes, and the woman smiled back, a radiant smile.

"Mrs. Atkisson owns the Northern Aire," Cook said.

"It's wonderful," Missie said.

"My family bought it in 1947 for forty-seven thousand dollars," Mrs. Atkisson said. "It's been through good times and bad times, but we all love it here. My son and grandson come up with me every summer to help." She handed Cook a key. "Your cabin is on the lake. Everything you need should be there. There's a little store in White Pines Junction, but a nicer supermarket about fifteen miles south. If you need anything, don't be afraid to ask."

"Are you busy?" Missie asked.

"The season is winding down. Everybody will be gone after Labor Day. We have twelve cabins. One has a young family; I put them at the other end of the resort, so you won't be bothered by the kids. The rest are couples, or fishermen. Two other parties will check out today. That's all for another week."

"We lucked out, honey," Cook said, and gave her shoulder a squeeze. "We just saw your sign on the highway."

"Things work out the way they're supposed to," Mrs. Atkisson said. "Always."

Missie put her arm around Cook's waist. "Did Cook tell you we're on our honeymoon?"

"No!" That smile again. Mrs. Atkisson had a beautiful smile, and with it came a twinkle to the eye. "Congratulations. The cabin on the lake is very private, and very romantic. I think you'll enjoy yourselves." She laughed. "Of course you'll enjoy yourselves. We've got boats. Row her across the lake some evening, Cook. Just because she married you doesn't mean you can stop romancing her."

Missie liked this woman. She might come up and spend some time with her. Have a cup of tea. Get to know her a little bit.

Missie walked down to the cabin with the key while Cook brought the car around. There were cobwebs on the doorframe, that's for sure, with old leaves and dead mayflies caught in them. She fitted the key and the deadbolt turned back smoothly.

The door opened into the epitome of an old, backwoods cabin. Missie felt as though she had stepped back into time. It was built of whole logs, as was the lodge, and filled with antiques, but there was no new Formica here. The carpeting was old, the framed prints on the walls were faded, the couch had definitely seen better days. Missie felt as though she knew about the hard times Mrs. Atkisson had gone through, just by looking at the interior of this cabin, and when contrasted with the remodeled loveliness of the lodge, she felt as though she knew about Mrs. Atkisson's hard-won prosperity as well.

This cabin was exactly the type of atmosphere she had hoped for. It was old, but it had charm. Character. Ambiance.

"Wow, look at this place," Cook said as he banged through the screen door with two suitcases.

"Isn't it great?"

He dropped the bags and went right to the front window that opened out onto a perfect, unobstructed view of the lake at sunset. "Let's move in here for good."

Missie wrapped her arms around his waist from behind. "Okay," she said. "Mrs. Atkisson could probably use the company. And the help. But first, let's unpack and make a fire."

Cook turned and gave her one of those hugs that cracked her back and lifted her an inch off her feet. She loved it when he did that. Then he was back into the car for the rest of their stuff and the cooler.

After Missie hung their clothes in the tiny closet upon hangers she had to untangle, and put their underwear in the magnificent old dressers, and unpacked their travel kits in the bathroom that was obviously an add-on, and not very well done, she popped the thawing pizza in the gas oven and came into the living room where Cook had lit the candles they'd brought and had a fire blazing. He was drinking a glass of white wine, sitting on a couch cushion that he'd pulled to the floor. Her glass rested on the mantel.

She knelt behind him and rubbed the back of his neck. "Good driving today," she said.

"Good navigating," he responded. "God, that feels good."

"Pizza in twenty minutes."

"Hmmm . . . time for. . . ."

"No," she said. "Twenty minutes, Cook. I need more time than that. I want more time than that. It's my honeymoon. I *get* more time than that."

He laughed, his teeth flashing, his dark hair sparkling in the firelight. Fire looks good on him, Missie thought. Everything looks good on him. She snaked around into his lap and they sat together, happily silent, watching the flames.

"Wife," he whispered into her hair, the concept new to both of them. She nodded. It was good.

They ate the pizza and drank the whole bottle of wine sitting in front of the fire, listening to the loons call to each other from across the lake, and rehashed all the funny things that happened at the wedding. Missie got a little giddy from the wine, but she knew it was all right. They were safely ensconced for the night, she was on her honeymoon, she was with the man she loved— her husband—and a few glasses of a nice Chablis to get tipsy was just fine indeed.

Eventually, of course, he led her to the bed that was too springy, but had a wonderfully soft down comforter, and he undressed her slowly with great tenderness and kissed all the places her underwear rubbed and then they made love to each other with excruciating tenderness.

Wrapped up in his arms, his snoring soft in her ear, Missie slept.

"I had the weirdest dream last night," Missie said as she spread apricot jam on his breakfast toast.

"Me, too," Cook said. "I dreamed the weather report."

"Weather report?" Missie looked out at the cloudless sky over the lake. Cook had moved a small table to the front window so they could eat with the view of the steam rising up off the lake and the quiet silhouette of the fishermen drifting in silent boats. "That is weird."

"Yeah. I usually dream the business news."

"You're kind of spooky, you know. What was the weather?"

Cook closed his eyes and pretended to remember. Sometimes Missie didn't know if he was kidding or not. "High pressure system moving in. Clear skies, high seventies to low eighties. Good golfing weather every day for the foreseeable future."

Missie wished she had dreams like that. She put the toast on his plate, shook out vitamins for both of them and let the high mood prevail.

At least she tried.

True to the elusive nature of dreams, by noon she could no longer remember the details, only the tenor of the dream.

Residue stained the back of her consciousness with the dark feeling that had come over her as she slept.

She and Cook played eighteen holes on a course with wildlife hazards. One fairway had geese, another fairway had ducks, one water feature sported a great blue heron they both thought was a statue until it took a step, and they saw a porcupine and a deer at the edge of the woods. It seemed as though the whole northwoods knew they were on their honeymoon and came out to congratulate them on their superb choices in mates. At least that's what she told Cook.

Somewhere on the sixteenth hole, they decided to fish the evening away.

After getting back to the cabin, showering and relaxing for a few minutes, Missie walked up to the lodge to arrange for the rowboat and to see if Mrs. Atkisson had any fishing tackle they could use.

"Oh, well," she said. "There's a tackle box, but I haven't looked inside it for years. It's right there in the boathouse. I'm afraid you'll have to take what you get. There should be a couple of poles in there, too, though I can't guarantee anything."

"That's okay," Missie said. "I don't really want to catch anything. It would scare them. It would scare me."

"They pull some mighty big fish out of this lake every year."

Missie shivered. "Maybe I won't even put a hook on. I'll just tie a worm to the end of the line and the fish can have it."

Mrs. Atkisson nodded. "That's my kind of fishing. How are you finding the cabin? Have everything you need? Are you warm enough?"

"Everything is fine, just fine," Missie said, that dream fading further into her memory, leaving her only the vaguest sense of something that she wanted to talk to somebody about, but she couldn't remember what or who.

"Don't forget we have breakfast here every morning. I know

you're on your honeymoon, but you don't have to worry about fixing him breakfast. You could sleep in an extra half hour." That twinkle again.

"Thanks," Missie said, resolved again to go back there when Cook was otherwise occupied, and spend some time making good girl talk with Mrs. Atkisson. Missie was certain Mrs. Atkisson would be full of fun information as well as excellent insights about relationships and how to forge a good marriage. But for now, she needed to report her findings about the fishing tackle and let Cook rig something up for them.

Neither had any luck at fishing, but they had fun. Being in a rowboat just in itself was fun, Missie discovered, as they took turns rowing so the other could troll some pretty pitiful-looking lures with rusty hooks. No self-respecting fish would bite anything they had to offer. But after golf and rowing, they were both ready to pack it in for the day.

Missie microwaved burritos, which they washed down with a couple of beers, then went to bed with a big bowl of popcorn.

Cook was asleep before he'd had his second handful.

Missie discovered she wanted to put sleep off as long as possible, to be as tired as possible, to perhaps sleep dreamlessly the night through.

But the time of reckoning was at hand, so she put the popcorn bowl on the floor, turned out the light, snuggled up to Cook's back, and succumbed to her exhaustion.

Wildflowers. Wildflowers everywhere. Beautiful, extravagant wildflowers with music to them, not just color and scent. She reveled in the magic of them, until she missed Cook. This was no fun without him. He'd love these flowers. They must be peculiar to the northwoods. Or maybe to honeymooners. She wanted to share the joy.

"Missie?"

"Cook, you goof, get down before you fall down. What are

you doing up there?"

"I'm stuck, I think," he said from the top of the tree. "I can't come down."

"You're scaring me, Cook." Something was pulling on Missie. She had to go, but she didn't want to leave him. "I've got to go."

"Go ahead. I'll catch up."

"No, come with me now." She had to leave, time was running out. "Come down, come with me now." She felt like she was going to lose him if he didn't come with her.

"Go on," he said with an exasperated grunt of exertion. "Go."

Missie turned and ran, tears flying out of her eyes, down her cheeks and into the wind behind her. She ran and ran, but seemed to make no headway. When she turned, she could still see Cook, stuck at the top of that tree. "I just found you," she said out loud.

"I just found you," she said out loud and woke herself up.

"Hmmm?" Cook turned over in the bed and his big hand found her hip and began rubbing it lightly, down the small of her back and up along her backbone. He didn't wake up. He didn't have to wake up to know that she was in distress and needed comforting.

Missie would never leave him behind. Never.

"Newlywed jitters," Cook proclaimed over his Grape Nuts. "It's an adjustment, Missie, marriage is. We're both a little tweaked by it. It's okay. The dreams will stop once we're settled in together. That wedding was a big deal. And now we're honeymooning, and when we get home, we'll have to move all your stuff into my place. Then we'll be settled, and life will go on until we get into a rut and you'll throw me out because I'm too boring."

She tapped his knuckle with her spoon. "That'll never happen." She wondered if he was right about that. Stress triggers nightmares. And migraines are prone to happen right after the stressful situation has resolved itself. Letdown syndrome, she thought it was called. Maybe that's all this is. "I just found you," she whispered. "I don't want to lose you."

"I ain't going anywhere," he said. "Except maybe hiking. There's a trail up into the woods. Let's go roll around in some poison ivy."

They spent the morning hiking, then stopped at a store for some fresh supplies. Cook grabbed a few handfuls of fresh lures to leave in Mrs. Atkisson's tackle box, and when they got back to the resort, Cook took a nap. Missie read for a while, and watched the lake, reluctant to sleep. Eventually, she wandered outside and into the sunshine.

Mrs. Atkisson was down on the dock, eating an apple.

"May I join you?"

"Missie! Please. Sit down. I was just hoping for somebody to come share this sunshine with. Isn't it exquisite?"

The lake was perfectly calm in the late afternoon. A couple of mother ducks trailing their babies hugged the shore. Missie took off her shoes, rolled up her pant legs and joined Mrs. Atkisson on the end of the dock. The water felt delightfully fresh yet warm on her feet. "You find time to come down here and enjoy your own resort," Missie said.

"Not easy. It gets very busy during the middle of the season. But if I can't enjoy it, I won't come anymore. How was your fishing excursion?"

"The fish were pretty safe, all things considered. Not so my rowing muscles. Seems the only things I'm good at catching are nightmares."

"Oh? You're having bad dreams?"

"Cook says it's newlywed jitters."

"Could be," said Mrs. Atkisson. She wrapped her apple core

up in a blue napkin and put it in her pocket. "Come to the lodge tomorrow morning at eight." She stood up and slipped into her sandals. She touched Missie on the shoulder. "We have dream reports over coffee. Sometimes they help."

Missie remembered seeing the sign. They really did hold dream reports. How odd. How so very odd. "Like interpretations?" she asked Mrs. Atkisson who was walking down the dock toward the shore.

"No," she called back. "Not exactly. Just come."

In the morning, Missie left Cook sleeping. She slipped out of bed, feeling sneaky and as if she were betraying him by keeping secrets. But the dream from the night before still held her in its grip, and if she could pry it loose by confessing it at the lodge, she'd definitely sneak out of her honeymoon bed to do it.

"Missie, I can't feel my feet," Cook had said in the dream. "I can't move my legs, Missie, I can't move my legs," all the while she's standing in a glorious field of flowers.

The worst part was that she knew she could just walk away. She could leave him there, pretend that she didn't know what happened to him, and start a new life. Ignore the situation and it would go away. "Cook?" she could say to her friends with feigned innocence. "I don't know. We grew apart, I guess. One day he just didn't come home." It would be easy. He was stuck in a tree and couldn't get down. She could waste her life trying to help him, or she could just go.

And then that thing pulled on her again. It was consciousness, she knew now, she was waking up, and she had to leave him there in the dream.

"Missie, I can't feel my feet." She could still hear him say that as she walked up the hill through a light rainfall to the lodge, and chills scraped her spine. She wanted to exorcise this sleep demon at this meeting and get back there, crawl into bed with her warm and sleepy husband and resume their honeymoon.

Mrs. Atkisson motioned for her to come in and sit down. She sat at a small table in the lodge dining room. A man and a woman sat at different tables and the man was speaking.

"Look at your hands. I think Carlos Castaneda said much the same thing in his Don Juan books, so I've been trying to do that, but I'm not very good at it. I get caught up in the drama of the dream and don't remember that I'm supposed to do something."

The woman spoke up as Missie poured herself a cup of coffee. "I read an article in *National Geographic* about dream research and how the researchers can contact the conscious mind of the sleeping person and help them control their dreams."

"That doesn't sound like *National Geographic* to me," the man said, clearly irritated with the whole business.

"Well, maybe it wasn't, but it was some magazine of repute," the woman said. "I remember they said that the signal for the dreamer to report to the researcher that they were back in control of their dream was that they clicked their eyes to the right three times."

"I don't know what good that does me," the man said. "There's no researcher here. Just this dream I need that I don't seem to be able to have." He sipped his coffee.

"This is Missie," Mrs. Atkisson said. "Missie and her new husband are staying with us for a while."

"Hi," the woman said. She was in her mid-thirties, Missie guessed, with hair dyed too dark for her age. It made her face look old. "I'm Canasta."

"George," the man mumbled. He was older, with multiple chins and a vein-sprocketed nose.

"Last night I dreamed a still life," Canasta said. "Apples and oranges and bananas and grapes all overflowing an ornate bowl on a table covered with purple velvet. That's all there was to the dream, except that it was somehow sacred, and not to be touched. What do you suppose that means?" She searched the faces of the others present, but nobody had a comment.

Missie was afraid that she either missed the point or misunderstood what was going on.

"I dreamed my husband was stuck in a tree," she said, and everybody laughed. Tears sprang up in her eyes as she heard their laughter. "This isn't funny. It's the second, no, the third, no, I don't know, anyway, I've been having this dream, and I have to leave him there, because . . ."—the words caught in her throat—"because I don't want to deal with it, I guess, and I could. I could leave him there and nobody would know."

Canasta nodded knowingly, and Missie wondered what the hell she thought she knew.

"He said, 'Missie, help me, I can't feel my feet.' " Missie's heart broke and along with it came the flood of tears.

Mrs. Atkisson handed her a tissue. "I dreamed of fire," she said. "An innkeeper's constant fear."

"We done, then?" George asked as he pushed his bulk up out of the chair.

Canasta crumpled her coffee cup and threw it into the trash, and the two of them left, Canasta touching Missie's shoulder on her way out.

A moment later, Missie looked up and she was alone. She wiped her eyes, blew her nose, put the tissue into the coffee and threw it all away. This had been a complete waste of time.

She walked back down to the cabin, through a harder, colder rain that soaked her through to her skin, undressed in the main room and slid naked and cold into bed next to her warm husband, who welcomed the coolness of her skin next to his in a very real and animated way.

Not a good day for the outdoors, they spent the day poking around in antique malls and tourist shops, looking at this and at that, learning each others' taste in everything. They laughed and hugged and spontaneously kissed, and told each other how much in love they were. They ran through the rain from place to place and lunched in a dark corner of an old pub where they held hands and tried to talk dirty to each other, but kept laughing instead.

Canasta was having lunch on the other side of the room with a man who looked to be her husband and three active, but well-behaved children. The adults were intent on a conversation and didn't see Missie, but what was most amazing was that on a shelf directly above them was a bowl of wax or plastic fruit in an ornate bowl sitting on a purple velvet drape. Ordinarily, Missie would never have noticed it. It was one of those well-conceived design elements that in itself was startling, yet went so well with the rest of the decor that all one got was an overall atmospheric impression, without noticing the individual items themselves.

Missie wanted to bring Canasta's attention to it, but then Cook made her laugh again, and the next time she remembered, Canasta and her family were gone.

They went back to the cabin and lazed the day away, Cook sleeping most of the late afternoon while Missie read, and then after dinner, they found an old dusty Chinese checkers game, and Missie whipped Cook's butt.

They made love after that, and Cook dropped immediately to sleep, leaving Missie alone to think about trying to control her dreams. Maybe she could remember to look at her hands, or take control and click her eyes three times to the right. But then what?

She didn't know. She just knew that she didn't want that same dream, because it made her feel so awful about herself. It made her feel dishonest. Worse than that, it made her question the commitment she had just made to Cook.

Overly tired, more from worrying than anything else, she dropped into a hazy sleep and stood instantly in the garden of flowers.

"Cook?"

"Up here," he said, and there he was, up in the tree.

"You have to come down. I can't do this anymore."

"I can't, Missie, I'm rooted."

She saw for the first time that he wasn't up in any tree, he had become the tree, or the tree was becoming him, or something. He was stuck, and she could see that it wasn't his fault. It wasn't his fault, it wasn't her fault, it was nobody's fault. She still had legs; she could walk away.

"Stay with me."

She looked around the landscape and saw the glorious flowers, the stumpy trees that surrounded Cook, the solitude and aloneness. If she stayed, she might as well be rooted too, and she wasn't.

"I don't want you to be here," she said. "This isn't how it's supposed to be."

"But this is the way it is. Come sit and talk."

"I don't know."

"Please don't leave me."

"I'm not rooted."

"I didn't ask for this."

"I'm sure you didn't," she said, and that cheating feeling, that failing feeling, that horrible feeling of cut-and-run-when-the-going-gets-tough feeling came over her again, and she knew deep in her heart that she was a loser. "You're better off without me, Cook."

"Oh god, Missie, please don't say that. Don't leave me now, not here, not like this."

Then she was blinded by her tears, and she turned and ran toward that which had begun to pull on her. She could hear him calling, "Missie. Missie, I can't feel my feet."

"Missie, Missie, wake up." It was Cook shaking her shoulder, and Missie came to consciousness in the cabin's bed with a heaving sob.

"Missie, I can't feel my feet," he said.

A whole team of specialists couldn't figure it out. Cook saw doctor after doctor, in clinic after clinic, city after city, and they all took more X rays and more blood and more scans, and conferred with each other while inch by inch, the numbness and paralysis crept up Cook's legs.

One long, sleepless night, while Missie sat in the uncomfortable chair next to Cook's hospital bed, she remembered the fruit bowl dream and the woman who took her name from a card game. Then she remembered the fat man who said he had something he couldn't manage to dream, or something like that.

She had dreamt Cook's woodenness before he got it. Was it a premonition? Or did her dream cause his paralysis?

She reached over and picked up the telephone and, with a series of calling-card transactions, got the number for the Northern Aire Motel. Missie knew it was five a.m. in the north-woods, but she didn't care.

"Hello?"

"Mrs. Atkisson, it's Missie."

"Missie, hello. How's Cook?"

"Not good, in fact"—she covered the mouthpiece with her

hand and turned away from the hospital bed—"he's getting worse."

"Oh, dear."

"Mrs. Atkisson, when we were there, I dreamed this."

"Oh?"

"I have a feeling that other people dream things at your place that come true. Is that right? Is this reversible? Did I cause it by dreaming it?"

"Oh, Missie, I don't know about any of that. Some say that this is a dream power place, and certainly enough of my business comes from those believers. But I don't know. I'm sure you didn't cause Cook's problem with a dream."

"Can I dream him well?"

"I don't know, dear. You could come try. Many do, but dreams are elusive and illusionary, and they don't necessarily conform to what you want, you know."

"You mean I could make it worse?"

"I don't know, Missie."

Missie looked at Cook on the bed and remembered the doctor's prognosis. When the paralysis reached his chest, he'd need a respirator. When it reached his heart . . . who knew? "It's worth a try. Do you have room?"

"Of course. You can stay with me in the lodge if nothing else."

Missie hung up, and by this time she was crying. She had so little time to do such a grand thing. Next she called Cook's parents and told them that she had to leave. His mother was aghast. Missie tried not to listen to the accusatory tone in her voice. Missie wasn't leaving him, she was trying to save him, but there was no making his mother see that. She didn't understand. She couldn't understand. But she agreed to come stay with Cook while Missie went back north.

Two hurdles down. Next: Cook.

The hospital was beginning to wake up, and Missie sat in her chair and looked at her pale husband, trying to figure out how to tell him what she was about to do. She hadn't told him about the dreams to begin with; how could she expect him to understand?

She couldn't expect, she could only hope that he trusted her enough to do what she had to do. The doctors weren't saving him. This might be a voodoo thing, but maybe it was her only chance.

He woke, and she helped him to wash and shave, and then sat with him while he had breakfast. When the doctor was due for his rounds, she kissed Cook's cheek and told him she'd be back, and then she scurried to the library and checked out everything she could on dream research.

It wasn't *National Geographic,* it had been *Scientific American,* and there was an article in there on dream research. The subjects could actually control their dreams with the help of a guide, and the sleeping person communicated with the guide by eyeball movements.

She wondered if Mrs. Atkisson would be her guide.

When she got back to the hospital, books in hand, Cook was reading the Sunday comics.

"Hi, baby," she said. She set her books and magazines on the floor and sat down on the bed next to him.

"I'm dying, Miss," he said. "I can't feel my butt."

"It's moving faster? Then I've got to hurry. I've got an idea for something I want to try." She picked up the *Scientific American* and showed him the article. He seemed to have no interest. "I dreamed this was going to happen to you, Cook, I dreamed you were turning into a tree, merging with it, putting down roots. I dreamed this when we were on our honeymoon up north. Now I find out that that's some kind of a dream power place, and things that people dream up there tend to come true. I don't know if my dream caused this or if I just had a premonition of it, but I've talked with Mrs. Atkisson, and I'm going back up there today to try to fix it. I'm going to try to dream you well, honey."

"You're going back up there?"

Missie nodded.

"When?"

"Right now. I don't think we have any time to lose."

"You're leaving me?"

Oh god, this was harder than she thought it would be. "I'm going to try to save you, Cook."

"By going on vacation? By skipping out on me while my chest becomes paralyzed and I either use a respirator or die?"

"No, it's not a vacation. Listen, I really think I can dream you well." It sounded so stupid when she said it out loud, but she really believed it. "I just found you, Cook, I can't bear to see you go."

"Well, if you go up north, you won't have to watch." He put the magazine down and turned his face away from her.

"I'm going to make you well, Cook. I'll be back"—she took a couple of sobbing breaths, the emotion hot and tight in her throat—"and we'll have our lives together. I'll be back, I promise."

"Go," he said.

"I love you," she said and kissed him on the cheek, but he was unresponsive, his eyes open and staring at something on the far wall.

Missie picked up her books, ran from the room, got into the car and headed north without even stopping to pack a bag.

If she didn't accomplish this in time, Cook would die before she could get back to him. If this was a stupid, irresponsible move, it was also irreversible, and that pain-filled little exchange would be their last.

No, she'd call him every day. She'd call him every day and report on her progress. She wouldn't be able to sleep twenty-four hours a day. She'd have to do something else some of the time. What would she do to fill her days?

Study about dreams.

Feel guilty about Cook. Feel guilty about the feeling of freedom she had by being away from him and not having to go through his death with him. Feel guilty about leaving him with his mother, when she was his wife and ought to be by his side, but instead, she was running away, being pulled toward something in the northwoods.

She drove all night, and as dawn grayed the cloudy sky, a soft drizzle began and she turned off the highway into the parking lot of the Northern Aire Motel.

Mrs. Atkisson greeted her with a long, warm hug, and showed her to a spare bedroom in the lodge. "You must be tired," she said, and Missie certainly was, although she was still too excited to sleep. She didn't even have anything to unpack.

Mrs. Atkisson put her to bed with a nice nightie, flannel sheets and a glass of warm milk, wished her well on her quest and closed the bedroom door.

Missie prayed again that she was doing the right thing, and then she tried to relax, willing her buzzing muscles to slow down. She closed her eyes, slowed her breathing, and listened to the rain on the edge of the roof right outside her window. Eventually, she fell into a deep sleep.

She dreamed she was dressed in a long, red satin ball gown, running through some antebellum southern mansion, looking for something, bumping into people in her mindless panic. She dashed as fast as her uncooperative and too-small shoes would permit, little strings of hair coming loose from her carefully woven hairdo and sticking to the back of her neck. She went from room to room, eyes restlessly scanning the crowd, then to the veranda, then back inside the hot, humid house, looking, looking, and she wasn't even sure what it was she was looking for. . . .

The next morning, Missie sat, vacant-headed, cradling a Styrofoam cup of hot coffee while at least a dozen people crowded the small dining room. George was back, or else he was still there, at the end of the season, and Missie heard a desperation in his voice that she hadn't heard when they were both there before. He had a dream to dream that he hadn't quite managed, and he'd been trying all summer.

Missie didn't have the luxury of all that time to have her dream.

There was much talk about controlling the dreams, especially the technique of looking at one's dream hands. "You program yourself at the beginning, before you fall asleep," one of them said, "to look at your hands, and then sometime during the dream, you look at your hands, and it reminds you. Then you're consciously dreaming."

"Yeah?" George challenged him. "Can you do that?"

"I sometimes get to see my hands in my dream," the other man said, "but then I wake up."

"I know it can be done," somebody else said. "Mrs. Atkisson, are people successful at controlling their dreams here?"

"Oh, I don't know about that," Mrs. Atkisson said.

Missie spent that day in the lobby, looking through all the books and magazines she had brought on dream research, and discovered, in talking with a few of the other guests, that the lodge bookshelves also held books, old books, on dream interpretation and research. She immersed herself in the topic, certain that it would have an effect on her subconscious.

It didn't. That night she had nonsensical dreams about things laughing at her from the dark.

She cried during the dream report the following morning, and of all the people who could have come over to comfort her, George was the one. "I believe in guided dreaming," he eventually said to her after he heard the whole story of Cook. "I'll be your guide if you'll be mine."

Missie dried her eyes on the sleeve of her blouse. "Really?"

"Sure."

She tried calling Cook to tell him the good news, but his mother answered and said that Cook was unavailable. Then she hung up.

That night, Missie went to bed with George sitting in a wing chair at the end of her bed. She was too excited to sleep at first, but George was absolutely silent. As soon as she fell asleep, he was to move into a bedside chair and begin speaking low to her, to guide her to Cook. She'd click her eyes to the right to tell him she was in control, and click her eyes to the left if she lost it.

She dreamed she was in an elevator, headed down. She was in an elevator with George. And George was telling her that she had control over the elevator, and she remembered her mission. She clicked her eyeballs, pushed on the elevator door and it opened into the field of flowers.

The musical flowers were closed with their heads hanging. They played a discordant tune as she walked through the rain-wet grass to the tree, where Cook slumped over, eyes closed, more tree than man. His needles were turning brown, falling off, carpeting the ground around him.

"I'm dying, Miss," he said without even opening his eyes.

"What can I do?" she asked.

"I don't know. Stay with me."

"I can't do that, Cook, you know I can't. I'm here to dream you well." Even in her dream, Missie was amazed that she remembered her mission.

"I don't know how you'll do that."

"I'm just going to dream you well. This is my dream, and I have control, so come on out of that tree and be my husband again."

"It's not that simple."

"Of course it is. This is my dream."

"But you're at the Northern Aire Motel, honey. You can't control the dreams there, because they're not really dreams. There is truth to what happens in your dreams at that place, and they control you, you don't control them."

"Is that true?"

Cook nodded, then slumped even lower.

The flowers wailed.

"You mean there's no hope?"

"Just stay with me, Miss."

"I can't, Cook, I'm asleep." She felt the tug on her consciousness. "I'll go back to the hospital."

"Hurry," he sighed, and she awoke to see George watching her with intensity.

"Cook said we can't change the things we dream here because in this place the dreams change us, we don't change them."

"How could that be?" George asked.

"I don't know," she said as she got out of bed. "But I have to go home. My husband's dying, and I need to be with him."

"Not until after you guide me," George said.

"He's dying, George."

"We had a deal."

"It won't do any good."

"Says the demon liar in your dream. A deal is a deal."

As much as Missie thought that her wedding vows superceded this agreement, she thought that spending a couple more hours at the motel wouldn't hurt. She'd already done irreparable damage to her relationship with her in-laws.

They went to George's room, where he changed into his pajamas and climbed into bed. As per their agreement, Missie sat in the wingback chair until he began to snore, then she moved to his bedside and began to talk to him, low and gentle, guiding him into control of his dream.

He clicked his eyeballs to the right, and she knew he was off and running. But she stayed in case he lost control. She stayed and waited with him with tremendous impatience.

Then the impatience began to diminish as she looked at his face. He was grossly overweight and had a popcorn nose, his remaining hair was graying and thin on top and looked kind of greasy, but there was something appealing about him, something little-boyish about his manner.

She found herself wanting to touch him, to smooth the hair from his forehead, to kiss his cheek, to climb into bed with him and cuddle up to his furnace warmth. She felt an overwhelming compulsion to hold his head to her breast, to rock him, to feel his closeness.

Very gently, she picked up the corner of the covers and slipped in beside him. Her nightie slipped up as she did so, but instead of risking waking him, she let it be. She kept watching his eyes for any evidence that he was waking up, or out of control in his dream, while she soaked up his warmth and enjoyed this weird closeness. She cradled his head and kissed the top of it.

Why am I doing this? she asked herself, a moment too late.

"Mommy?" he said. Hands like paws grabbed at her, ripping her nightie, then clenched her throat. With as much agility as she could muster, she parried his move and fell out of bed onto the floor with a loud thud.

He was still asleep.

Had he wanted sex with her? No. Had he wanted his mother? Had he wanted sex with his mother, or to choke her to death?

91

Something weird along those lines, and she had willingly crawled into his bed. No, not willingly. She had been manipulated by the dream forces of the motel.

She ran from his room back to her own, showered, and left, leaving a quick note for Mrs. Atkisson.

She cried most of the way home. Why had George been able to achieve his dream when she couldn't achieve hers?

She only hoped she wasn't too late to be with Cook when he died.

God, she'd given up precious hours to be with that George creature.

She hated herself.

It was rush hour before she got to the hospital, and traffic crawled. Exhaustion was the only thing that kept her from shrieking.

Finally, she got to the hospital, parked in the ambulance parking spot and ran in, ran to Cook's room, and ran right into his mother as she was coming out.

Her face was a white grotesquerie of grief, and she didn't even recognize Missie.

Missie knew she was too late. She pushed past the nurse who followed her mother-in-law out and went into Cook's room, which was filled with machinery, all silent.

Another nurse was busy disconnecting tubes and hoses and when she saw Missie, she quietly left the room.

Cook was dead, his face dull gray like a weathered board. The stub end of a plastic tube stuck out of his mouth. Grief so enormous that she couldn't contain it squeezed Missie until she didn't know if she was going to scream or faint.

If only I'd. . . . If only I'd. . . . If only I'd done a million things differently, she thought.

She sat in the chair his mother had just vacated and picked up his hand. It was cold and lifeless. "Oh god, Cook," she said between hiccupping sobs. "Oh god, Cook."

She cried until she could cry no more, and some attendants came to see to her husband's body. She watched them take him, and then she didn't know what to do, or where to go, or how to make arrangements. Maybe his mother was doing all of that. How could Missie ask her? Talk to her? Face her?

She couldn't.

She went home to their apartment.

But it wasn't really hers yet, because hardly any of her stuff had been moved in. They'd gone straight from the wedding to the northwoods, and straight from there to the hospital, and all her stuff was still in her old place, boxed up and ready to move. This was clearly still Cook's apartment. They'd never had a chance to make it theirs.

She went into his closet and smelled him on all his clothes. Then she pulled his shirts off the hangers and got into his bed with the smell of him on the pillow and finally fell into a dreamless sleep that gave her tortured psyche some rest.

The phone rang in the morning, waking her up to bright sunshine streaming through the windows as if nothing had happened. She lay in bed, surrounded by a profusion of Cook's clothes, and listened to his mother talk on the machine. She talked fast and low, as if she had written the message down and had to read it fast before she broke down.

"Missie, it's Luann. Cook is dead, honey, and I've made arrangements for the funeral to be at Charles Brothers on Tuesday at three o'clock. I didn't know what else to do, dear, because I don't know where you are or what you're doing. Call me when you get this, or I'll see you there."

Tuesday at three.

Grief was still a stomach cramp, and Missie didn't know how she was ever going to ease it. She remembered in a long trail of advices from a variety of sources: Live each day as if it were your last. Never go to bed mad. You never know where the merry-go-round will stop. Life is but a day's work; do it well. End each meeting as if you will never see that person again.

She felt like she had so much unfinished business with Cook. What had their last exchange been? "You're leaving me? Go."

Oh god, Cook, I'm so sorry.

Maybe there was a way she could bring some kind of closure to the hell she felt burning inside of her.

She got up, showered with his scented soap, brushed her teeth with his toothbrush, toweled with his towel, combed out her hair with his comb, and then jumped back in the car and headed north.

She walked through the field of dead flowers. They were crispy and fried in the hot sun.

Cook, now completely turned to deadwood, stretched over the path like a droopy dead snag. She had to look hard to recognize him.

"Cook?"

No answer, of course.

"Oh, Cook, I'm so sorry," she said, feeling rational and in control. She realized she was in total control of this dream, and that she could do whatever she wanted.

There was only one thing she wanted to do, and that was to be in charge of Cook's remains. To grow up, take responsibility for herself and her actions, and do that one duty for her dead husband that she ought to be doing, instead of leaving that to his mother as well. His mother didn't understand.

"I need a chainsaw," she said, and in the way things work in the dream world, a chainsaw appeared at her feet. She cut down his tree, then cut it into short lengths. Funny, it didn't seem like Cook at all anymore. She piled it all up and lit a match.

He went up with a whoosh, wood so dried out and ready to

burn that it took but a minute and he was nothing but a pile of smoldering ashes in the middle of what had once been the most beautiful meadow she had ever seen.

"I loved you, Cook, I loved you like nothing and nobody else. Ever." She reached down and picked up a handful of his ashes.

When she woke up, she was shivering, still in her car, parked in the parking lot of the Northern Aire where she'd given into her exhaustion the night before. She hadn't wanted to wake Mrs. Atkisson in the middle of the night. It was still night.

Her hand was full of ashes.

She didn't know exactly why she felt better, but she did, and she put the ashes into a tissue, and tucked it into her purse. Then she started the little car and headed for home, to work on fixing her life.

She thought she saw smoke in her rearview mirror as she left, but chalked that up to dream residue. Two miles further down the road, a half dozen fire trucks roared past, but by then it was too late.

Just as well, she thought, and, with a newfound confidence, she headed home to take care of her husband's affairs.

Shooting Rats

When Jimbo saw the lights still on at the police station, he pulled over and killed the engine. Not much waited at home except an exhausted Margie and her endless grieving, a son too occupied with his computer to communicate with his parents, and a house that was one son shy of a home.

He saw those lights at the police station and hoped that it wasn't Sheriff Withens in there burning the midnight oil. Jimbo and the sheriff got along just fine, but it wasn't the older man's company he wanted to keep. Jimbo thought that hefting a few beers might be a good thing to do, and he'd like to do it with Paulie Timmins. He hadn't been out drinking with anybody, much less Paulie, in what seemed like years. Jimbo was ready for a boys' night out.

Paulie had been a fullback on the White Pines Junction High School football team, and he hadn't ever lost any of that size. Nor, at thirty-three years old, had he put on any fat. Jimbo didn't know how Paulie did it, but then Jimbo sat behind the editor's desk at the newspaper all day now that he had a reporter to do the running around, and he had definitely gained a few. But Paulie, in his tailored police uniform, still looked fit and trim.

"Jimbo!" Paulie looked up when he heard the door open, and the smile on his face was genuine. Jimbo's heart immediately warmed. This was a good idea.

"Thought maybe you'd be up for a few beers, Paulie," Jimbo

said. "It's been too long."

"Bear with me a few minutes while I finish up this paper-work," Paulie said, "and we'll go do just that."

Jimbo relaxed in Sheriff Withens' big, loose desk chair, and swiveled back and forth while Paulie shuffled papers. He picked up the phone to let Margie know he'd be home late, and left a message on the answering machine. He suggested that she take Jason out for a burger or something so she wouldn't have to cook. He was still mindlessly swiveling back and forth when Paulie spoke.

"You look bored and sad, my friend."

Jimbo looked up and gave what felt like a wan smile.

"I know what you need, and it ain't no beer."

Jimbo raised an eyebrow. Paulie knew Jimbo would never fool around on Margie, so it had to be something legal as well as exciting.

"I'm going to change," Paulie said, grabbed his gym bag and went into the men's room. When he came out, he wore jeans and a gray T-shirt stretched tight over his muscled chest. He picked up his car keys from the desktop. "C'mon," he said. "I'll drive."

Paulie had a tricked-out muscle truck, a big Chev pickup with plenty of horsepower and an oversized bed. He popped in a CD of some new music Jimbo hadn't ever heard, and they headed out into the night. Jimbo felt young again. He felt the years of responsibility, grief, and routine melt away. He didn't envy Paulie's single lifestyle, but he realized he needed to revisit those carefree days, if only for an hour or so now and then.

Paulie took a few familiar turns out on the county roads and then pulled inside the gate that never closed, the one to the county dump. He stopped about fifty feet from the edge of the debris, turned off the lights and engine, turned off the music, and they sat in the quiet, in the dark.

"The dump? That's what you think I need?"

"Not the dump itself," Paulie said, and pulled a gun case from behind his seat. "Target practice."

Jimbo shook his head. It had been ten years, maybe fifteen since he'd been shooting rats at the dump for fun. He wasn't sure he wanted to do it anymore. But he was along for the ride, and what did it hurt?

The Vargas County Landfill was a sight to behold in the daylight. It started out as an enormous pit, an acre or more in size, and had been filled over the years to a gigantic mound. The snow fences around it were covered with paper and plastic bags that had been blown off the top of the stack. In the daylight, it was full of crows and other raucous scavenger birds. In the night, the rats ruled. Big as pups, they had been moving targets for pubescent boys since probably long before Jimbo was born. But he didn't know that grown men still took pot shots at them.

Jimbo watched Paulie load the clip with a single .22 round, talking easily the whole time. "The rats are smart," he said. "You won't have a second chance." He handed the gun to Jimbo. "I'll turn on the headlights, and you nail one. If you can."

Jimbo opened his window and leaned out, feeling the heft of the gun in his hand. It was a lightweight thing, surely no kick at all. He'd been challenged. And he was up for a challenge. Hey, he thought, this might be fun.

Paulie hit the headlights, and a thousand pair of eyes turned to look at them. Jimbo took careful aim at the king of the heap, a big fat thing, but he missed. He kept clicking, wishing the clip was full. But it wasn't. He had used up his chance.

The gun emptied, the headlights went out, Jimbo pulled back inside the cab and Paulie rolled up the window. "That was pitiful," Paulie said.

"Doesn't matter," Jimbo said, feeling a little adrenaline rush. "It was fun."

Paulie nodded and reloaded one round. "How are things at home?" he asked.

"Okay, I guess. We'll get past it."

"It's been, what, a year since Micah disappeared?"

"Seven months."

"Takes a while," Paulie said. "I guess."

"Yeah."

"Margie doing okay? You two getting along?"

"Yeah, I don't know what I'd do without her."

"And vice versa, I suppose."

"I hope. Jason's doing better, too. We've all got the guilt, you know."

"Yeah."

"What about you?" Jimbo asked. "Dating?"

"Nah. Think I'll be single all my life. Don't think a woman is what I need."

"Really?" Jimbo was amazed. "You gay?"

"Nope. Just not much interested."

"Wow," Jimbo said. "Margie's my best friend. My partner. I can't imagine not having her. Or someone in that role. You know. Cook. Sex. Laugh at *The Simpsons.*"

"Maybe if I had it, I'd miss it," Paulie said, "but I do all right on my own. Now watch."

He opened his window and the dump smell came back in. He turned on the headlights and popped a big rat at the edge of the trash. Paulie smiled at Jimbo, turned off the headlights and rolled up the window.

Instead of reloading, Paulie fired up his big truck and slowly backed away from their target area.

"That's it?" Jimbo asked, disappointed.

"That's it."

"I was just warming up."

"Save it. We'll do it again another time."

Jimbo smiled. Paulie had been right. He felt a hundred percent better, and he was ready to go home to Margie and Jason.

The next night, Jimbo just happened to drive by the police station, and was disappointed when he didn't see Paulie's truck out front. The office was dark. Jimbo was surprised at how disappointed he was. He thought about going out to the dump himself. Maybe Paulie was out there.

Nah. He'd better go on home. They'd do that again some other time.

The next night he stopped in again, but Paulie didn't seem interested. He was preoccupied, and Jimbo felt silly for even suggesting such a juvenile pastime with such earnestness.

That night, too, he went home, but when Margie reached for him in the dark, he had nothing of himself to give her. He was busy thinking about all those rats and how he wanted to nail just one. Just one.

The next day, he took a walking lunch break and wandered on down to Doc's. Doc had the tackle shop, and in the back he sold a few weapons. A couple of handguns, a couple of hunting rifles, a couple of shotguns was all he had, but he could order anything.

"Thinking about a .22 pistol, Doc," Jimbo said. "Been wanting to do a little target practice."

Doc locked up the cash drawer and Jimbo followed him through the store, past the mounted Muskie in a glass case, past the rows of tackle, past the live wells full of bait fish, to the door marked "Office." Inside, Doc dialed the combination on the big steel safe, opened it and brought out a blue plastic box with S&W embossed on its top.

"Semi-automatic, perfect for target practice. You going to be taking Jason out?"

"Yeah," Jimbo said.

"Perfect gun for a kid to learn on."

"Smith and Wesson, eh?"

Doc nodded.

Jimbo ran the action back and forth a few times, figuring how it all went together. "Great," he said. "I'll take it."

Doc closed up the safe, and they went out in front to fill out the requisite paperwork. Jimbo bought a couple of boxes of rounds, and when he left the tackle shop, he had a very scary feeling of power in his gut.

Back in his office, he loaded the gun and put it in his desk drawer, just like in the movies. He had a loaded gun in his desk. It kind of scared him. All day long it pulled at his consciousness. He was never unaware that he had a loaded gun within reach. He liked the eerie feeling.

He called Margie and told her he'd be home late, and then fabricated work to do until the sun went down. Then he took his loaded gun out of his desk drawer, stuck it in his jacket pocket, got in his car and headed for the dump.

Paulie's truck was parked where they had parked before.

Jimbo turned off his headlights a fair distance away, coasted to a stop and turned off the engine. He walked over to Paulie's truck, but there was nobody in the cab.

It was creepy, being out there in the silent dark, the night obscuring the stench of the garbage. He heard the rustling of the vermin in the acre of trash, and didn't know what to make of Paulie's disappearance.

And then Jimbo saw him, by the light of the moon, just standing, bent like an old man, head down, a good hundred yards away, and a fair distance into the dump itself. He walked over, and Paulie didn't twitch a muscle, not until Jimbo got right next to him and said, "Paulie? What's up?"

A rat lay dead at Paulie's feet, a small rat. Paulie nudged it with the toe of his tennis shoe.

"Got'cha one, eh? Good going," Jimbo said, mystified at Paulie's behavior.

"Yep," Paulie said. "Got me my quota."

They stood there for a long moment, then Paulie lifted his head. "Gotta go," he said, "gotta go see my sister." And head still down, he walked back toward his truck.

Jimbo watched him go, watched him fire up his truck, watched him drive slowly through the gate and on out to the road. Paulie was a strange duck, that was for certain. Enthusiasm dampened, Jimbo went home too, his new gun still pristine.

The next night, though, as the moon came up, Jimbo felt the urge and followed it all the way to the dump. He pulled up to where they had parked before, and took a deep breath. Then he rolled down the window, clicked off the safety, turned the headlights on and blasted away. He got three big damn rats with the first clip. He turned off the lights, rolled up the window, and reloaded.

One box of rounds later, he figured he'd nailed a bunch. What a feeling! He was high, his blood pressure was down, he felt as if he'd just had the best sex of his life.

And speaking of sex . . . it was time for Margie.

He drove home with a song in his heart.

But when he got there, what he found was a tearstained Margie and an emergency at the paper.

The Northern Aire Motel had caught fire while he was out at the dump, and the paper's publisher wanted to know who was covering it.

"Mrs. Atkisson was my mother's best friend," Margie said. "She came into the diner all the time. What could have caused this?"

Jimbo was a little bit confused as to which metaphorical fire he should put out first. Console Margie, call his boss, call his reporter, or run out to the fire. He decided to sit down and tend to his wife first. "It was an old building, honey. These things happen. Wiring, propane, lightning, who knows? Did Mrs. Atkisson die? Do you know that for certain?"

"No," she sniffed, then wiped her nose. "But even if she didn't, that place was all she had."

"I'm sure she had insurance. Are you all right? I've got to get somebody out there to cover the story."

"I'm okay," she said. "You can go."

Jimbo got back in his truck and headed for the Northern Aire. He could see the glow in the sky from the blaze.

Paulie met him at the drive. "The firemen are just letting 'er go," he said. "They're watching the trees to make sure we don't have a forest fire on our hands."

"Mrs. Atkisson?" Jimbo asked.

"Don't know yet. Probably inside, along with her guests. Seemed to come on real sudden like."

"Jeez."

"Where were you tonight?" Paulie asked.

Defensive fear grabbed hold of Jimbo's chest. "Why? You ask that like I was a suspect."

"Just asking," Paulie said.

"Don't treat me like I'm an arsonist." Jimbo pulled a reporter's pad from his glove box. The blue plastic of the Smith & Wesson box seemed to glow neon in the light. "Do you suspect arson?" he asked in his best reporter voice, hoping the switch of subject would bring Paulie back to the task at hand.

"Got yourself a new gun?" Paulie asked.

"Yeah, Jason and I are going to do some target shooting."

"Let me see."

"Let's talk about the fire," Jimbo said.

Paulie leaned down and put his official police face in Jimbo's window. "Let me see the gun, Jim."

Jimbo pulled it out of the glove compartment, opened the box and handed the gun to Paulie. Paulie opened it, slid open the chamber and sniffed. "Were you at the dump tonight?"

Jimbo felt strangely ashamed. "Yeah," he said with what he thought was righteous why-shouldn't-I-be-at-the-dump? calm.

"How many rats'd you kill?"

Jimbo shrugged. "A few."

Paulie nodded, handed the gun back to him. "There's not going to be a story here until the thing burns down, cools, and we can get inside to determine the casualties, if any, and the cause of the fire."

Jimbo nodded. "I'll grab a few hours of sleep and come back."

Paulie rapped his knuckles twice on the roof of Jimbo's car and walked off.

Jimbo drove away, feeling guilty as hell, and he didn't know why.

By the time he'd driven five miles toward home, his guilt had turned to righteous indignation. What the hell, he thought. Why should Paulie be asking me what I was doing? What kind of a friend suspects the editor of the newspaper of arson, for cripes sake? His fingers gripped the steering wheel until they hurt. And then they automatically turned the wheel toward the dump, where Jimbo knocked off two more rats and felt vastly better afterward. Then he went home, showered, shaved, took Margie for a tumble in bed, set the alarm for two hours hence, and took a nap.

The full story didn't come out until mid-day. Eight people killed in the fire itself, including Mrs. Atkisson. A blazing tree fell on two firemen trying to keep it from spreading, bringing the total to ten.

Jimbo printed a Special Edition.

For the next week, he was busy keeping the local folks apprised of the situation out at the Northern Aire, documenting the funerals, the human-interest stories of who had been killed, and dogging the ongoing investigation into the cause. By the time he could actually go home with a desk cleared of urgent work, he was exhausted.

All he wanted to do was go to the dump.

Odd, he thought, as he sat at his desk and loaded his .22. It used to be when he was this tired, he'd want to go home, have a beer and snuggle on the couch with Margie. Guess those days were gone. The years had given him enough of a security envelope in his marriage, and now what he wanted was a little adrenaline rush.

He drove slowly by the police station, but Paulie's truck was gone. He was a little disappointed. He thought he could probably do a little bit better in competition with him now. So he drove on out.

But Paulie's truck was blocking the drive. Just inside the gate, Paulie had pulled it up diagonally, and Jimbo couldn't get past. So he parked in the ditch, got out, stuck his pistol in his pocket, and walked on in.

Paulie was walking back to his rig, nothing more than a sauntering shape in the thin moonlight. "Hey," Jimbo said.

"Hey, yourself."

"You blocked the gate."

"Yeah."

"What's the deal?"

"It's either you or me, Jimbo," Paulie said. "We can't both do it. I don't know why I ever brought you out here. It was stupid. Unless . . . unless maybe it's time for me to quit. Maybe you ought to take over. My sister's kid . . . drowned the other night."

Paulie's big, meaty, healthy face looked hollow and gaunt in the unfiltered light. Jimbo chalked it up to the fire and the ensuing investigation.

"Yeah, maybe. I took over for Lars Boynan, and maybe now it's your turn. I'm pretty tired of it."

"I don't understand what you're talking about."

Paulie clamped a big paw on Jimbo's shoulder. "One a day, that's all, Jimbo. You want to control the population, not eradicate it. One a day." Then he climbed up into his big truck, blinded Jimbo with the headlights, turned around and drove off.

"Jerk," Jimbo said. Paulie took all the fun out of coming out here and blasting away. He walked toward the moonlit mass of confusion, pulled his gun from his pocket and planned to kill his one for the day. He wanted a good shot, a steady aim, he wanted to blast its damn rat brains all over somebody's discarded sofa. Nothing left for the crows to eat.

He was mildly surprised at himself for that attitude. He'd always been such a pacifist.

But look at that. Right there, standing on the top of what looked like the corner of some appliance protruding from a sea of busted black garbage bags. One big rat, staring right at him.

Jimbo kept walking toward it, and it didn't twitch a whisker. He stopped, raised his pistol, took careful aim, and thought it was a little bit too easy. If he was only going to shoot one, why the easy one?

Yet it begged to be shot, the way it stared at him with its beady eyes shining like ball bearings. This rat had attitude. Jimbo motioned at it to go away, but it stood its ground.

The rat dared him to shoot it.

Jimbo felt his lip curl up in distaste, aimed again and fired.

Between squeezing the trigger and seeing the little body flip into the air, Jimbo had a terrible feeling in his gut, a recognition of sorts. It was a horrible, wrenching, sickening elevator-drop feeling. He turned and ran back to the car.

The next day when he heard that Paulie had dropped dead

from a heart attack, he was barely surprised. That rat had reminded him of Paulie in its last nano-second of life. Jimbo just sat at his desk in the newspaper office, waiting for the kid to finish Paulie's obituary, where it would go right next to Paulie's nephew's obituary in the weekly paper. Jimbo sat there with sudden wisdom and an ageless feeling of responsibility, cleaned his gun and resolved that one a day would be all he would kill. One a day. No more, no less. Until the day he saw Jason's face or Margie's face in the balance he was to keep. And then he'd get rid of the gun, walk straight away and damn the consequences.

DOC'S BIG CATCH

Doc stepped into his bass boat just as the sun was coming up over the treetops to the east. A light mist covered the lake, the brisk air smelled October-fresh. He set the thermos of sugared and creamed coffee and a Styrofoam cup of worms next to the extra gas tank, then motioned for Cane, his Samoyed, to join him if he wanted. He wanted.

Doc turned the key, pushed the button, and the motor caught immediately. He inhaled the smell of the gasoline, the lake, the morning, and the dog. He didn't stop to savor it, that's what the fishing was for. Savoring. He was in his element. He was home, and he was grateful every day of his life for it.

The dog settled in the passenger seat, where he could look out the windshield. Doc untied the bowline, engaged the motor, and they putted away from the dock and out toward the far side of the lake. When far enough from his neighbors, he pushed on the throttle, and they raced across the glassy surface. He looked back and saw his house and lawn recede, the picnic table and barbecue standing where he'd last left them. Home was a comfort, though it was a lonely place without Sadie Katherine, and the prospect of being alone all winter was not a good one. Sadie Katherine was good for many, many things, but one of her best qualities was her skill at games. She played chess, Scrabble, cribbage, gin rummy, and poker, and she played them about on a par with Doc, which always meant fierce competition, all winter long.

He missed that. Good god, he missed that. He couldn't imagine a winter without her.

Doc put those thoughts aside and concentrated instead on the tackle he was going to need. This was a walleye morning, and he had about two hours on the water before he had to get back, eat breakfast, shower, dress and drive into town to open the tackle shop.

When he reached the right spot, he killed the engine, then sat in the gently rocking boat, listening to the awakening morning as he rigged his line and then poked the weighted hook three times through a nightcrawler. Cane got down from his seat, sniffed the cup of worms, then took his customary place forward, next to the trolling motor. He sat, his white fur fluffing in the slight breeze, sniffing the air and looking natural and regal. A tug of affection pulled on Doc. Cane was not a young dog. One day Doc would be fishing without Cane, too.

Doc dropped the line over the side of the boat, and immediately it felt as if a giant hand had grabbed his hook and pulled it down. He jerked the rod back to set the hook, but it didn't budge. It was like a snag, but they weren't moving. There was nothing for the hook to snag on.

Then it released, and Doc reeled it in, an eerie feeling of déjà vu accompanying it.

He felt life on the end of the line, and, when it came up, he had a white fish on the end. It was a Northern Pike, a long one, close to thirty inches, its markings faded and yellowish but still visible on its queer white scales, and it was giving him no fight.

He'd hooked the fabled albino pike, and this was the second time he'd caught it or one of its kin.

He didn't want to touch it. He remembered what had happened the last time he'd touched it. He brought his line up taut, but let the fish undulate slowly in the water. It ought to have red eyes like a normal albino, but this one had golden eyes. Golden eyes that looked right at him.

He looked at the fish. It looked back at him. He remembered that look. The last time he saw it was the first time he fished this lake after he got back from Vietnam.

It had all happened about the same way. He'd come home from Vietnam, given his mother a kiss, his father a handshake, and then jumped in his car and come up to the northwoods. He'd been camping for about a week, trying to cleanse the Army and all its war-related nastiness from his soul. He borrowed a little boat, and went out early one fall morning to fish for walleye, a dozen worms he'd dug himself in the bottom of a rusted coffee can he'd scavenged out of the park trash. He caught an albino pike, but it was the strangest strike he'd ever felt. Like someone had grabbed his line and held it tight while they put the fish on, then let the fish passively rise to the surface.

He reeled the odd fish in, but it didn't thrash, it was calm, so he didn't feel like he needed his landing net. He reached down and grabbed the fish, brought it up to eye level, and that's when it happened.

He looked into those golden eyes, they looked at him, and Doc realized he had an option. Two paths stretched before him in his mind's eye. On one path lay his NFL dreams, riches, big house, football glory, lots of women, beautiful women, but the vision had a shallow feel to it. There was ease to life, but no meaning. No love. No warmth.

The other path, as clearly sign-posted as a fork in the road, had a little house here on the lake in White Pines Junction, a small tackle shop, a dog, a wife, and never enough money. A struggle, but filled with heart.

There was never a doubt in his mind. He would choose the northwoods lifestyle, even though he knew that rearing children in Vargas County was not an option for him. He'd still opt for the simple life, with one woman he could love and take care of, and a community that he could be a part of because of who he was, not because of the money he made.

The fish blinked, or at least Doc thought he saw the fish blink. He took the hook out of its lip, took another moment to marvel at the wondrous colors that swirled along its mutated skin, then bent over to release it. It slipped out of his grasp and went deep into the water, leaving barely a surface ripple.

Within a month of catching that golden-eyed fish, his father had died, and with the small inheritance his mother passed on to him, he bought a rundown storefront on County Road B and opened his tackle shop. Within the year, he'd found a naked and chilled-to-blue Sadie Katherine laughing on the dock. He pulled a blanket from his truck, wrapped her up and took her home for some hot tea, and for the next thirty years they walked side by side through life. She never exactly told him her history, and he'd never exactly asked, but she knew how to guide for fish as if she knew the way fish thought. Uncanny. With her as his partner, his life was in order.

Over the years, he heard legends of an albino strain of pike in the lake, but he never told anybody that he'd caught one. He assumed that eventually all the Indians would spear them out; surely the albino held a tribal significance.

And now he'd caught another one.

Doc looked at the fish in the water and didn't want to touch it. He never regretted his life as a husband and homeowner, with a dog and a tackle shop. The finances had been a struggle for years and years, but now that the house and inventory were paid for, there was a little more money, a little more time, a little more leisure. He'd had a succession of good dogs, and he'd had one spectacular woman. He'd had a good life.

Of course, he'd wondered about his choice over the years. He wondered if the choice had really been put to him or if he'd had some kind of a brain fugue that morning on the lake. He and

Recon John had spent hundreds of hours discussing fate and the illusion of control that folks thought they had over their lives. But in the final analysis, when Doc went to bed every night, he believed he had made a choice, that somehow the fates had allowed him the opportunity, and that he had done the right thing.

And now here was the fish again. Was he ripe for another decision? Or was it just his lucky day?

He lifted up on the line. The fish wasn't tightly caught.

He reached down with his pliers, hoping to grab the hook and twist it out of the fish's mouth without having to touch it. But just as he got there, the fish thrashed and swung away from him. On reflex, he grabbed it.

And he saw two paths.

One was a long life of fishing and living at the lake. He saw himself old and bent, thin and coughing, taking his boat out every morning, worrying about surviving every winter. He relied on the kindness of friends and strangers to see to his needs, and every morning that he woke up, he wondered why.

The other was an instant of terror and regret, and a life well-lived came to a brutally quick termination. Perhaps soon.

Which would it be, Doc?

He brought the golden-eyed fish up to eye level, and plucked out the hook. He didn't want the responsibility again. He'd lived with it once, he didn't want the burden of it a second time.

"You decide," he said, and tossed the fish back into the lake.

Then he sat down, poured himself a cup of coffee, and wondered if there would have been some kind of relief in making the decision himself. Some kind of soul settlement in knowing.

Cane wandered back from the bow and rested his big head on Doc's knee. Doc scratched the dog's scalp and sipped his coffee. "I think something big just happened here, boy," he said. "Or maybe not."

He sat for a while longer, trying to decide which he would have chosen if he had. He couldn't see that one way would be better or worse than another. But for the moment, he'd lost his taste for the walleye chase.

"Time to go to work," he said to the dog, who hopped back up into the passenger seat. Doc threw the dregs of his coffee over the side, started the motor and headed back across the lake to embrace his fate.

The New Kitchen

Howard Leppens raised the crowbar over his head and with a whack so violent it made Louise sick to her stomach, he buried the claw end in the kitchen wall, then tugged, putting his considerable weight behind it. The ancient plaster and lath exploded outward, sending white shrapnel zinging across the room.

Louise left her husband to do the demolition work and went for a walk. She'd pick out the new cabinets, appliances and wallpaper later. She was happy the remodeling project was finally under way, but not so happy about doing dishes in the bathroom for the next three weeks. Oh well. A new kitchen would be worth the inconvenience.

She took the cell phone along to tell her best friend Julia that the work had begun in earnest. The whole kitchen remodel had been Julia's idea. She was the realtor who sold them the house and she was Louise's new best friend.

A half hour later, she walked back through the front door to find Howard's sweat-soaked back to the door. He stood staring at the exposed studs in the wall where the refrigerator used to stand in front of that ugly wallpaper. Plaster dust hung in the air and coated Howard, and rubble was thick on the ancient linoleum.

"Look," Howard said, leaning on the crowbar. Louise looked. Written on a two-by-four in white chalk, big as life, was the name Pursley. She caught her breath. "What does that mean?"

"Means he built this house is what it means," Howard said. "They wrote his name on the shipment of lumber."

"That doesn't have to mean *Lawrence* Pursley," Louise said. "There could have been other Pursleys."

Howard threw down the crowbar and left the room. Louise began sweeping up, taking sidelong glances at the evil name inscribed within the walls of her home. Soon, she heard the shower. She was afraid this would put Howard off so much he'd want to sell the house. If they did that, he'd want to move back to Boston, and she wouldn't be able to stand that. No, now that Kevin was grown, they had their final, permanent retirement home in White Pines Junction. And it was paid for, thanks to their son Kevin's good fortune, and no thanks to Howard. So what if their dream house was built by the notorious Lawrence Pursley. That was not her fault and she would not be punished because of it. This was her new home. She had new friends. She had a new life. She would not go back to Boston. Kevin had settled here, and she would never leave Julia, the best friend she'd ever had.

Howard tossed and turned in his sleep all night, and he rolled around so violently and sighed so loudly that he made sure Louise didn't get any sleep either. At the crack of dawn, he was up and into his work clothes. Louise, bleary-eyed, got up after him and went down to plug in the coffee pot that was currently on the screened front porch. She'd had Howard put the storm windows on before he started ripping the kitchen apart, but the November cold was not to be kept out. When she got back inside, Howard was in the kitchen again, staring at the name on the stud.

"Just paint over it," Louise said.

"We're moving," he said, then put on his work boots. "I'm going to get breakfast at Margie's."

She watched him slam out the porch screen door, get into his truck and drive down the lane. *We are not moving,* she said to herself, and poured herself a cup of coffee. Then she went to the kitchen and looked at that name again. Pursley. "We are not moving," she told it. Damn Howard and his righteous indignation based on nothing religious or moral that she'd ever seen. Howard had no particular moral code that he lived by, at least nothing he had ever exhibited to her in all their years of marriage. Howard was the first to grab a great deal, no matter who he screwed, and he justified it in a million different ways.

Howard. A master of justification, that's what he was. And now he was trying to justify going back to Boston. Well, Louise would not leave Kevin here by himself, and she would not be bullied by her husband and his meaningless pseudo-ethics.

An hour later, Louise had drained the pot of coffee and still Howard hadn't come home. He was probably gambling at one of those Indian casinos. Gambling away money they didn't have. She picked up the crowbar and started prying plaster. They had to fix the kitchen anyway. Howard would change his mind about moving, once the new kitchen was in.

Demolition was kind of fun, she discovered, especially when the big hunks came loose and she could see real progress. She felt a kind of freedom in forcing the destruction.

Instead of plaster behind the pantry, the wall was plywood. Louise stuck the crowbar in the edge and pushed with all her overly caffeinated strength. The board splintered. She pried up the nails all the way around, and when it came free, she looked with amazement at what lay inside the wall. On a shelf was a small caliber pistol, a half-full bottle of whiskey, a carved wooden heart, two sealed envelopes, and three bullets lined up in a row. Two of the bullets were whole, and one was just an empty casing. Written on one sealed envelope was one word: *Marcy.* And on the other: *Louise.*

When Howard returned home, he found Louise sweat-soaked and covered with plaster dust, crowbar in her hand. One whole wall of the kitchen lay open to the studs. Where Pursley's name had been was now a white streak of paint, and, on the stud next to it, she had painted LEPPENS.

"Good work," he said, then pointed at their name on the stud. "But we're going back to Boston."

Louise took another whack at the plaster and let her anger vent there instead of where she really wanted to put it.

"I'm not going to live in a house built by a murderer," he said.

She turned to face him. "You've *been* living in it."

"But it's different, now that I know."

Louise remembered Howard's obsession with the Pursley case. Lawrence Pursley had been charged with the murder of his wife, but no murder weapon had ever been found and, in fact, no body. No body, no crime, the jury effectively said, and let him go free. Howard had raged. Louise had privately cheered. She was always one for the underdog, and there was no evidence at all that Lawrence Pursley had murdered his wife. She wanted to see the evidence before convicting him, rock hard evidence, not mere circumstantial, innuendo-based rumor. Some knee-jerk jerks she knew were satisfied with that, but not Louise. She figured if you were going to put someone away for life, you better have solid evidence.

"You're just looking for a reason to go back to Boston, because you miss your bookie," she said, "and this isn't a good enough reason. Pursley was never convicted of her murder."

"He bragged about it," Howard said. "He was evil. I remember the case. It happened while we were in school."

"I remember. So?"

"So he slept in our *bedroom,* Louise. She may be buried under the floorboards up there."

"Don't be ridiculous," she said, and took another whack at the wall.

"Regardless," he said, and put a hand on her shoulder. "The movers are coming tomorrow. I found a contractor to finish the kitchen and called Julia to list the house. We're leaving."

"I'm not," she said, and buried the crowbar once again in fresh plaster.

In the morning, Louise dismissed the movers when they showed up. She called Julia and told her that she and Howard had had a big fight. She'd taken him to the bus station that morning, and put him on the bus back to Boston. He'd get himself another car when he got there—she needed to keep the one they had—and that they had agreed to a trial separation before making any real decisions.

Julia sounded very practiced in her words of comfort. Realtors had seen other marriages go belly up over a remodeling project.

Two days later when the contractor arrived, there was a fresh piece of plywood on the wall where the new pantry would go. Louise had learned a few skills—the art of saw, hammer and nail being among them.

She had learned those skills by following the very specific instructions Lawrence Pursley had left in his letter to her. He must have been evil, Louise decided, or at least psychic. He knew her by name, and he knew the problem she was up against. After reading the letter at least a dozen times, she decided he was right. She'd tried it her way, and she'd tried it Howard's way. Neither of those had worked. Maybe she should try it Lawrence Pursley's way.

The evening of her discovery in the wall, she had showered, powdered and perfumed, took Howard to the screen porch, sat in his lap, gave him the carved heart to soften him up and a glass of the drugged whiskey to make him woozy. When the time was just perfect, she shot him in the head with one of Pursley's two remaining bullets. Then she dragged him to the basement and laid him to rest alongside Pursley's former wife, or what was left of her, inside the wooden casing of the old sump pump. It was a nice fit. Louise took off his clothes, opened him up, and emptied a bag of quickset cement on him. Then she re-nailed the old boards back into place. The cement would draw out his moisture and harden in place. He'd become a desiccated, petrified statue in no time, just like his very unattractive roommate. Ugh. No wonder Lawrence had murdered her.

Then, on the shelf inside the kitchen wall, she placed two empty bullet casings, one whole bullet, the whiskey bottle, the carved heart, the gun and the remaining envelope. She nailed the plywood down good.

The relief she felt was beyond amazing. She felt young, invincible, and completely at ease. She wondered why she hadn't thought of that simple solution to all her problems before. She was going to have an amazingly simple life from now on, a life without Howard and his debts. It would be a few years before she could file for Howard's life insurance, but all good things come to those who wait.

Julia stopped by a week later to see how the remodel was progressing. Her eyes were puffy and they had dark circles under them.

Louise, feeling like the epitome of the counseling neighbor, put the pot of coffee on and they sat in the screen porch, where the air was a little fresher, and talked while the contractor installed the kitchen cabinets.

"It's my son," Julia said. "He's a drunk and a druggie and I'm afraid his wife is going to divorce him. I'd hate to lose her. She's the daughter I never had. They live downstate, where he's been in and out of treatment facilities. I'm thinking of having them move closer so I can keep an eye on him. Otherwise, I'm sure Marcy will leave him, disappear with my grandsons. I don't think I could bear that."

"*Marcy?*" Louise said.

Julia nodded as she dabbed her napkin at smudging mascara, then wiped at her nose, completely ignoring her coffee.

Louise felt a surge of affection for Julia, and wanted to help her grieving friend. The thought flitted through her mind that it was a well-justified offer.

She felt a flush of pleasure in the freedom of accepting that which has been preordained.

"I don't think Howard's coming back," Louise said, trying to sound matter-of-fact without sounding pleased, "so I'm thinking of moving to a smaller house. Think Marcy'd like a place with a new kitchen?"

Just a Foot Away

The first indication Cara Trenton had that all was not right at The Tickled Bear was at nine a.m. when Isaac Knotts gave the door a brisk knuckling, and Babs didn't come to open it. Isaac waited, knocked again, and, by that time, Cara had come out of her gallery next door to sweep snow off the sidewalk before it turned to ice.

"Where's Babs?" Isaac wanted to know, and he took the heavy box from his shoulder and set it on the step.

"Haven't seen her yet this morning," Cara said. "Was she expecting you?"

"Delivery every Thursday at nine a.m.," Isaac said. "Christmas jam and mincemeat today."

Cara shrugged. Isaac pounded so hard on the shiny blue door with the closed sign that the miniature sleigh bells that Babs had hung on the inside of the door jangled. He waited another minute, then shouldered his heavy box and turned toward his truck.

"Want me to hold on to that until she gets here?" Cara asked. "She might just be running late."

"That'd be great," Isaac said. "I've got a full morning of deliveries across county."

Cara held her gallery door open and Isaac put the box down on her countertop. "What kind of jam?"

"Today? Cranberry banana. My granddad's special holiday recipe."

Mike, Cara's parrot, squawked and Isaac gave him a scratch on the back of his neck.

"I'll have to try some."

"Buy it from Babs," Isaac said. "I don't compete with my retailers."

Isaac left, and Cara and Mike had a long talk about him that would sound like nonsense to the uninitiated. But Babs's doorway was busy, and Babs was nowhere to be seen. By ten o'clock, Cara had taken in a two-box delivery from UPS; three hand-spun, hand-knit sweaters and a tote from a hippie kind of woman wearing Birkenstock shoes and smelling faintly of patchouli oil; and a slim letter package from FedEx. All for Babs. By ten after ten, a small group of women, surely the wives of ice fishermen, stood around in their down coats waiting for the lights to go on, the sign to flip and Babs to open the door, revealing her bright, cheery and perfectly made-up smile.

But the sign said it would open at ten, and, by ten-twenty, the women wandered away, muttering to themselves, adjusting their earmuffs and tossing their scarves. The payoff money their husbands had allowed them in exchange for guilt-free fishing time was clearly burning holes in their uptown tiny purses, and Babs had just the right kind of expensive trinkets, clothes and accessories they wanted to buy. But they didn't have too much time to whine, because Kimberly had opened the dress shop across the street, so they could go waste a little time over there and then come back. Babs must have had some kind of emergency. Spilled coffee on her lap on the way to the shop or something. Who hadn't had *that* happen at least once?

Cara Trenton, who owned the photography gallery next door to The Tickled Bear, knew Babs would have even opened early, had she seen that group of well-heeled women. Nobody in White Pines Junction would ignore free-floating tourist dollars. Especially winter dollars. She tried calling the shop, in case

Babs was counting receipts or restocking and had lost track of time, and when she still hadn't opened the door by eleven, Cara called the house. When there was no answer, she called Gordie at the taxidermy shop. Gordie answered with his big voice, which always surprised Cara, because Gordie was not a big man. He was small and meticulous, good at his art, but perhaps the big he-men who fished these lakes for gigantic fish needed to deal with a big-voiced man, so Gordie gave them one. But when you met him personally, in his studio filled with exquisitely mounted fish and wildlife, he was soft spoken and soft-handed. A gentle man with a gruff telephone voice.

Cara told Gordie that Babs hadn't opened the shop yet, which seemed to be news to Gordie. He said he'd put the "Be Right Back" sign up at his shop and then run home to check on her. He sounded sufficiently worried, or so Cara told Sheriff Withens later.

By noon, Gordie was at The Tickled Bear. Cara wandered over, as the group of women was still at Kimberly's, trying on hats and things, and Gordie asked Cara to call the sheriff while he searched the shop. Babs was not at home, Gordie said. Her empty coffee cup was in the kitchen sink, as usual, her car was gone, her purse was gone, the bathroom smelled like shampoo and perfume, just like normal. Her car hadn't broken down on the usual route between home and the shop—she always drove the straight route down County Road K into town—and Gordie was starting to worry.

Cara called the sheriff while she watched the women exit Kimberly's, each with a shopping bag, and look toward her gallery. They squinted at The Tickled Bear and its "closed" sign, then started across the street to her. She welcomed them in, and told them there had been a family emergency next door, and Babs wasn't likely to open that day. They grumbled, but Mike the parrot charmed them, and they spent enough time talking with him and listening to him crack jokes, that a few bought framed photographs. Photographs of the local herd of albino deer were always a popular choice. Those and anything with a bald eagle in it.

About two o'clock, the sheriff drove away. Gordie came out of The Tickled Bear, locked the door behind him, came into Cara's gallery, and collapsed into a hand-hewn pine-log chair. "I'm a suspect," he said with a mix of awe, surprise, and regret. "I'm worried sick, and the first person they look at is a spouse for a murder—murder, Cara! The second most popular theory is a lover that she might've run off with."

Cara shook her head. Hard to imagine what Gordie was feeling.

"Hi, Gordie," Mike said, and flapped.

"Hi, Mike."

"I love you, Gordie," Mike said.

"I love you too, Mike," Gordie said and gave the parrot a wan smile. Then he turned back to Cara. "A lover! Do you think Babs had a lover and has run off with him? Tell me, Cara, please, god, tell me if you think you've seen her carrying on with somebody. Has she confided anything like that?"

"Of course not," Cara said. "You've got to be kidding."

"Well? Then what? Where is she? I got up at five, ran, showered, and headed for the studio. She was still in bed."

"Did she have to run into the city for anything? Did she have an appointment that you didn't know about? Was Cindy or somebody supposed to open the shop for her, forgot, and it's all a big misunderstanding?"

"We've been over all that. We called Cindy, and she didn't know anything. There was nothing in Babs's appointment book. I don't get it." He shook his head and ran fingers through his hair. "I'm scared to death."

"Is the sheriff getting up a search party?" Cara asked. Mike started to fuss, so Cara picked him up and put him on her shoulder, where Mike pulled strands of Cara's curly red hair through his beak. Mike loved to preen his friends.

Gordie nodded, his head low, his eyes filling with tears. "Tomorrow. He wants to wait twenty-four hours for her to show up. I'm scared to death," he whispered.

Cara fiddled with a pen on her countertop, not knowing how to comfort her friend, feeling inadequate, and oddly blessed that she lived alone with her camera gear, darkroom, and Mike, whom she had inherited and who would outlive her by about fifty years.

Gordie sat in the pine chair for another ten minutes, head in his hands, and finally, without a word, got up, got into his truck and drove away. Cara started sorting and cataloging negatives, a mindless job she hated.

On their way home, Cara and Mike stopped at Margie's for a chicken Caesar salad, and the diner was abuzz with the latest news. A foot had been found at the edge of the ice at Minnow Lake by little Katarina Svensen and her dog Chewy. Sheriff Withens had Lexy identify the toenail polish color as Porn Star Pink, the last she'd put on Babs at her most recent pedicure, and while the evidence was being sent out for official DNA testing, the sheriff had taken Gordie into custody and ordered a dive team to search the lake.

Cara lost her appetite, pushed the salad away, and cradled her mug of hot black coffee as Mike greeted the other diners, and took bits of salad and meat from Cara's plate. Babs Van Rank was dead. It was inconceivable. Even more inconceivable was the idea that Gordie could have done it. But if not Gordie, then who? Who would kill Babs? Cara's gallery had been open next door to The Tickled Bear only since spring, but she'd never seen anything untoward or suspicious. Ever. Babs sold handmade items from all over the northwoods, and took deliveries from the craftsmen, the knitters, the jam makers, pickle canners, the wood carvers, and from UPS almost every day. There was a constant stream of people in and out of that shop, and during the off-season, Babs's shop was the hub for shipping White Pines Junction goods to stores farther south. She did well at it, too. There was something special about the northwoods stuff, and specialty shops all over the midwest, maybe all over the country, wanted it.

Babs was bright and cheerful, had a low, pleasant voice, was perfectly made up at all times, every long brown shiny hair in its proper place, and she knew how to put together an attractive package, whether it be herself or The Tickled Bear. She was a member of the White Pines Junction Chamber of Commerce, acted as lively auctioneer every year for the grade school fundraiser, donated to local charities, did her work for the Heart Association and was an all-around wonderful woman and loyal wife. Cara didn't know Babs all that well, but she liked her, and couldn't imagine anyone killing her. And cutting off her foot!

There was still a chance that it wasn't Babs's foot, Cara knew, but it was a slim chance.

She put a ten on the table for Margie and went home with Mike. She was ready to flop on the couch, stroke some soft feathers and feel Mike's tiny little heartbeat. She needed some normalcy in a community never known for it.

The next day, Cara took an alternate route to work because she didn't want to see the divers in Minnow Lake. It was bad enough having the gallery next to The Tickled Bear.

Town was full of tourists because the weather had turned cool and overcast, and the gallery had a constant stream of lookers and a few buyers. At three-thirty, the familiar FedEx guy came with a shipment of mat board and frames.

Cara thanked him, spoke a few words of courtesy about the weather, then watched as the guy swung back up into his truck, clipboard in his hand.

"Hey," Cara called out her door. "Where were you yesterday? Day off?"

"No," he said, "I didn't have a delivery here yesterday. Why?"

"No reason," Cara lied. "I was just expecting this stuff yesterday."

They waved good-bye at each other and Cara went inside her gallery to stare at the FedEx envelope she had accepted for Babs yesterday. It sat on top of the sweaters and the boxes from UPS. Cara wished she could remember what the FedEx guy yesterday had looked like, and now that she thought about it, she wasn't even sure it had been delivered by a guy in a FedEx uniform, or even by someone driving a FedEx truck. Cara was starting to have a bad feeling, and not only that she was a pretty poor observer, for a photographer.

FedEx always came to White Pines Junction late in the day unless it was an expensive priority delivery. Cara checked the label on Babs's envelope. Nope. Standard overnight. That meant delivery at three-thirty p.m., as usual.

She hefted the envelope. Light. If she opened it, she'd be messing with evidence, maybe. Besides, wasn't it a felony to open somebody else's mail? Was FedEx mail? She couldn't call Gordie for his permission, and the sheriff was busy at Minnow Lake. Maybe Cara ought to call Pastor Porter to come over and witness her opening the envelope. Maybe Babs did have a lover. Maybe he killed her, then posed as a FedEx delivery guy to give himself an alibi.

No, Cara, that's stupid, she told herself. You and Mike have been watching too much television, but not even a television studio would buy that script.

She looked outside and saw the FedEx truck down at Doc's, so she picked up the envelope again, flipped over her sign to the "closed" side and trotted across the street.

"Would you scan this for me?" Cara asked at the door to his van. "Tell me when it was sent?"

"Sure." The driver passed his hand-scanner over the barcode, and then pushed a button, frowned, scanned it again, and handed it back to Cara. "Never was," he said.

"That's what I thought. Thanks."

To hell with Pastor Porter, she thought, and ripped open the envelope.

Inside was a single sheet of paper, a model release for an ad to run in the northwoods real-estate locator magazine, signed by Viktor Haas, the playboy who owned the marina just outside of town.

Cara knew Viktor, and it hadn't been Viktor who delivered the envelope. Besides, the return address on the FedEx envelope was not White Pines Junction, it was Minneapolis. None of this made sense. She closed up shop and went to find the sheriff at Minnow Lake.

But the sheriff didn't have much time to listen to Cara's theories. He was busy zipping into a body bag the second dead female with missing body parts that the divers had found that day. Neither one of them was Babs Van Rank. Both women had their heads shaved bald.

Cara sat at the picnic table with some of the other locals, and, as they speculated about the identity of the found women, a diver surfaced through the hole in the ice with a thumbs-up signal, and soon Sheriff Withens was zipping up a bald and leg-less Babs.

The sheriff sent the coroner's car on its way down to the city with its miserable cargo, then he stopped by the picnic table. Cara had never seen the sheriff look so worn and haggard. "I've lived too long," he said. Cara moved over and the sheriff settled down onto the bench. Jimbo Benson, who edited the weekly newspaper, offered him a cup of hot coffee from his thermos.

"Who're the others, Sheriff?" Jimbo asked.

The sheriff shrugged, sighed, then got up. "Tourists, I think. I've heard no missing persons reports up here lately, other than, well . . . I've got to go tell Gordie," he said.

Cara stopped him and told him about the weird FedEx package. When she said that the model release was Viktor's, the sheriff nodded toward the divers. "That's Viktor down there," he said. "Go ahead and interrogate him for me." Then the man, bent by his burdens, got into his cruiser and took off, spitting gravel.

Cara waited for Viktor to unsuit, talk with his search and rescue pals for a while, then she approached him, and asked about the strange FedEx delivery. Viktor, ruggedly handsome and the perfect model for the specialty clothes that Babs sold, explained that Babs needed the release before the ad was to run, and he'd left it at his mom's place in Minneapolis. She was going to FedEx it back to Babs, but then his kid brother came down to help in the garage and dropped it off instead. Then Viktor looked at Cara as though she smelled bad for asking about that at a time like this, and turned his back.

Cara went back to her gallery to tidy things up, thought she might stop at the jail to say hello to Gordie, if she could get in to see him, maybe take him some magazines or something, find out what Gordie wanted her to do about Babs's shop.

She moved the UPS boxes from the countertop to the back of her frame shop, and then the box of jars of jelly and mincemeat. Hmmm. Cranberry banana jelly. She took a pint jar out of the box, held it up to the afternoon light. Beautiful deep red color. Not clear like a pure cranberry would be, but clouded because of the banana addition. She pried open the lid and scooped some out with her finger and tasted it. Yum. She'd have some on her toast in the morning, and slip an IOU into the box. Then she moved the tote and the sweaters. Two of them were obviously for a man, but the other was nice. Very nice. Cara's colors of brown and blue, and her size, too, with a little picot stitching around the neck. She tried it on and admired himself in the mirror. The wool had a nice sheen to it with what looked like a reddish highlight. Very nice. It would be perfect for the winter.

She thought about that little hippie girl who had brought this to Babs. She probably had kids and expenses. Cara hated to see her stock sit in Babs's closed shop, or worse, kick around the back room of her gallery while the whole Babs mess was handled. Her address was on the tag.

Cara put Mike on her shoulder and headed home. She'd just make one brief stop on the way.

The winter sun went down early, so when Cara pulled into the woman's driveway, she could see her through the lighted front window with her spinning wheel. Cara carried all three sweaters and the tote, planning to buy one and return the rest.

The girl stopped her wheel, opened the door and took a couple of steps onto the front porch, hugging herself against the cold.

"Hi," Cara said in greeting, then held up the sweaters. "I've come to talk to you about Babs Van Rank. You know, from The Tickled Bear?"

"No," the woman said and backed toward the door. "I don't know nothing. You better get off my land, or come back with, you know, a warrant."

"A warrant? No, you don't understand, I've come about these sweaters."

"Isaac!" she screamed and backed into the house.

Isaac, the cranberry banana jam man, came out holding a shotgun.

Cara dropped the sweaters in the snow and raised her hands. Mike flapped his clipped wings and floated to the ground, landing on top of the sweaters.

"She's a redhead," Isaac said.

The girl peeked at Cara from around his back. "That's good," she said, "it looks natural."

"Hey, listen," Cara said, but nobody listened to her, they listened to Mike, who was pulling hairs from the sweater and saying, "Hi, Babs. I love you, Babs."

Cara saw the taillight of Babs's car hidden around the funky old garage about the same time realization hit her, and her last thought was of Gordie, poor Gordie, who had always loved the way Babs made those mincemeat pies.

HOUSE ODDS

Julia owned way too much property in White Pines Junction. As she sat with her accountant's report for the year end, she was appalled at how much property she owned, how much she paid in taxes, how much she got back in rents, and what her net worth was. She was pleased, there was no question about that. When her husband had taken off with his tart, she had strong-armed him for most of his wealth, and she'd had a little tucked away herself. It hadn't taken her long after the wedding to realign. He'd evidenced his snaky ways the minute the honeymoon was over. So while Julia was pleased with the bottom line of her investment portfolio, she wasn't all that crazy about being overly invested in real estate. In Vargas County real estate, anyway.

Marcy needed a helping hand, and Julia had no spare cash. The only thing she could offer her daughter-in-law was real estate—a little cottage or an apartment—for her and the boys, but Vargas County and kids . . . not a good match. She could move Kevin Leppens out of his cottage and into—no, he was a good tenant. Too good to lose.

She wanted Marcy and her boys nearby, but far enough away to be safe.

This was the price, she thought, as she had every day since her son—Marcy's druggie husband—had become a problem. This is the price one pays for populating a place out of the mainstream. Vargas County was a sportsman's paradise, an investor's dream. It had pretty much everything anybody needed, including wonderful summers and exquisite winters. Everybody in Vargas County prospered, including—she consulted her financial statement—her. And the down side was . . . well, the down side was that Marcy couldn't move next door, not with those little boys, because those two sweet little things would be vulnerable to the down side. And Julia would never forgive herself for sacrificing them in order to prosper.

She could move. She could set them up in a close-by town. She could send Marcy some money and let Marcy make her own decisions. Ultimately, Julia thought, it wasn't up to her. It was up to Marcy. And Marcy had her own parents—she wasn't really Julia's responsibility. And if Marcy decided to bring her boys to White Pines Junction, well, that was between Marcy and her conscience. Julia would advise her of all the pros and cons.

She set the financial statement aside and picked up her appointment book. She was to show property to a young couple at two p.m., and just had time to finish dressing before her appointment at the hair salon. She'd be finished there just in time for a lunch date with Mitch, and be ready to show property at two. Life was good. And if she really admitted it to herself, having Marcy and the boys close by would cramp her style a little bit. Julia wasn't crazy about living the rest of her life alone, but she was having fun being single, even in the limited local social scene.

Julia tried not to think about Marcy, and put her mind on Mitch instead, and dressed appropriately, then bundled up and headed out for the Shear Pleasure and a little girl talk with Lexy.

Lexy, true to form, had multiple levels of hair piled on top of her head, and exaggerated cuts on the side, so they were asymmetrical and off balance, much like multi-layered, asymmetrical, off-balance Lexy herself. Her hair was a flaming red, bordering on purple, and she wore Kelly-green eye shadow. She was dressed in her signature white lab coat over tights. Today her tights were purple, and there was a hole in the thigh of one, where white skin protruded, attesting to the tightness of the tights and the generous proportion of Lexy's thigh.

"Hey, baby!" she greeted Julia, as she opened the door to the salon, which used to be a garage attached to Lexy's little house. Julia wanted to believe that Lexy knew her name, but, in reality, she believed that Lexy didn't know anybody's name, she just marked her appointment book with X's.

Julia took off her coat and unwound her scarf. It was too hot in Lexy's place; it always was. But it was festive with tacky Christmas decorations that were still up two weeks after New Year's, and that made Julia smile.

"Oooh, so dressy, Miss Sassy," Lexy said. "Looks like you've got a date. Go take off that dress and put on a smock."

Julia did as she was told behind the Oriental screen.

"Wash and set? Perm? Color touch-up? Nails? Pedicure?"

Julia smiled. She'd like all of that, but wasn't sure she could put up with the company for all that long.

"Wash, trim, blow dry," she said. "That's it for today."

She got her wash, then Lexy examined her roots and pronounced they were good for two more weeks before she would be so obvious people would be able to see her gray part approach long before they saw her face.

Julia appreciated Lexy's idiosyncrasies. She was fun, for a while.

As the ends of her hair were beginning to coat the floor in little dark commas, as the tiny silver scissors flashed around her head, a cold lick of wind blew in and the jingle bells on the door handle jangled.

"Hey, baby!" Lexy said.

Margie came in, and pulled her stocking cap off her head.

She rubbed her reddened cheeks with mittened hands and sat down in the other swiveling chair. "Hi, Lex. Hi, Julia. I thought I'd come by and see if you had time to give me a trim."

"Hmmm," Lexy said, "let me look." She left Julia and consulted her appointment book on the table by the phone. "If you don't need too much, I can squeeze you in quickly right after her."

"Great," Margie said, and unbuttoned her coat. "I'll wait."

Julia tried not to stare at Margie, but whenever she looked at the once-beautiful young woman who pioneered the area by opening the best diner in the county, all Julia could see was the grief she held onto so tightly it showed in her face. Margie had never recovered from Micah's disappearance. Would Julia be able to recover if she encouraged Marcy to move her boys to town and one—or, god forbid, both—disappeared in the same way? Would Julia be able to recover if she were merely silent in her encouragement to Marcy?

The thought gave her a hot flash.

Lexy blotted Julia's forehead with a tissue, and with it came most of her makeup. She'd have to go home again to repair the damage before meeting Mitch.

Lexy went back to trimming Julia's hair while Margie watched, and Julia watched Margie in the mirror. Lexy hummed, the heater fan wouldn't stop, and the three women were otherwise silent. Then Margie spoke.

"How do you stand it?"

Lexy stopped clipping and they both turned to look at her.

"How can you live here?"

Lexy dropped Julia's strand of hair and pulled up a chair. Julia looked at the clock. She'd never have time to go home to primp for Mitch. Oh well. She'd have to make do.

"It's where we live, baby," Lexy said. "Why? What's the matter with you?"

"I've been thinking about trying to get pregnant again," Margie said with a catch in her voice, "but I could never have another child and keep living here."

"It's been what, two years since Micah?" Julia asked.

A tear tripped down Margie's cheek. She nodded. Lexy handed her a tissue. "I know your kids are grown, Julia," Margie said, "but what about your grandkids? Don't they ever come to visit you? And you, Lexy, don't you want to have a couple of kids? Don't you think we sell our souls to live in this place where they steal our children?"

Julia was disappointed that she hadn't followed this train of thought through earlier in the day, and then maybe she'd have some answers.

Margie dried her eyes and her sorrow was immediately replaced with anger. Righteous indignation. "I make a good living here, just like everybody else. We prosper, Jimbo and me. And you, Julia, hell, you own more real estate in this county than anybody else. We know you're rich. Lexy, your appointment book is full. It's the same for everybody up here. Everybody does well. There isn't an unemployed, poor, street person in this whole county, except for maybe Recon John and Chainlink Charlie, and they *want* to be that way. They aren't poor, they're just weird."

Lexy looked like she'd like to have a cigarette, but of course she wouldn't while there were customers in her shop.

"So doesn't it make you mad? Don't you think we're all guilty?"

Lexy squinted up her face and clipped her scissors a few times. Julia felt as though she were the responsible adult in the room, she ought to be saying something. "It's a thought I'm sure we've all had, Margie, but I don't think we're guilty of anything but doing life well. Lexy works hard for her prosperity. So do you. So do I."

"And look at the dues we pay to belong to this club. It costs us a child a year, just about."

"People die everywhere," Lexy said, and stood up, ready to tackle Julia's head again. Julia was ready for her to resume. She glanced at the clock. She was going to be late for Mitch.

"These kids don't die, that's the point. We just give them away, and give lip service to what a shame it is, and go on with our lives."

Lexy turned and gave Margie a full-frontal look. "You didn't leave when Micah left. You are still here, reaping the prosperity."

"I've paid my dues into this little club of the damned. More than you will ever know."

"You knew about this place before you settled here. You knew it happened, but you never thought it would happen to you," Lexy said.

Julia had never seen Lexy this confrontational before. Margie started to cry again. "Yeah, sure," Lexy went on. "I want to have some kids someday. I kind of hoped that I'd get together with Paulie Timmins. But then, you know . . . he died. One of these days I'll snag me a nice fisherman, though, and we will have some kids. Will we stay here? I don't know. I think it'll never happen to me."

"It could."

"Yes. It could. And to you it did. We make our choices, Margie, and we live with the consequences." Lexy grabbed Julia's head and, with hard fingers, turned her face to the mirror and went at her hair again, quite viciously, with the comb.

Margie shrugged into her coat and left without another word.

"Jeez. She's still blaming us." Lexy pulled on Julia's hair hard enough to make her wince.

"Got any tea?" Julia asked.

"Sure, baby," Lexy said, brightening up immediately. "Lemon Zinger?"

Julia smiled.

When she left Lexy's, she went straight to Mitch's office, where the waiting room with a gold garland over the reception-ist's window was empty and the receptionist told her the doctor was expecting her. Then she pushed the intercom, announced Julia, and soon Dr. Mitch Kardashian, the amazingly handsome dentist, came out looking like he was ready for the opera, wear-ing a full-length black wool coat and a white silk scarf. Julia knew it wasn't going to be long before he whisked her off into the land of carnal bliss, but she was going to hold him off for as long as she could. She was hoping for a wedding ring, or at least she thought she was. It had been a long time since she'd fallen for a man, and she wanted to be sure. If she wasn't sure she wanted to marry him, she didn't want to bed him.

But he sure was handsome. He smiled at her with genuine pleasure, and nothing made her feel sweet and feminine like a man who was eager to see her.

"Darling," he said.

Another point in his favor.

"I had an emergency this morning and had to put off a cli-ent. I've squeezed her in at the end of my lunch, and I'm afraid we're not going to have time for the lunch I hoped. I intended to take you"—he pushed the door open and held it for her to step into the frosty air—"for a *leisurely* lunch, but I'm afraid it's Margie's for us today."

Julia was surprised at how disappointed she felt at the change of plans she didn't even know about. He made it sound so intriguing. She waited for Mitch to unlock his Mercedes and open the passenger door for her. He treated her like a queen. Leisurely dining or fast food, it didn't matter to her. With his swarthy, hairy good looks and those milk-white teeth and deep brown eyes with the whiter-than-white whites, he was all hers.

"I'm sorry you had a stressful morning," she said.

"Not as stressful for me as for the sheriff," Mitch said. "He was the emergency. A tootsie-roll pulled off an old crown and exposed the root of a molar."

Julia shuddered.

"Said he saw God."

They both laughed. Mitch had a deep, hearty laugh that matched the rest of him. Julia loved it.

Two minutes later, they pulled into Margie's crowded parking lot. Mitch opened the car door for Julia, then he opened the diner door, and escorted her to a booth in the far corner. There was something special about being the date of the most eligible, handsome professional man in town. Julia felt remarkably well-tended and pampered within Mitch's protective aura.

Margie came over with the perennial coffee pot in one hand, and two menus in the other. She wouldn't meet Julia's eyes, and Julia knew that Lexy had hurt her feelings, had hurt them deeply. "Margie," she said, and, when Margie did look up, Julia could tell that Margie had been crying. Had cried off all her mascara and her eyes were a little bit puffed. "You know I don't share Lexy's opinions about things."

"Doesn't matter," she said. "Forget it." Margie took a ragged breath, and her mouth tightened against a new serving of tears. "She's right."

"She is not right," Julia said, maybe a little bit too forcefully, because Margie turned and walked back into the kitchen.

"What the hell is that all about?" Mitch asked. The concern in his face made Julia feel bad that she'd made Margie cry all over again. She briefly related the incident, and Mitch looked down at his fingernails.

"Lexy's right, you know," he said. "I'd never have children here. I think about it a lot, the kids that I see, their parents. I think they all live on the knife's edge of hope versus fear, and I think it's a conscious decision they make. They're gambling."

Julia gasped at the concept.

"Sometimes you win," Mitch went on, "and sometimes you lose. But the constant is that the house takes its percentage from every single bet. Ultimately, the house always comes out on top. Winning and losing is just an illusion. When you gamble, the house wins."

Just then, a composed Margie came back from the kitchen, and when she filled up their coffee cups, Julia touched her hand with a fingertip. Margie managed a weak smile, then took their orders. Two salads with vinaigrette.

"What about me?" Julia asked Mitch. "I'm not gambling."

"But you will. That's the uncanny thing about this place. It's a giant casino. Odds are, you will eventually place a bet. Even the UPS guy is bound to plug a quarter into a slot, just on the off chance."

That just settled it, Julia thought. No Marcy, no grandkids. She would put her foot down. She felt her face grow hot that she had even considered bringing them here.

"What's so amazing to me is that Margie and Jimbo, bereaved and bitter, continue to live here, even though they've got another son."

Julia had that plunging elevator feeling. "And she's even considering another. You think they'd take two kids out of the same family? Don't you think they've paid their dues?"

"Flip a coin and it comes up heads ninety-nine times in a row. What are the odds of it coming up heads the hundredth time?"

Julia shrugged. "Astronomical."

"Fifty-fifty," Mitch said. "The coin doesn't care what happened before or after."

"What about you?" she asked him.

"I'm a compulsive by nature," he said, leaning close to her. "I've done drugs, booze, gambling, sex, food, even exercise . . . you name it, I've indulged in it to excess. And now I don't do any of that anymore. Now I'm a moderate. I don't drink, I don't smoke, I don't gamble, I won't have sex outside marriage, I exercise like a normal person, and I eat right."

"You keep a tight rein on yourself?"

"My world has become more black and white," he admitted. "There are things I don't do, places I don't go."

"Isn't that terribly restrictive?"

"Actually, it's liberating. I can do anything I want to now. Anything I want. It just so happens that I don't want a martini. I'd rather have a Diet Coke. Or a cup of coffee."

"And you live here because . . . ?"

"Because it's so beautiful. And it's a fine dental practice. And there's you."

"Think you can live inside the casino without plugging in that quarter?"

"I'm not smug about it. I'm just not interested. Besides, I'm not here for the long term. I'm here to put in my time, get my stake, and get out." He reached across the table and took her freshly manicured hand. "In the meantime, there are healthier things around to capture my interest."

"But what about the house's percentage?"

"I can afford it," he said, and kissed her fingertips.

The whole time Julia was showing property to the young couple, she wondered what her responsibility was in informing them of the pitfalls of living in the area. They were newlyweds, sure to want to have children eventually, maybe sooner.

She didn't mention it.

When she got back to her home office, she kicked off her shoes, changed into jeans and a sweatshirt and busied herself in the kitchen making her annual apricot jam for the library fund-raiser. But her mind couldn't leave Mitch and his theories of Vargas County. Was he kidding her with all this stuff? Was he kidding himself? Was he right? Was Lexy right? Should she move to firmer soil?

Why would she? Because she's living the good life, funded by the sacrifices of grieving parents?

Boy, that was sure an ugly thought.

And another not-so-great idea was hitching herself up to a compulsive for the long run. Mitch could drink again, gamble away all she had built up over the years, snort it up his nose, gain three hundred pounds. . . . He was not as attractive now as he had been hours earlier.

Julia had a lot to think about.

When Marcy called just as Julia was filling the jars with lava-like boiling apricot jam, she let the machine get it. She listened to the message later, as the cooling canning jars pinged with a tight seal, and she was having her ceremonial bagel with a taste of the fresh jam on it.

Marcy was crying. Hysterical. Julia threw the bagel into the sink and tried to understand what Marcy was saying. She was at the hospital with Seth, the oldest boy. It sounded as if Jack, Marcy's husband—Julia's son—had beat her up and when little Seth tried to come to her rescue, Jack broke his arm.

It was way past time for Julia to act. *Jack had broken Seth's arm!* The boy was only eight. That bastard. She grabbed her coat, purse and keys and jumped into her car.

The hospital was two hours south. By the time Julia got there, she was even more confused than she had been before she started out. Driving left too much time to let thoughts tumble around in her head like laundry in a dryer.

But when she saw Marcy's face, bandaged and bruised, one eye swollen closed, one ear stitched up where she'd taken a kick to the head, all Julia's good ideas about anything fled and she was filled with compassion, remorse, guilt, love and sympathy. How could she have ever raised a son that could do something like this to a sweet girl like Marcy?

Marcy fell sobbing into Julia's arms. Julia knew that Marcy's parents lived in squalor down south in Mississippi or somewhere, and that Marcy would never go back. Julia was her mother now. Julia comforted her daughter-in-law and asked about Mikey. He was upstairs in the hospital day care. He was physically safe, if traumatized. Seth was having his arm set.

By the time the social worker talked with Julia, and she'd helped Marcy with the police, the forms, and had met with a counselor, it was late. Julia loaded up Marcy and her two silent children, Mikey, six, and Seth, eight, and took them to Mc-Donald's, but it didn't help much.

"Okay," Julia said, putting a French fry into her mouth and trying to appear positive, "here's the deal. You're all going to come up and stay with me at the lake for a while. And as soon as we can, we're going to get your stuff from your house and move you all up to the northwoods."

"With Daddy?" Mikey said.

"No, honey," Marcy said with a hitch in her voice. "Daddy can't be with us anymore."

"Good," Mikey said. "I hate him."

It was like a stab in Julia's heart to hear her grandson state hatred for her son, but under the circumstances, she could understand it. Truth be told, she wasn't too far behind Mikey on that one.

The boys fell asleep in the backseat as they drove back to Julia's house. The closer they got to Vargas County, the more agitated she got, trying to think of alternate locations they could stay until Julia figured out the finances. She was real-estate rich and cash poor, and she just didn't have the money to put Marcy up in a hotel or a motel or apartment. She'd have to get rid of a tenant, which would take time, or they'd have to stay at her place. Either way, the boys would be in the casino.

But anything was better than sending them back to Jack. Jack would likely kill Marcy next time. And Seth too, if he got in the way.

Marcy was silent on the way home. Julia wished her daughter-in-law would talk—either nervous chatter or confessions or just tell the story of what had happened—but Marcy was deep into her own thoughts, letting Julia stew in hers.

She was actually bringing the boys to Vargas County. Julia didn't even want them to visit, although they did regularly. They loved the lake. They swam like little fish, they made friends easily and probably this summer they'd learn to water-ski. Seth would, anyway. They would love it. She found herself trying to bargain with God. *They've been through so much,* she found herself praying. *Please let them live with us in peace. Please protect them and don't let them disappear. Don't take them away from me, please, I've been a good girl.*

It was temporary. She'd find them another place to live, and she'd do it right away. Some place outside of Vargas County, before Marcy found work, the boys got settled in school and all. She'd get them out. They'd only stay with her for a little while. Just a little while. *Just a little while. They're not really residents. Just guests. Temporary guests. Surely they can't be subject to the house take.*

But as Julia pulled into the driveway of her beautiful waterfront house, her mind busy with who would sleep where, whether or not the beds were made up, and if there was enough food in the house for breakfast, she very clearly heard the sound of a quarter dropping into the slot.

A Totem for a Time

The day that Recon John lost his lucky jawbone was the first time since Vietnam that he was afraid for his life. It was the jawbone from a monkey that took a bullet for him by jumping on his back as he stood on top of his tank just as a sniper fired from the outside limit of his rifle's range. The monkey hit John hard and just as he grabbed at it to toss it off of him, he felt the slug, heard the monkey's "oomph," as the breath was knocked out of it, then it went slack. A moment later, it fell from him, eyes wide with wonder, arms and fingers working weakly, grasping at nothing. The bullet had stopped in its spine. A buddy stepped on it and finished the job the sniper started, and John had cut out its jawbone to take as a souvenir.

Those were rougher days.

But in the thirty years that followed, he'd taken that small polished piece of jawbone with him everywhere, and he had always got along well in life. It was as much a part of his gear as his toothbrush, dental cleanliness being the only aspect of his personal hygiene that John was truly fastidious about.

Accordingly, he hung the jawbone on the birch branch where he kept his toothbrush, and he kissed it every morning after his breath was minty fresh, and said his thanks to the god who made that monkey act in such a strange manner at such a crucial moment. It started his day out right, thinking about the curious drift of things and how little control mortals had over their lives.

145

John lived in the woods and fended for himself, denying the government and bureaucracy any illusion of control over him. His one nod to civilization was dental floss, toothpaste, and a fresh toothbrush every year on his birthday.

So when his jawbone went missing, John went through what he later considered quite a strategic series of emotions.

First, he got mad. Who came to his place and messed in his stuff?

Then he got scared. He must be letting his guard down. If somebody could find his place, they could find him, and being found was not one of his favorite things. The last time he was found, there was trouble in town, and he didn't want any part of anything like that, ever again.

After anger and fear came the feeling of vulnerability, and that both scared him and made him mad. If he didn't have his lucky jawbone, he wasn't invincible.

But of course that was crap. It was just a bone. It had no power. No real power.

And after that series of emotions came the question, the most important part of the process. What did the universe want to tell him, teach him or prove to him? Taking that important memento, that piece of bone that was nothing in and of itself, was a radical act, and only the universe knew what it meant to him. Whoever took it didn't know that sometimes he sat for hours, looking at the lake or the sky or the woods, rubbing his thumb across the mandible until it glowed with a patina from the oils in his skin. Nobody else knew that he understood that piece of monkey jaw the way few people understood anything in their lives. In the Zen of it all, he not only *knew* the bone, but many times he *was* the bone. It was everything and it was nothing. John knew it was just a stupid bit of animal that he had to smuggle out of Vietnam, but it was the one irreplaceable artifact in his cache. An important factor when trying to second-guess the gods and their inscrutable methods.

He had to look beyond the camouflage.

He began his search, of course, right under its perch, then knowing the ways of squirrels, chipmunks, rats, raccoons, porcupines and the like, enlarged his search in a widening spiral. He was able to set aside the more philosophical aspects of the situation as he conducted a thorough reconnaissance. The snow actually made it easier, because the bone had been there on its perch the day before, and it hadn't snowed since. He didn't bother with the undisturbed white stuff.

By the time John got to what he considered the perimeter of his camp, he was back to considering the metaphysical implications, because the jawbone was flat-out gone.

He began to make plans to: A. move; and B. watch his ass like never before, because sure as that monkey had saved him and kept him all these years, there was just no telling what was about to happen without it.

But before he did anything, he needed to relax and consult the inner self.

So he rolled a joint and sat in the center of his place next to the fire pit and took a deep, cleansing breath.

Then he contemplated smoking the joint, but decided it would leave him too vulnerable, so he set it on a rock, and felt mildly resentful that he could no longer relax.

He tried to be calm. He tried hard.

But calm was as elusive as the jawbone, and John had the jangles, so he put a fresh T-shirt on over his dogtags, shrugged back into his fatigue jacket, brushed his teeth, set his snares, booby traps and trip wires, and went to town. There was only one place he could find some calm today, and that was at Doc's.

The tackle shop was empty when John peered through the glass door, then he gently opened it to keep the bells tied onto the handle from rattling.

Doc, half glasses set on his nose, was grinding his teeth over some bookwork and stabbing at a small calculator with the eraser of a pencil.

"Doc," John said.

Doc looked up, started to smile, then frowned instead. "What the hell?" he asked. "You look. . . ." Words failed him.

"Jawbone's gone," John said, and to his surprise, he felt like crying.

"Whoa," Doc said, and dropped his pencil. "Coffee."

John nodded and watched as Doc put the "Be Right Back" sign in the window, then the two of them walked in silence across the street to the diner.

Doc had been a young lieutenant working with the medical unit when John showed up in Nam. They met hard and fast under terrifying, screaming circumstances. When it was all over, John arranged to get out at the same time and followed Doc home. Doc had people, had a place, eventually had a wife. He also had demons, but only John knew about those.

Doc knew John's demons—could call them by name if he wanted—and that's why John could never go back to Cincinnati. So he lived in the woods and he counted on Doc for more than the occasional odd job for extra money. Sometimes he just needed somebody.

Now and then Doc came out to his place, too, and the two of them would smoke a joint and stare into the fire for hours in silent companionship. Like they had when Sadie Katherine left. That time Doc had brought Jack Daniel's. John, who didn't drink, watched Doc drink, cry, fall asleep, and then in slow motion, fall off the rock he'd been sitting on. John covered him with a sleeping bag, and, in the morning, Doc's equilibrium seemed to have returned.

Margie had coffee set up for them in a corner booth when they walked through her door.

John put four packets of sugar in his, Doc used one and some cream.

"You look like hell," Doc said.

"I can't think."

Doc nodded and stirred.

A few minutes later, Margie refilled their cups and set down a sugar dispenser.

"Sandwich?" Doc offered.

John shook his head and watched the white granules stream out of the dispenser and into his cup. "Shit's gonna hit the fan," he said. "I can feel it."

Doc nodded and stirred.

"Might move," John said.

Doc nodded.

"Who stole it, do ya think?"

"Don't know," Doc said. "Shit happens."

John nodded and added more sugar to his coffee syrup.

The bell on the door dinged, and John tensed. As he did so, the top of the sugar dispenser fell off, splashed into his cup, and the whole cylinder of sugar followed.

John stared at the white mountain for a long time before he righted the empty glass dispenser and set it gently on the table. Chills ran up his spine as he read in the spilled sugar, as sure as any gypsy read in a cup of tea leaves, that this was only the first instance of his bad luck run. He looked up at Doc, but Doc didn't get it.

Didn't matter. The message was for him, anyway.

Margie rushed over with a damp white towel and a tray and scooped the mess off the table, all the while chattering about her carelessness and mumbling I'm sorries. John tried to smile kindly at her to show her there were no hard feelings, because he knew it wasn't her fault. He saw Doc make small talk with her while he wondered where he could go to hide so that the bad luck couldn't find him.

Nowhere, he decided. Just go home and ride it out.

Margie brought fresh cups of coffee and a big peanut butter cookie for each of them, but John had no appetite. Doc ate both cookies and drank his coffee, then said, "Come stay with me at the house for a night or two."

It was a good idea. John didn't want to visit his bad luck on Doc, but he didn't think that was part of the deal. The bad luck was his, not Doc's. He nodded and, having accepted, felt a little bit more at ease. Somehow the bad stuff was easier to handle when there were two to share it. At least Doc's company would help ease him into his new life of living doom.

Natasha looked at the timer on the bread machine for the fourth time in two minutes. It had eight minutes to go, and she had nothing to do but wait for it, so she tapped her long nails on the old Formica counter and waited for the red numbers to count down. Eight minutes, it turned out, was a long time.

But when the machine beeped, she took out a sweet-smelling loaf of wheat bread and set it on the counter to cool. Then she cleaned the bread machine, wiped it dry, wiped down the countertop and sat on a stool, looking around her perfectly groomed kitchen and felt a gnawing hunger inside her that homemade bread would never satisfy.

Worse than that, she knew exactly what she needed, and she hated the thought of it. She hated what it did to Mort when she satisfied her cravings, but she was as subservient to her hormonal needs as he was to his appetite for food. They had come to an understanding over the years, and he had accepted the inevitable terms of their unconventional relationship, maybe better than Natasha had. She wished the restlessness would just go away, but it wouldn't. And she'd rather bed some local and just get it over with than to let the restlessness run away with her, all the way to Nashville, or San Francisco or something, somewhere far away from Mort, whom she loved and cherished above all else.

So now it was eleven o'clock in the morning, and all she had on her schedule was to make dinner. All that free time was trouble. Maybe she better take care of the problem before it took care of her.

She'd keep her eyes open, but White Pines Junction was a tiny place, and she couldn't afford to ruin Mort's reputation. Discretion was everything, and that was part of the problem. Desperation didn't honor discretion.

Waiting for Doc to close the tackle shop and go home was excruciating for John. To kill some time, he left the diner, went back to his campsite, tucked his toothbrush in his pocket and looked around. No sign of the jawbone. All his traps and snares were intact. The bad luck didn't seem to want to get him there. He wrapped his rifle in his waterproof poncho and buried it under the tent where the ground wasn't frozen solid. He walked carefully, warily, stepping lightly, nervousness in his stomach, through the woods to the road, feeling as if there were a sniper around every tree. He walked a mile down the road, dodging into the woods whenever a car went by—an old habit he saw no reason to break—then walked through the woods again to the lake shore, and there he sat to contemplate life and luck and to wait for the shop to close.

That night, Doc broiled summer trout and corn on the cob from the freezer and mashed up some potatoes, and the two of them sat at the little kitchen table to eat. John felt better just having a heartbeat within speaking range, though they didn't talk much.

"I think it's a wake-up call," Doc said around a mouthful of potatoes. "I think you've been leaning on that bone like a crutch and now you're well and don't know it."

John thought about that. He was well? He didn't know he'd been sick. Had he been sick? Doc seemed to think so.

"I think you will come to find that losing that jawbone is the best thing that ever happened to you."

John hadn't known Doc to be capable of such psychobabble clichés, but it felt good to hear him talk. It felt good to be considered. It felt good to be counseled. "Think?" he said.

"Yep." Doc wiped the corn off his face and threw his napkin and his paper plate into the garbage, then opened the door and tossed the corncob to Cane, who scooped it up and happily trotted off with it.

"So what now?"

"Coffee," Doc said.

John was sad that Sadie Katherine wasn't here to be serving the coffee with her own brand of corn muffins and some of that homemade cranberry jam from Babs Van Rank's Tickled Bear on them.

"This is what I think," Doc said, leaning across the table and drilling John with his brown-eyed stare. "I think it's time you came out of the woods, got a job, got a house and got a woman. I think it's time you left your voodoo juju out there in the woods, and brought your dental floss to a real house with a real goddamn toilet and a real kitchen and made a life like a normal goddamn human being. I think you've been doing this damaged vet thing long enough, and the gods have decreed you fit for society."

John was stunned. He'd never heard Doc speak like this to anybody, and had no idea he felt this way. But Doc being his best friend, his comrade, his brother, his big brother in a sense, John listened and considered.

"So you go home and pack up what things you think you need, and you move here into the spare bedroom. I could use the company. I'll give you a few months to get a job, get acclimated, then you can start paying rent."

"I don't—"

"*Listen to me,*" Doc said, and leaned over the table in seriousness. John listened. "You took a big hit back in Nam. We all did. You're more fragile and took longer to recover. But now you've recovered. If you don't step out and take advantage now, *right now,* you're going to twist too far the other way. This bone thing, losing a simple goofy monkey jawbone, has thrown you for a loop, and that's a strong indication that you've gone too far, John. Come back to reality, boy. Do it now."

John sat back. If the universe had taught him anything, it had been to listen, to pay attention, and that Truth came from many sources. Perhaps Doc was speaking the truth right now.

"Okay," he said.

"Fine," Doc said. "Go get your stuff and tomorrow we'll buy you some clothes."

"I guess I don't need any of that stuff," John said, thinking about his belongings out there in the woods. Ragged sleeping bag, tent with mildew in the corners, dented saucepan, a few sets of faded fatigues, probably three dollars in change, some dental floss—everything else he had gathered to make his campsite a home he had gathered from the woods, and to the woods it could return. None of it was important. Only the jawbone, and its disappearance had left him naked. If he was going to begin a new life in a new place with a new code, he might as well do it complete.

"Good," Doc said, and pointed the way to the guest room. "Hang out here for a while, and when you're ready, I've got work."

"Thanks," John said, went into the guest bathroom and ceremoniously set his toothbrush in the holder. It felt like a religious ceremony. The start of a new life. He looked in the mirror and decided it wouldn't hurt to be warm, shave regularly, get a haircut, bathe in warm water for a change. There was an edge to his looks that he had admired in years past, but now he just looked like a graying old man, sharpened to a point by life's rasp. Doc didn't have that edge. Doc looked softer, and while John never wanted to lose his reaction time or instinct to stand with his back to the wall at all times, he could use a little softening.

He barely slept that night, in the luxurious bed with sheets and pillow. He felt too vulnerable, sleeping in a box with hard walls. He couldn't relax. When Doc got up to go to the toilet several times in the night, John heard every sound. When Doc got up to make breakfast, John followed, and ate heartily of bacon and eggs and drank filtered coffee. "Think I'll get a haircut," he said.

Doc nodded. "Extra razors in my bathroom," he said.

Natasha slipped out of her silk lounging pajamas and pumped a palmful of moisturizing lotion from the bottle on her night-stand. She creamed first her elbows and shoulders, then arms and hands, then pumped out some more, and did her feet, her heels, calves and shins. When she got to the meaty part of her right calf, it felt sore. Bruised. She angled the nightstand light on it, but, because of the awkward angle, she couldn't see anything. Must have bumped into something, she thought.

"Something wrong?" Mort was reading a magazine, propped up by a half dozen pillows.

"A bruise or something on my leg is all," she said, then she slipped out of her lace bra, and wearing only pink bikini pant-ies, got into bed next to him and turned out her light.

She watched him read, wearing those goofy little half-glasses, his eyes going back and forth across the page. "Baby?" she said.

"Hmmm?" He lowered the magazine and looked at her, then

smiled. It was as if he couldn't help but smile when he looked at her, and that made her feel very good.

"You know I love you, don't you?"

"I do indeed," he said, and kissed her forehead. "You're my chocolate delight," he said, "and I'd be less than nothing without you."

She smiled at him. He always said something like that at bedtime, but though it was ritual, it wasn't insincere. She turned away on her side to get a head start on sleep before he turned out his light and started to snore. She tried to think about the act that she was surely soon to commit, and tried to justify it, tried to get up a head of righteous indignation in order to justify it, but none of that was in her anymore. She just felt sad about it, in spite of the tiny bit of excitement she always felt in the face of a new adventure. Sad for herself, sad for Mort.

When Doc went to the tackle shop, John filled the bathtub with hot water, threw in some of the scented salts Sadie Katherine had left on the shelf, then climbed in and soaked until the water turned chill. Then he rummaged around in the drawers in Doc's bathroom until he found fresh razors. He shaved, clipped his fingernails and toenails, and plucked a few eyebrow hairs that had sprouted on his nose. He smeared deodorant under his arms, spritzed on some musky scent, then, reluctant to get back into his tattered fatigues, he fumbled in Doc's bureau until he found a pair of sweatpants and a T-shirt he could wear.

Doc had left forty dollars on the kitchen table.

John went shopping, and when he came home, he had a haircut, two pair of jeans, a long sleeve wool shirt, new underwear, socks, shoes and three T-shirts. He felt good, and when he looked in the mirror, he looked like the average guy on the street. He was still gray-haired and too thin, but without his mustache he looked younger. He looked like he could be an executive. He'd be invisible in White Pines Junction, because nobody would recognize him.

He washed his old clothes, folded them and set them on top of his boots in the corner of the closet. He was going to give this new life a serious go.

When Doc came home, John had washed the whole kitchen, including the floor, and had vacuumed the rest of the house. Clearly, Doc approved of the way John utilized his forty-dollar investment in both his appearance and his actions. Doc broiled steaks for dinner, and a domestic partnership was born.

Over the following week, John got up with Doc, they breakfasted, then John went around the house, fixing things. Doc was handy, but he was busy with the shop and didn't have much time or energy left over for the details that needed attention at home. John stacked the firewood, and fixed the leaky garage roof. He installed a new toilet, fixed the faucet in the kitchen, caulked windows and finally painted the whole interior of the house.

It didn't take long for John to get used to his hot showers and warm bed and the nice fleece slippers Doc brought home for him one day. He also got used to the companionship when the two of them would eat a satisfying meal then sit down to watch television together.

When the nights turned warm and the leaves began to bud, John dreamed about the winters he spent in the woods—cold and alone—and he would marvel at himself and his stubbornness.

Now and then he would think of the monkey's jaw and wonder if he'd been wrong about it all these years, or if the jaw was still working its juju on him, from wherever it happened to be. He preferred to think the jaw was still working. To think he had been wrong about it would mean that his whole philosophy of life had been faulty; that he had lived for all these years standing on a false floor. While he thought he might one day be willing to accept that, living in a house instead of his tent was adjustment enough for now. He enjoyed the good luck the jaw continued to provide, but worried that the other shoe was about to drop. He tried not to dwell on it, however. It didn't really matter, whether or not the jaw was more than just an old bone, he decided. He was about as happy as he'd ever been, happiness being the illusion it mostly was. He just went about trying to earn his keep.

Then the snow began to fly again, and Doc kept short hours at the shop. Nobody fished on the weekdays, and only a few went ice fishing on the weekends. There wasn't enough money for him to hire John, but it was clear that John was out of projects around the house.

Over breakfast, Doc casually mentioned that he saw a Help Wanted sign up at the Fish Haven Motel. John got the hint.

It was off season all over Vargas County; the tourists begin to swarm a couple of weeks before Memorial Day and the crowds die out seriously after Labor Day, but old Mort and his beautiful, much younger black wife Natasha were wanting to do some remodeling on the rooms at the motel before the new season. Gotta keep up with the competition, Mort said.

John signed on, and began work the next day. It was hard, sweaty, satisfying work, and he, by arrangement with Doc, spent his first couple of paychecks accumulating tools. He didn't like accumulating possessions, but figured that was part of the package of living as a contributing member of society. After he bought a certain number of things, he'd start paying rent, and that suited Doc just fine.

He noticed the way Natasha looked at him whenever he went into the office, which doubled as a part of their living room, to talk over materials or details or what have you with Mort. They were an odd couple, Mort and Natasha. He was in his sixties, balding and kind of greasy and chubby; she was in her forties, tall and statuesque, always made up and dressed in a wardrobe that she hadn't acquired in White Pines Junction. John often wondered what she saw in Mort and life up in the northwoods, but he never asked and didn't much care. He found most things having to do with personal relations so far out of his arena of understanding that he didn't even question them. Like Sadie Katherine coming into Doc's life and then leaving just as mysteriously so many years later. Unfathomable. What Natasha could see in Mort also mystified John, but then that wasn't his knowledge to possess, either.

Natasha liked what she saw when she looked at John, though, that was obvious, and as he worked, he began to dwell on her. His curiosity began to sprout—always a danger—and he wondered how she smelled up close, and what that dark smooth skin tasted like. It had been years since he'd had a woman. It had probably been twenty years since he'd been close enough to one to even fantasize. His hands grew callused with the hard work he did at the motel, and yet he longed to run those hands over her smooth inner thighs. At night, he would lie in bed and stare into the dark, wondering what it would be like to have a woman breathing softly next to him, warm and gentle, someone whose back he could rub in the night when the moon wouldn't let him rest. Little by little he began to think of a mate, and since Natasha was visible on a daily basis, he plugged her into that role in his mind.

The second dangerous step.

So when she came in to him with a hot cup of coffee one day, sat on an overturned bucket and smiled that ruby-lipped smile, it was only natural that he stop work and fix his attention on her. So began a daily ritual.

Step three.

He didn't normally like talking about himself, but for some

reason she drew him out, laughing at his ideas about life, but not ridiculing him. And then one day, he said, "How about you and Mort?" He didn't know exactly what he meant, or what the question was, but he figured she'd answer whatever her answer was.

And so she did. "I love Mort," she said simply, and that was that.

But, as it turned out, loving Mort was not synonymous with being faithful to him, and the daily cup of coffee turned into daily caresses, then kisses, and soon frenzied coupling on the floor.

John didn't mind that too much. Although it wasn't exactly what he wanted, it seemed to suit Natasha just fine. John wanted someone in his bed, someone to make leisurely love to, someone he could get to know from her ankles and toes to the back of her neck and the tips of her earlobes. He wanted warmth and friendship and companionship and love. Natasha wanted sex, and John came to believe that Mort was either unable or unwilling, but happy to hire John for the job.

The sex was nice. A warm, juicy, sweet-smelling woman moving and moaning under him was far better than him taking the edge off himself out by the lake, but when it was over, she cleaned herself up, he zipped up his workpants, and they both went back to their daily routines. She went back to the office to Mort, and John went to his daydreams at Doc's place.

John dreamed about romance. He lay in bed at night and dreamed of a romantic dinner with Natasha. He thought of buying her flowers, and kissing her fingertips at just the right moment. He thought of taking her to a movie, sitting in the back row and brushing that long, statuesque neck with his lips during the love scene. Though she was actually under his fingertips every day, there was no romance involved. It was an animal release that was barely even pleasurable.

When John was finishing the tile on unit thirty-four, Mort popped his head in to see him. "I'm headed for the city," he said. "Be back in a week. Help Natasha out if she needs anything, will you?"

My chance, John thought, and felt his face grow hot with deception. "Mind if I took her out to dinner?" he asked.

Mort straightened up in the doorway as if a casual bit of information had just turned into a conversation.

"Sure," he said slowly. "Do whatever you want." Then he looked at John with a disappointed expression, as if John had just forced Mort to admit to knowing about the two of them. If John didn't rub Mort's face in it, then Mort could claim innocence, and it would all be a plot against him. But by making him complicit, he was responsible and couldn't blame Natasha for it all.

Interesting, John thought, as he went back to work, that instead of romancing the beautiful Natasha and dreaming about bedding her, he had as much sex as he wanted with her, but what he longed for was the rest of her. The important part.

Recon John had been a folk legend in White Pines Junction as long as Natasha had lived there. Who'd have thought he'd come out of the woods, clean himself up and be ripe, randy and ready for a daily discrete romp? Never in a million years would Natasha have considered Recon John as her necessary diversion, but, as it turned out, he was perfect. He was a little on the thin side, but still looked good in a pair of Levi's, his equipment was in excellent working order, and he seemed to appreciate her the way she wished Mort would. It was good, if she could keep it to just the two of them, and not be obvious in front of Mort. She hadn't had that talk with John yet, but knew she had to soon.

When she brought him coffee an hour later, he kept his distance and invited her to dinner.

She turned coy. "When?"

"Tonight. I'll pick you up at seven."

"A date?" She smiled slyly and trailed a finger down the buttons on her blouse.

"Dinner," John said, and it was hard to resist her, but he managed it. "I got permission from Mort."

"You didn't." All her coy seductiveness vanished.

"It was my attempt at honor in this situation," John said.

Natasha stared at the floor for a time, then looked up at him. "Seven," she said, turned and left the room.

When he came out of the bathroom, dressed in fresh jeans and T-shirt and smelling of Doc's aftershave and mouthwash, Doc gave a low whistle. "Date, eh?"

John nodded.

"She's married, John."

"I know."

"This is a small town."

John didn't know how to explain to Doc the complicated mess his relationship with Mort and Natasha had become, so he just let it be. The thing was, he didn't want more sex with Natasha. Hell, he didn't even know her.

He shrugged into his old fatigue jacket which was worn and threadbare, and took the time to trim the threads that hung down at the cuffs. At least it was clean, now that he had access to Doc's washing machine, then he walked the short distance to the motel. The night felt mild. The snow had melted, and spring was so close he could hear it.

Natasha was a good two inches taller than he in her spike heels, and she wore a silver slinky dress that was low cut in front and cut low in the back. She wore a plain black ribbon around her throat and diamond studs in her ears. "I ought to be taking you someplace fancy," he said.

"I'm not dressed up for any place," she said. "I'm dressed up for you."

Good answer.

They walked across the street to the diner where Margie giggled her little girly laugh when John asked for a wine list. She brought back two mugs of coffee and the sugar dispenser and left them to their talk.

"Do you believe in luck?" Natasha asked.

John had been admiring her beautiful teeth when she asked that question, and a sinking feeling in his gut replaced his feeling of good will. He had just about gone beyond the luck thing, gotten over the missing jawbone, successfully put aside the superstitions that a solitary life in the woods had led him to develop. He wasn't sure he wanted to revisit that place that was so newly raw inside him, that wound where his belief system had been so freshly ripped away.

"Why? Do you?"

Long fingers with red nails felt aimlessly around the coffee cup. "Not really, but if there is such a thing, I think I've hit a bad patch," she said. "But I'm sure it's only temporary. And I'm not sure it has anything to do with luck, good or bad. I think it's just life."

"Tell me."

They talked until the diner closed at midnight, telling each other their life stories, and when John walked her home, he took with him her history of abandonment and foster homes, her experiences with drugs and alcohol and living on the street, then being rescued by an idealistic priest and finishing high school at a Catholic girls' school when she was twenty-four, getting a job at a deli and meeting Mort. They'd been married for over a dozen years, locked in an unconventional but close and workable relationship.

John felt a profound affection for her. He kissed her cheek, inhaled deeply of her scent, then said good night. He walked toward Doc's place without looking back to see if she was watching him.

Sleep didn't come at all that night. They should have stuck to impersonal sex, because now that the personal had entered into it, he wanted more of her, and he knew that couldn't be.

Doc was right. She was married. She loved Mort, and he loved her. They were a good match, and John had no right to come between them. Impotent Mort didn't mind if John serviced Natasha sexually, but Mort didn't want anybody falling in love.

And John was afraid that was what was happening to him. For some reason, he had never felt such an understanding of another person before. Had he never looked beyond their shells? No. Not since Nam. You fell in love with people and then they died right in front of your face. Perhaps this was more of the getting well part that Doc talked about. He was well enough to want to fall in love with someone again. But then maybe it wasn't Natasha he was falling in love with, it was people.

And perhaps that was worse. Personal entanglements. He'd just scratched the surface, and he didn't know if it was going to get better or worse. Would he become more practiced at it, more comfortable with it? Or should he retreat now before he got in too deep?

John was no fool, but he was unaccustomed to such feelings. He felt as if he'd lost his internal compass. In the woods, he knew the sounds, knew the meanings of the sounds. Here in the real world of people and emotions and relationships, he couldn't even tell if his back was to the wall. And without the jawbone, he had nothing to hold that he knew was real.

He tossed and turned, and eventually the bed became uncomfortable, because it meant he was becoming indebted to Doc, and he didn't know the social ramifications of that. He felt he was flying blind, and when you didn't know where your buddies were and didn't know who your enemies were, people got hurt. People got killed.

He thought about waking Doc up and talking with him, but he knew what Doc would say. He'd say that if John wanted a woman, he ought to practice being with them first, and then find himself one that was available. Easy to say, but that didn't help John out of his current feelings.

He got up, opened the closet and put on his old clothes and boots. He grabbed his fatigue jacket, tucked his toothbrush in his pocket, picked up the high powered flashlight and went outside.

Natasha couldn't sleep in their big bed without Mort. He went away so rarely that she never became accustomed to his absences, and she never slept well when he was gone.

And now there was John to keep her awake. Maybe that's why Mort left, she thought with anguish. He left so I could work this thing out.

John had a vulnerability that was very attractive to the frustrated mother inside Natasha. No kids was part of the bargain she had struck with Mort, and usually that was fine, but lately the baby hunger had returned in earnest, and even though she was pushing menopausal, thoughts of becoming accidentally pregnant by Recon John had overwhelmed her and her better judgment. She knew that most of the feelings that were coming up for her had to do with mothering him. She just wanted to press herself to him and suck out all the hurt. She couldn't make Mort better; he was a happy man. But John needed somebody, and Natasha just had to make sure it wasn't her.

Automatically, her hand reached down to rub the sore part of her calf. The bruise—or whatever it was—wasn't getting any better, it was getting worse. It was sorer by the day, the skin blackish purple in an egg-sized oval, and sometimes it flat-out hurt, with a stabbing pain. Mort would be worried, if she told him, so she thought she might want to see the doctor before Mort got back, just so she'd be able to put both their minds at ease.

She tried massaging it, but it was too sore, so she lay back and thought about how young and carefree she felt having dinner with John.

Honorable John, who had asked her husband if he could take her to dinner.

She better leave him just exactly the fuck alone, before she did something really stupid.

And then a sharp pain in her calf hit her so fiercely that she yelled.

Natasha was sitting on Doc's picnic table, wrapped in a down coat and a blanket, rubbing her calf when John stepped outside.

He was surprised to see her there, but then again, he was not. He thought he recognized her vulnerability. "Hi," he said.

"Hi," she said. "I've been looking for the courage to knock on your door."

"Come on."

She climbed down from the table, wrapped the blanket around herself and followed John to the water's edge and along the path through the woods. Shining the flashlight, he preceded her, and disconnected the snares, trip wires and booby traps. Squirrels and raccoons had got into his stuff and strewn it about. John made a small fire, opened the tent, shook out his sleeping bag and lay it next to the fire. Natasha sat down and wrapped him up in the blanket with her. A cold moon rose through the trees.

"I had a good luck piece for a long time," John said. "Then I lost it."

"Did your luck turn?"

"I don't know. It's hard to say. Yesterday I would have said no. Now, I think maybe yes."

"Because of me?"

"You're married."

"Yes."

"Life is complicated."

"Yes."

"It was simpler when I was out here." John clicked on the flashlight and slowly spotlighted the arc of ground in front of them. Shadows grew long and moved as the beam traveled. "I thought I might leave Doc's place and come on back here."

"Solitude does nothing to enrich the soul," she said.

He looked at her in the firelight. She still had the diamond studs in her ears, but had changed to black sweatpants and a red sweatshirt. Her fire-lit profile looked suddenly wise to him, noble, serene, uncomplicated, self-assured. Her rich skin glowed.

Almost against his will, he felt his hand creep up under her sweatshirt to hold a perfect, braless breast.

She smiled at him and gently pulled his hand away. "No more of that, I'm afraid," she said. "I can't risk it. We're beyond the physical, and that's too dangerous."

He understood completely. Maybe this was the other side of that mysterious relationship thing. Maybe he'd broken through. He felt special. It was a feeling he thought he could come to like. "Does it get easier?" he asked. "Can I learn to navigate society?"

"You will," she said. "But I'm not certain it gets any easier. The subtleties grow ever more complex. Mort and I—we've worked out what works for us. Generally speaking. This is the first time that . . . something has happened."

Again, John understood. Again that feeling of being special. In the Zen of it all, they were all perfect, but in the reality of the firelight, he was a child and she was the wiser. And he wanted to learn the ways of the world. For the first time, he felt as if there were value in being among people. Maybe, he thought, I'm not falling in love with Natasha or with people. Maybe, in fact, I'm falling in love with myself.

"I think that I've made too many excuses for myself over the years," Natasha said. "I think it's time I grew up and made forward progress. Like you."

"Me?"

"Yeah, you. Look at you. You've been out here how many years? And now you've pulled yourself up and reentered the land of the living. I need to do that."

"You *do* do that."

"Not with Mort, I don't. I think I kill him a little bit every day. And I'm going to stop it, because he is, without question, the love of my life."

Doc's right, John thought. I want to hear a woman say that about me.

Natasha started squirming. She wiggled around and wiggled around and finally pulled up the sleeping bag they were sitting on and dug around underneath it. She pulled out a length of old dental floss, threw it on the fire, and then went back to digging. "Jeez," she said, pulling something out of the dirt. "No wonder. I was sitting on this."

It was the jawbone.

John was afraid to touch it for a moment. It hadn't brought him luck, he realized in an instant, it had insulated him from life.

"What kind of an animal was this, do you suppose?" she asked, turning it over in her hands. She looked at John.

He shrugged, unable to speak, incapable of telling her about its power over him.

"Oh, my god," she said, uncrossed her legs and pulled up the leg of her sweatpants. On her calf was a bite mark, still red and imprinted, though no skin was broken. "This woke me up tonight. It felt like a bite. Hurt like bloody hell. Look." She held the monkey's jaw to the bite mark on her calf. It fit exactly. "Jesus," she said. "That's creepy." She tossed it on the fire, and John repressed the urge to jump up and grab it out. Instead, he willed the panic to subside, insisted that his muscles relax. He thought for a moment that he would cry. Instead, he closed his eyes and tried to be one with the universe, to know that the evaporated particles of the jawbone were being returned to their natural elements. He breathed deeply, hoping to breathe some of them in.

"I need social tutoring," he said.

"I'm only available tonight," she said, and rested her head on his shoulder. John put an arm around her and realized that the monkey and its jawbone had sent him out into the world, and started him on the path of showing him the things he ought to be knowing. He breathed in the delicious, perfumed scent of Natasha and realized that that monkey and its jawbone had just saved his life for the second time.

A CHICKEN TOMATO
SANDWICH ON TOAST,
PLEASE, HEAVY ON THE
GUILT-FREE MAYO

Margie dried her hands on the dishtowel, then threw it into the laundry bag for the service to pick up in the morning. She did one last walk-through of the diner, checked that the front door was locked, turned on the nightlight behind the counter, turned off the overheads, and walked into the quiet kitchen. She paused, listening to the quiet hum of the refrigerators.

She was hardly ever the last person here anymore. Someone else usually closed up for her. When she was here, the place was a bustle of noise. But it was nice when it was closed, and instead of putting on her coat and heading home, she put a teabag into a cup of water and stuck it into the microwave. Then she sat down at the big baking table and warmed her hands around the mug.

This had been the single worst day in all the years she had run the diner. A crew of actors, actresses, camera people, directors, makeup artists and whole trailers full of stuff had arrived in town to film a commercial, and they were going to be around for a week.

By the end of the lunch shift, Margie's two cooks and two waitresses wanted to put a "No Hollywood Types" sign on the door. The Californians were driving them nuts. By the end of dinner shift, Margie wasn't sure who would be willing to show up for work the next day.

Nothing satisfied those people, and it was mostly because what was on Margie's menu wasn't on their diets. They wanted low-fat this and vegetarian that, half-caff this and with a twist of that. They asked for substitutions with virtually every meal, because nobody liked what she had to offer. They shrieked with laughter when they saw Margie's specialty, fried cheese curds, on the menu. Margie always liked to accommodate when she could, but two people yelled at her girls, and at least a dozen more left their meals on the tables and walked off without paying their checks.

Margie cried in the ladies room twice. Something she tried never to do.

This was her diner's worst day ever and those people were going to be here for the rest of the week. Maybe she should recommend to them that someone cater their food. Margie was certain she lost money, and she hoped she hadn't lost good employees.

Margie folded her arms and rested her head. She was tired beyond tired. She was past exhaustion. She was fed up. She was overwhelmed.

Overwhelmed.

She and Jimbo had done all right in White Pines Junction. They owned the diner free and clear, along with the land it sat on. They had only a little mortgage left on their home. Jimbo was almost finished with the novel he was writing, little stories and anecdotes about living in Vargas County and the strange things that were always going on. Jason was growing up to be a fine boy with an incredible intelligence. He'd get scholarships to the university of his choice, there was no doubt about that. Except for today, life was good.

Except.

She looked up at the calendar on the wall. Micah would have turned seven in another month. She'd be shopping the catalogs for his presents already, and party preparations would already be under way. He'd be excited as any little boy could get, having a hard time sleeping as the time drew near. He'd be in school now, she thought with a pang. Bringing home art for the refrigerator.

She blinked twice and then wondered how she could ever have thought that life was good when they were without their son. It made her angry to think that she could be getting over him. She should be pining for him every moment of every day, like a decent mother.

"Stop it," she said out loud and then took a long sip of the chamomile tea. She'd been to enough counseling sessions to know that grief eventually fades, and life goes on. Everybody dies.

If only Micah had died. But he hadn't.

"I would give this whole building, this whole business, my happy home life and my good health to just see him one more time," she said to the silent kitchen. "I'd give up Jimbo and Jason and my right hand just to know that he was all right." A sob caught in the back of her throat, and she made the conscious decision to indulge herself for as long as that cup of tea lasted, then she'd regain control with her iron grip, and carry on with life. In the morning she'd order some nonfat yogurt and milk and buy some turkey sausage and some of those non-cholesterol fake eggs.

But before the tea was cold in its cup, Margie had gone to the office and fetched the small white paper pharmacy sack from the back of the bottom file drawer and sat with the two bottles of blue capsules. She had kept the leftover narcotics from when Jimbo cut his hand, and again when he had that hernia fixed. There was more than enough here to end her misery and her grief and her horrible, horrible guilt. Yes, she believed that suicide was a mortal sin, and that she would choose the finality of death as her choice, but she also believed that Jesus would give her one more chance to hold her little boy in her arms before she said good-bye to him, and that's all she was asking for, really. She'd gladly give up her eternal life for one more hug and a whiff of his sweet tousled head.

Margie sipped the tea and knew that tea wasn't part of the program. Beer was. Drink two beers to slow the metabolism, eat a sandwich to slow the absorption, and then start taking the pills, slowly, two at a time, until she felt so sleepy she couldn't stay awake. Then she'd go lie down on the couch in the office, pull the afghan over her, put her head on a pillow, maybe take a few more just to make certain, and then go to meet her little boy and her doom, both together, perhaps in that order.

The thought of it was the only thing that gave her peace. As she sat at the big table in the dark diner with only the humming of the giant coolers to keep her company, she wondered why she hadn't done it already.

It was time.

Knowing that, she felt the exhaustion of the day slough off her shoulders, and the excitement of a new adventure began to fuel her.

She popped the top off one of the pill bottles and spilled the capsules out onto the tabletop. Then she opened the refrigerator and got herself a Michelob. It had been hours since she'd eaten, so she opened the bread and pulled out the cold chicken and tomatoes and made herself a big, sloppy sandwich, then set a place for herself at the table. This was a ceremony, not anything to gulp standing up at the sink. Before sitting down, she went back to the office for a piece of paper. She needed to leave a note for Jimbo.

Then she drank her beer, ate half of her sandwich, took a couple of capsules, and tried to compose her note.

Forgive me, Jimbo, she wrote. *I know Jesus does. I can't go any longer with this burden of guilt. I need to see my baby.*

Margie read it out loud to herself, and it sounded stupid. Oh well. Suicide notes were not supposed to be great literary works. This would get the job done. She finished the beer and opened another. *Be good to yourself, my love, and take care of Jason. He'll need you now the way Micah needs me.*

That was pretty good. She took two more capsules and started in on the other half of her sandwich. Two more pills from the pilfered stash and she'd be beyond the point of no return. She could survive four, or maybe even six of these narcotic caps after a long sleep, but, beyond that, there would be no coming back. If she came back, it would be brain damaged, and she couldn't do that to Jimbo.

She counted out six more. That would be what she would take as soon as she had the other half of the sandwich down. Then she'd take the rest to the couch. They'd dissolve slowly and do their work over the long haul of the night. She wouldn't puke them up, she wouldn't wake up in the morning in the hospital. She had it all figured out. Babcock would find her in the morning when he opened up to start the coffee and heat the griddle. The diner would close for the day and the staff wouldn't have to deal with the out-of-towners, and those people would have to find their dietary accommodations elsewhere. Fat chance.

This was a fine sandwich, she had to admit. She put a little Tiger sauce on it, and, as she did, the phone rang.

She looked at it, hanging on the wall, surrounded by yellowed pieces of paper taped up with all kinds of phone numbers and messages on them. It was Jimbo, it had to be. She had to answer it, because if she didn't, he'd be worried and come looking for her, and that could foil her plan.

She let it ring three times, then stood on surprisingly woozy legs to answer. "Hello?"

"Hey, babe," Jimbo said. "It's late. You coming home soon?"

"I'm buried in paperwork," she lied, and felt the hand of God waving its finger in her face. *Naughty, naughty.*

"Well, don't be too late. You know I can't sleep without you next to me."

"I know." Her tongue felt thick and she hoped he didn't notice a slur in her speech.

"Okay, then. Get home as soon as you can. Drive safely. Don't forget that Jason and I love you."

"Love you too," she said, a sob catching in her throat.

She hung up the telephone and looked at the table. A plate with juicy tomato/mayo drippings and a few crumbs, one empty beer bottle and another half empty, and a pile of blue pills.

This had been an excellent idea merely twenty minutes earlier. Now Jimbo had interrupted her and made her think about how he always complained that he couldn't sleep if she wasn't in the bed next to him. Yes, it chained her to him, particularly at bedtime and when she wanted to take off for the weekend with one of her girlfriends, but that was okay. Those were easy things to give up, considering.

And he had mentioned Jason, her first born, her eleven-year-old boy genius who had a brain so big his thought processes had long since passed both her and Jimbo, and that wasn't easy, considering how smart Jimbo was.

How many of those blue pills had she taken? Four. She had sixty to do the job, but had only got to four, and had been about to take another six, the amount of no return.

She poured the rest of the beer down the sink, rinsed the plate, bottled up the rest of the pills and put them safely away in the little white sack in the back of the file cabinet. If she hurried, she could get home before getting too woozy and then she could fall asleep next to Jimbo and he need never know. She'd wake up in the morning just fine, come to work and deal with Hollywood tastes and appetites.

She'd wake up just fine, as long as the grief and the guilt and

174

the hurt and the never-ending, god-awful pain was just fine. Now she couldn't indulge herself in that sweet, blissful, guilt-free, pain-free rest in the arms of Jesus that she had so desired, so longed for, so deserved. No, she had to go sleep next to Jimbo.

And she would do it, too, goddamn him. She would raise that remaining son to be a good man, and she would see Jimbo through to his old age and death, every stinking day resenting the fact that she couldn't have her own peace as they had somehow found theirs. She resented the shit out of it, and she resented them for it.

But maybe she'd feel different in the morning.

Margie turned out the last light and went home.

RECLINING YEARS

Mrs. Teacher was so eager for the fishing season to begin that by the time the tourists hit town, she had acquired a whole new spring and summer wardrobe, and had everything ironed and hanging, perfectly coordinated, in her closet. New shoes were stacked neatly in their boxes on the floor, her hair was freshly colored and permed and she'd bought new combs to keep the curls out of her face.

The locals began to arrive with the snow melt, coming up on weekends to open their cabins and air out the bedding. They repaired the damage the squirrels had done during the fall and winter, and checked to make sure their pipes hadn't frozen. They flushed the toilets and inspected the roofs and checked in on their garages, full of boats, fishing equipment, jet skis and dirt bikes. This was recreation country and Mrs. Teacher was ready for a little recreation.

Easter Sunday she put on a new frock and hat and shoes and went to church. She sneaked out a little early to beat the crowd, such as it was—Pastor Porter never quite filled the sanctuary— and headed directly to Margie's.

Margie rolled her eyes when she saw Mrs. Teacher come in, but Mrs. Teacher was above that and politely ignored her. She also ignored the warning glance that Margie threw her way. Margie didn't understand. She didn't know what it was like to be a widow. Margie may have lost a son, but that wasn't the same. She still had Jimbo to warm her bed at night. Mrs.

Teacher had nothing but a fading memory.

She successfully ignored Margie's scorn with head held high as she scanned those assembled. At a table for two, over by the window, a man in a ball cap was sitting by himself. He had his coffee and some kind of a tabloid newspaper, which meant his breakfast hadn't arrived yet. Mrs. Teacher made a beeline.

"Excuse me," she said politely, putting a hand on the empty chair opposite him. "May I join you?"

He wasn't a local; at least Mrs. Teacher had never seen him before.

He looked around as if prepared to see that the restaurant was packed; that there was no place else for this woman to sit except at his table, but that was not the case. "Sure," he said, then returned to his paper, then put it down, then picked it up, then finally folded it and set it next to his silverware.

"Thank you," Mrs. Teacher said. She held out her hand. "I'm Emily Teacher. I so dislike eating alone. Especially on Easter."

"Fred Kramer," he said, shaking her hand. "Is it Easter?"

She nodded. "Have you ordered yet?"

Just then, Margie came with his ham and eggs. "What can I get for you, Emily?"

"Oatmeal and tea, please," Mrs. Teacher said without looking up. Margie whirled and was gone.

"I don't recall seeing your face before," Mrs. Teacher said.

"I'm just up checking on my brother's place," Fred said, and dug into his breakfast.

"Please go ahead," Mrs. Teacher said, disappointed in his manners. "Who's your brother?"

"Tom Kramer," Fred said behind a mouthful of eggs.

"I see your parents weren't much with names," she said.

He stopped chewing and squinted at her for a moment, then washed down his mouthful with a swig of coffee, white with cream.

"And what do you do?"

"I'm a friggin' brain surgeon," he said.

She laughed. "Me, too!"

He scowled. "Actually, I work for a concrete sawing company down in Moline."

"Actually," she said, "I'm a retired switchboard operator. I live here all year round."

"Through the winter?"

"Yes," she said with a little pride. She knew not too many people lived in the northwoods year round, and almost all of those who did were young, hardy outdoorsmen. "It takes a little planning, is all. That's why we love spring so much."

"Huh," he said, and went back to his breakfast.

"So will you be in town for a long time?"

He shook his head, and then swallowed. "Just the weekend. My brother and his family will be up in a couple of weeks." His eyes kept straying toward his newspaper.

Margie brought Mrs. Teacher's oatmeal and tea at the same time she brought Fred Kramer's check. He stood up immediately, put two dollars on the table, and smiled down at her. "Have a nice day," he said.

My ass, she thought. She waited until he was out of the parking lot, and then disappointment weighing her down, she paid for her oatmeal and went home to her lonely house.

She didn't want romance, she just wanted someone to talk with. She would have been desperately happy for the rest of the day if Fred Kramer had only asked her a question about herself. Shown a smidgen of interest. Or if they had made some kind of a human connection. Couldn't he see how starved she was?

She threw her keys into the bowl on the table by the door and, without taking off her coat, sank down onto her overstuffed chintz chair. Everybody thought she was out husband hunting, but that was not it, and if anybody ever took the time to ask her, she'd tell them. "I just want someone to talk to," she said out loud. "Someone to do for. Someone to laugh at David Letterman's show with." And then the tears came again, and ran mascara rivulets down her powdered cheeks. She was glad Henry wasn't peeking in the windows to see what had become of her. She was a disgrace. Starving and ashamed of it.

Eventually, she slid out of her coat, and then out of her clothes, leaving them in a puddle on the floor, and climbed back into bed, pearl earrings and necklace still in place. She didn't care.

Sometime in the mid-afternoon, a call to the bathroom roused her, and as she walked through the living room, it struck her. "There's no room for a man in this house," she said. Over the course of the ten years since Henry's death, she had feminized the place and filled it up with fancy crap. A man needed to be comfortable. A man needed a recliner and a remote control. If she bought one, maybe a man would come to fill the space.

Maybe a man like Yul Brynner.

Yul Brynner had been the man of Emily Teacher's dreams since she saw him in *The King and I* when she was still a girl with youthful lusts. She liked a bald head on a man. Some men wore them better than others, but she had always found it to be an attractive look.

She put on the kettle, took off the pearls, and got to work, filling boxes with candy dishes, figurines, glass animals, and trinkets. She rearranged a few things in the living room and made a pile in the spare bedroom for the Goodwill. Then she got out the JCPenney catalog and made a phone call.

The delivery truck came before the neighbors arrived for the season, so she didn't have any explaining to do. The men carried in the big leather recliner and the large-screen television set, then installed the dish on her roof and ran all the wires. She rushed around fussing after them, but they had no time to talk with her, either, and they declined her offers of tea and cookies. They just made man conversation between them, while Mrs. Teacher luxuriated in the smell of men in her home.

When they left, she was surprised to discover that she was not at all inclined to turn the television on. She knew she got lots and lots of stations, especially sports, but she had been so used to just the two stations, one of them snowy, that she didn't even know what was on to watch. So she left it dark. A big, dark, blank presence.

When she went to bed that night, exhausted from all the unaccustomed activity, she felt a disappointment she was ashamed to admit, even to herself. Somehow, she had it in her head that with the leather recliner and big-screen television, she'd get something else. A new life, maybe.

But no.

She washed her face and got into her nightie and tried hard to say her prayers, but there weren't any words for how she felt inside. She didn't know what she wanted, so she didn't know how to ask. It was a difficult time, but she curled up under her down comforter that didn't warm her, and waited for blessed unconsciousness.

The light woke her. The unmistakable blue light that comes from even a color television set, even a big-screen television set, bounced off her open bedroom door and shone right into her face. For a moment she felt disoriented, then she remembered the huge television that sat like a monolith in her living room. There must be some sort of a timing device on it, she figured, and it had turned itself on.

She got up, pulled her robe over her nightie, stuck feet into slippers, and wondered if she'd be able to figure out how to turn it off. She could always pull the plug if there wasn't a simple power button on the remote control.

But the television hadn't turned itself on. Yul Brynner sat in the leather recliner watching Letterman.

"Did I wake you?" he asked when she came into the room. "I turned it down."

"No," she lied. "I was awake."

"Oh," he said, then clicked up the volume.

"Can I get you something?"

"Do you have any popcorn?"

"No, but I can get some in the morning."

"Okay," he said, and went back to the television.

"How about a sandwich?"

"Sure."

She went to the kitchen and made him a peanut butter and honey sandwich with raisins and sprinkled cinnamon, poured a big glass of milk, added two cookies to the plate for fun, and took it out to him. There was no place to set it, so he put the plate in his lap, and set the milk on the floor.

"I'll get some TV trays while I'm out tomorrow."

"That's good, dollface," he said, and switched it over to Jay Leno.

She watched him for a time, amazed beyond words, and then she went back to bed.

In the morning, the plate and empty glass were in the sink, the television was off, and there was no sign of Yul. In spite of herself, she smelled the headrest of the new recliner, and while it smelled mostly of new leather, she could detect the presence of aftershave. Old Spice, if she wasn't mistaken, and strong enough for her to believe that it wasn't just a handprint from the delivery guy. Yul Brynner had been there, had watched her television, eaten her sandwich, drunk her milk. And he wanted popcorn. Well, by god, he'd have it.

She dressed and drove all the way to Wal-Mart.

By the time she had all her purchases unloaded and set up, she was exhausted. But the house had been transformed. A lava lamp sat atop the television; there was a TV tray on each side of the recliner. She had beer mugs and cold can keepers. She had beer and pretzels and chips and popcorn and cheese and chili and hot dogs and salsa and onion dip. She had frozen pizzas and man-sized bulky sweaters and slippers and fresh towels. She decided against buying cigarettes, Yul's history being what it was, and for the same reason she passed on cigars and pipes. But she bought lollipops and candy canes. The candy canes had been on sale.

She arranged everything, and then carefully bathed, powdered, shaved and perfumed, and despite her efforts to stay awake to welcome him, she fell asleep on the sofa, cozied up in her afghan.

When she woke, he was there, watching Letterman.

"Hi," she said, sleepy-eyed.

He laughed at Letterman's monologue.

"I got popcorn."

"Got any cheese and crackers?"

"Sure," she said, and got up to prepare it. On the way past him, she couldn't help herself, but reached down and touched his shoulder. He was warm. Solid. Muscular. And his head shone in the light of the television.

She made him a big plate of three different types of sliced cheese and crackers, and included a cold beer, then put it all down on the new oak tray table between their chairs. Then she sat down in hers, pulled the afghan over her lap, and they laughed at Letterman together.

It was the closest Emily Teacher got to heaven since Henry had died.

When Letterman signed off, Yul picked up the remote control, looked at her and said. "Thanks, sweet cheeks." He clicked the button. The picture on the screen flashed off, and he disappeared as well.

Emily rubbed her eyes. She looked at the decimated tray of food, at the half-gone glass of beer. She looked at the impression his body had made in the chair, and then she wrapped the afghan tighter around herself and snuggled up as tiny as she could.

She was losing her mind.

Loneliness was giving her hallucinations.

And then as if to prove it, he didn't come again for a week. Heartbroken, she let the food spoil in the refrigerator, and left the cracker box open, so the crackers went stale. No fool like an old fool she said to herself over and over again a thousand times a day. She thought about calling her daughter who lived down in Tampa to come get her and put her in an old folks' home.

Yul Brynner. Good lord. What had she been thinking?

And yet . . . who drank half of that beer? She hadn't. She didn't like beer.

Just as she was about to call the Goodwill to come and get the television and the recliner, Regina Porter called and invited her to lunch. Emily knew that Regina called her out of parish obligation, but she was just as happy to have something to look forward to, so she accepted, and they met at Margie's the following Sunday after service.

"How have you been?" Regina asked.

Mrs. Teacher regarded the odd young woman sitting across the table from her. She yearned to bare her soul—to cry and wail and talk about Henry and his passing and how lonely she was, how that terrible, debilitating loneliness had led her to accost tourists regularly in Margie's diner, how she, in her wanton

183

desperation for companionship, had conjured up a beer-drinking apparition which couldn't exactly be a Christian thing.

But Regina would never understand that kind of loneliness. Regina had her husband and their church. All Mrs. Teacher had was a new leather recliner and a big-screen TV.

"I've been well," she answered.

"We've worried about you," Regina said. "We'd like you to come to a potluck now and then. Maybe help out with Vacation Bible School this summer."

"Maybe," Mrs. Teacher said, already wanting to get home just in case her mysterious visitor decided to pay a day visit. Yet that was ludicrous. She ought to get involved with local things, but she never had. She'd had Henry, then she'd taken care of Henry, then she'd mourned Henry in solitude. And now . . . and now she had her insanity to keep her company.

"It's not good to be so alone," Regina said. "Trust me on that. Things happen inside your head."

Mrs. Teacher smiled. "I'm fine, but I appreciate your concern and will consider your invitation."

That night, she tried to wait up for Letterman, but dozed off, and when she awoke, it was to Yul's hearty laughter in the chair next to her. She was so grateful she felt like crying.

She fixed him a snack, and watched while he ate, strong jaw muscles chewing, sensuous lips smiling, piercing dark eyes full of humor as he watched television.

When Dave's musical guest came on, Mrs. Teacher grabbed the remote and found the mute button. "We have to talk," she said.

"Already?" he said. "Usually, I get a year's worth before this crap."

"I beg your pardon?" Mrs. Teacher was offended and justifiably so.

He took a long, exaggerated sigh. "What is it?"

"Are you going to keep coming around?" she asked, her voice trembling.

"Maybe," he said.

"Maybe?"

"I don't seem to have much to say about it." His eyes strayed back to the television, and he reached for the remote.

She pulled it away from him. "Who does? Who has the say?"

He shrugged. "You, probably."

This was not the answer she had expected, yet it rang with truth. She handed him the remote. He blew her a kiss, and turned up the volume.

Mrs. Teacher went to bed and left him alone. In the morning, she cleaned up his dishes then sat in his recliner and did some serious thinking.

Ever since Henry's death, all she thought she wanted was someone to watch Letterman with. That was what she said, what she thought. That was what she thought she missed the most—doing for someone and laughing with someone.

However, that wasn't exactly the case.

She wanted more.

The following night, she stroked his tan, muscular forearm while they watched TV and he stayed through Conan O'Brien. The following night she massaged his shoulders and kissed the top of his smooth head. He didn't seem to mind. She moved the TV tray from between their chairs and began holding his hand. He allowed it.

But he didn't respond. Didn't react. Didn't pick her up and carry her to the bedroom for a wild, passionate romp. He never returned the affection. The closest he got was to ask her to pick up a jar of pickled herring the next time she went to the store. And then he called her "Babycakes" as if that made up for it.

She began to understand that her influence was limited. He was what he was, he did what he did, and that was that.

Well, fine. It wasn't enough.

So one night she fixed him a pizza and followed it up with a hot fudge sundae, and when Letterman was signing off, she took the remote and turned off the TV. Yul looked at her in surprise, with those soft lips and those penetrating dark eyes under thick brows and she almost lost her resolve. But he wasn't what she wanted. She thought he was, but he wasn't.

"It's over," she said.

He frowned. "You sure?"

She nodded.

He reached over with one finger and touched her face. "Bye, cutie pie," he said, and was gone.

Typical, she thought. Not even a thank-you.

In the morning, she donated the TV and recliner to the Goodwill. Then she started making a list of what she really wanted.

When it was all down in black and white, and all the details were firmly cemented in her mind, she bought champagne, caviar, a cabinet full of expensive imported cheeses, a wide array of expensive wines, a special edition Scrabble game and fresh sheets for the bed. Then she sat down to wait for Alex Trebek.

Fred Kramer's Regrets

Fred Kramer tied his brother's boat up to the little dock and pulled in his basket of panfish. He was sorry the long days of summer were almost over, especially since his brother's kids loved to come up to their summer home as much as Fred did. When the kids were there, Fred wasn't. Fred, single, overworked, underpaid, lonesome and prone to sit in his chair with his beer and his sports on a weekend, was all too happy to run up north to take a look at the place and make sure it was secure.

He liked his brother all right, and the wife and all those kids, but they had seven of those kids, and each one had to bring up a friend, and it was just too much activity for Fred, who preferred his own company, for the most part.

He didn't recognize the boat he tied up next to, but he recognized the man in the fish-cleaning shack. Mooseface Tyler. Fred didn't have much use for Mooseface.

The shack had two cutting boards and two basins, and Fred hoisted his basket to the countertop and began to sharpen his knife on the honing stone that was tethered to the cabinet. "Hey, Moose," he said.

"Hey." Mooseface stopped cutting fish long enough to wipe a bloody, scaly, slimy hand across his forehead, then lift his beer to his fleshy lips. Fred noticed the stringer of fish he was working from, and he noticed the number of fish heads in the basin, and, by quick reckoning, he realized that Moose was about double his limit.

187

"Nice catch," Fred said. "Aren't you about double your limit?"

Mooseface fixed him with an ugly stare, took another swig from his beer without taking his eyes off Fred, and then scowled and went back to work.

Fred hated guys like Mooseface Tyler. They broke the rules, broke the laws, and because they were so mean and ugly, people just let them get away with it. Nobody ever confronted them.

"Illegal catch," Fred said. "Guys like you make it rough on those of us who play by the rules."

Moose picked up his empty stringer and his bucket of cleaned fish, left all the fish guts in the sink, and walked away.

"That man don't deserve a place up here," Fred said to the next crappie he filleted. "He don't deserve a nice boat like that, he don't deserve to have fishing luck like that, not when I obey the laws and try to do right and live from paycheck to paycheck. Shit," he said. "Life ain't fair." He turned the fish over and expertly separated the meat from the bone.

Filled with disgust and resentment, Fred finished his work, threw a few fish scraps to the cats that circled the shack like sharks, wrapped all his mess along with Moose's mess in newspapers and threw it into the garbage can. He threw buckets of lake water onto the counters, cleaned up the shack, took his fillets and headed back to the house. He wasn't going to let Mooseface Tyler ruin his weekend. He carefully bagged the filets and tucked them into the freezer.

Man, he'd like to have a little piece of the northwoods. He'd like to have a little cabin, not nearly as expansive or as much to maintain as this place of his brother's. He'd just like a little cabin, well-insulated with a wood burning stove and a decent kitchen. He'd like to have a place that was his own, where he didn't have to worry about messing up cupboards by putting things in the wrong places, or folding the linens the wrong way.

Even though he was family, he always felt like a guest at his brother's place. It was the wife made him feel that way. The wife and all seven of them kids.

But even that was okay. He'd take what he could get. And right now—he checked his watch—he needed to pack up and get back to the city. And he needed to do it before the sun went down.

It was a month before he again got back up to the lake; it was a month before his brother and family had other obligations and Fred could go up and stay in the peace and quiet. He stopped at Doc's to hear the latest gossip and found out three important things. First, that the crappies were biting on those stinky orange cheese balls that Fred hated to use; second, that Babs Van Rank had died; and third, that Mooseface Tyler had turned over a new leaf, come to Jesus, perhaps, and had taken it upon himself to start picking up litter around town. Which, of course, included the fish shack. Doc about split a gut telling Fred about Moosie buying the local Superette out of Arm and Hammer. Fred got a chuckle, but not nearly the belly laughs that it brought Doc and apparently the rest of town. Fred thought Moose had it coming, and that it was about time he paid a little back.

Turned out that Mooseface hadn't had that change of heart all by himself. The local magistrate had a little something to do with it when Moosie was caught helping himself to a whole box of Twinkies while he waited for Slim Nottingham to fill up his car and his boat with gas. Slim saw the box of Twinkies, fresh delivered that morning, sticking out of Moosie's jacket when he reached in his wallet for his credit card. That was enough for Slim. He called Sheriff Withens while pretending to process the card, and the sheriff pulled up just in time. Slim pressed charges, because it wasn't the first time Moosie had done a little light-fingering in his mini mart, and that made Slim a popular guy with the owners of most of the retail establishments in Vargas County.

Fred didn't like to feel smug, but he enjoyed the smugness he felt when Moosie pulled fish shack cleaning duty as his community service. It was only fair.

The idea of Babs Van Rank being dead was a different matter. There wasn't any fairness in that. Fred sat for the rest of the day with Babs's death stewing in his innards. He took his stinking cheeseballs and got into his boat and spent the day contemplating the death of a spouse, and waited in vain for a crappie to find his bait attractive.

Gordie, Babs's husband, was a good guy; he'd done nothing that Fred knew about to bring this upon himself. Life was a mystery as to why something like this happened to mild Gordie and not nasty old Mooseface. Fred didn't know if Mooseface was married, but he assumed that he was, and that his wife was either wrong in the head or as ugly a woman as ever lived. But Babs was very pretty, and she and Gordie had a nice life. What would it be like, Fred wondered, to have a spouse just up and die?

Or maybe Gordie was a bad guy, or Babs was cheating on him. Chances are, things weren't as nice and as pretty as they seemed on the surface. Chances are, the two of them had dry rot in their marriage, and Gordie was probably relieved to be rid of her. She probably nagged him day and night.

Fred had never married, and it was probably a good thing. He liked his freedom. A wife would resent his fishing. And sports. His whole lifestyle.

When he came off the lake, after not catching a single fish with those stinking cheeseballs, he went to Margie's to have himself a meal and see if he could overhear some fishing news from a source a little more reliable than Doc.

The news was hot. Mooseface Tyler had caught the famed albino pike, killed it, and taken it to Gordie to be mounted. That news made Fred seethe. Mooseface, that disgusting waste of human skin. Fred should have been the one to catch the pike. Now that was a trophy.

Fred ate some of Margie's chicken fried steak, then went on home to his brother's place. Tomorrow he'd try worms. They were almost a sure thing. He didn't know why he'd wasted his whole day on those stupid cheese balls. When he got back to the cabin, he threw the jar into the trash and mildly resented Doc for recommending them.

Fred sat on his brother's couch and watched the blazing color of the sunset out the picture window. He knew what he was going to do that evening, and he relished the anticipation, in spite of the creeping feeling inside him that one of these days he was going to get caught.

One half hour after dark, he put on a black knit watch cap, grabbed his brother's dark windbreaker, and went out the door.

He parked two blocks from the Svensen house, then turned the lights off and waited.

The light went on in Katarina's bedroom. He opened the car door and got out, eyes riveted on his destination.

He walked around the side of the neighbor's house and quietly through their backyard. Their house had the look of emptiness, and, for a moment, the thought crossed Fred's mind that he should stay there while they were gone. Live right next door to Katarina. But he wasn't stupid. He walked slowly and quietly around the house, watching his step, and took up his place next to the pine tree.

There she was. Beautiful Katarina, dancing to some music only she could hear, wearing a T-shirt and panties. Her blond hair swung back and forth as she moved, her budding breasts making small braless mounds under the tight shirt with thin straps and a little pink satin rose right in the middle of the neck. Her lips moved, and Fred could see, or imagined that he saw, lip gloss.

It was all he could do to keep his distance. He loved Katarina, had loved her since she was about eight. He wanted to take her in his arms and smother her with kisses. He wanted to take her home, marry her, and just sit and watch her all day, every day, walk around in that sweet little girl underwear. He wanted right now, to run up to the window, press all ten fingertips against it and watch her up close. He wanted her to see him. He wanted her to invite him into the warm yellow light of her bedroom, into the warmth of that down comforter, those pure white sheets, that tight, flawless skin. Fred's erection grew hard and uncomfortable in his trousers, but that just made him angry with himself. He just wanted to admire her, he told himself. Some of his thoughts were sick, he knew, but he thought pretty much everybody had some kind of sick thoughts.

"Whatcha doin? Looking at the gurl?"

Fred whirled around at the voice that came from right behind him. Chainlink Charlie. A big, meaty, mentally deficient bum who lived off the good graces of the townspeople, Chainlink Charlie carried all his possessions in an old Army duffel bag. He was snaggletoothed and scraggly bearded and smelled god-awful.

"No," Fred said.

"Yes, you were," Charlie said, and his lips curled up into a grin. "Yes you were, yes you were."

"No," Fred said, his face growing hot. "I'm looking after this house while the owners are gone. Just doing a walk around the property is all."

"You were lookin' at the gurl," Charlie said. "She's pretty. I like lookin' at her, too."

Just then Katarina's light snapped off. Charlie made a sound of disappointment, and Fred made fast tracks toward his car, hoping to escape without further incident. He hoped Charlie didn't talk and that people wouldn't believe him if he did.

No such luck.

The next morning, Fred was awakened by a pounding on the cabin door, and, when he opened it, wearing T-shirt, boxers and his brother's plaid robe, big Tryg Svensen filled the doorway.

"You fucking pervert," Tryg said quietly. "I would expect something like that from Charlie, because he's not right, but not from the likes of you."

Fred held up a hand, as if that was going to keep Tryg from ripping his head off. Tryg didn't even notice it. He took a step across the threshold and into the kitchen.

"I have one suggestion for you, Freddie boy. Pack your shit and get out of town, and I won't have to call the cops or tell your brother about what you do when you come up here to use his place."

"Listen—" Fred said, but Tryg took another step toward him, and he was forced two steps back.

"You best save your breath," Tryg said, his voice still horribly quiet amid the anger that tightened his face, "and just do as I suggest."

Fred nodded.

"And if I ever see you within shouting distance of my daughter again, I'll feed you to the crabs." He took another step forward. "Do you for *one instant* doubt what I'm telling you?"

Fred shook his head. He felt like a child. He felt like a fool. He felt like a guilty pervert.

Tryg turned and stepped out the door. "Have a nice drive home," he said.

Fred closed the door and locked it. He took a deep, ragged breath, then started to pack.

But the more he packed, the more indignant he got. He

hadn't done anything wrong. He'd never touched Katarina. He didn't hang out at the schoolyard, he didn't offer the kids dope or booze. He hadn't done anything wrong, besides walk through the neighbors' yard when they weren't home and avail himself of the eye candy that happened to present itself through her window. She should pull the goddamn blinds, he thought.

Still, he packed.

On his way home, he stopped at Gordie Van Rank's taxidermy shop to pick up his mounted walleye. He hoped it was ready. He didn't really want to see Gordie, but it was unavoidable.

A tasteful little bell rang when Fred pushed open the door, and Gordie's weird low voice called out from the back room. "Be right with you," he said.

Fred nervously looked at the rack of brochures by the front door. He didn't know what he was going to say.

"Fred?"

Fred turned, and there was Gordie, looking the same as always.

"Heard about Babs," Fred blurted out. "Came by to see you. And pick up my mount."

A soft smile crossed Gordie's face. "Thanks, Fred. That means a lot. They got the folks who killed her, you know. They killed her and Cara Trenton and a bunch of tourists. I did a couple of days in jail before they found the scum who did it, but it's all behind us now."

"Bummer," Fred said.

"I'm still kind of numb, actually. Funeral was just Saturday. Can't believe it. Still expect her to come walking through the door." Gordie lifted Fred's beautiful walleye down off its peg and handed it to him.

"Wow," Fred said. "Nice work, Gordie."

"Thanks. It came out real nice."

Fred paid him, collected his receipt and made ready to leave.

"Well, take care."

"Thanks, Fred," Gordie said with sincerity. "Next time you come up, let's have a beer together."

"Yeah, okay," Fred said, and escaped.

As he left, he saw a dark-haired man escorting a beautiful woman across the street into Margie's diner. They were both dressed nicely, and Fred was slammed with an envy that tumbled out of his guts and threatened to overcome him. Everybody else had the good stuff. Fred Kramer had nothing.

Tryg Svensen had his beautiful daughter. Fred's own brother had all that love, all those kids, all that money, that beautiful summer home at the lake. Gordie had his amazing talents, memories of his lovely wife, two shops to run. Gordie even had his grief and a widower's respect. Doc had his big laugh and spotlessly tidy tackle shop. Even Mooseface had the lord, or some such, and a queer gleam in his eye. All Fred had was a nice mounted fish that he'd put up over his phony fireplace in a tacky little apartment in the bad side of town, a dead-end job and a lot of lonely nights. Why couldn't he catch a break? Why couldn't he get the good stuff? A nice place to live, a nice woman, a nice faith, a nice little business to run?

Because you're a fucking pervert, that's why.

Fred turned away from the handsome couple, got into his car and headed down the road toward the interstate. He gripped the steering wheel tighter and tighter, as an airless, breathless feeling grew in his chest. Why them? They're not so much. There was nothing, *nothing* that Fred could see that made any one of them more special than he, yet they seemed to have it all, while Fred had squat.

Oh god, his chest felt like an elephant was sitting on it. A tingling went down his left arm and a fiery pain began to crawl up his jawbone.

He pulled to the side of the road, turned on the emergency

flashers and cut the engine. He concentrated on breathing. Just breathe, he said to himself. Just breathe.

He spent the hour or so bargaining with God. If God would just let him live through this, he wouldn't be jealous anymore of other people's stuff. What was the sin? Covetousness? He had it, and he'd get rid of it. He'd be nicer to his brother's wife, he'd be more tolerant of their kids, he'd be more grateful for the things that he had. He'd be nicer to people. He'd give to charity. He'd go to church—well, maybe not. He waited it out, praying hard and fast and with uncommon earnestness. The pressure in his chest eventually eased, the fire slid down his jaw bone and extinguished somewhere around his clavicle. His left arm remained detached in a strange way, but he wiped the chilled perspiration from his forehead, muttered a heartfelt thank-you to the universe power controllers, turned the key and pointed his truck back onto the highway toward home or the hospital—he'd decide once he got back to civilization.

He decided on home.

When he opened the door to his apartment, he felt as if his eyes had been opened for the first time. It was a messy hole. How could he ever bring a nice-looking lady like the one he saw with that dark-haired guy to a place like this?

You clean up your act, he told himself, and perhaps a woman like that might come along. You live like a pig.

Tomorrow, he thought. Tomorrow he'd get to work on his life, cleaning up all the messy areas, but now he thought it might be best to go to bed. His heart was upset, and he being fifty-two and not in the best shape or having the best of nutritional habits, thought he ought to give it a little rest.

No sleep came to him, and he lay in bed tormented all night long about the things he'd done, things he'd said, things he'd thought about other people, when he himself had never held to any great moral or ethical standard. Looking over his life with his new perspective, he remembered things that made him cringe, made him moan out loud. All in the past. All history. All things he could not change, could not take back. He lay in the night, smelling the stink of his dirty clothes in the overflowing hamper, the overflowing garbage sack, and the mildewed towels in a heap on the bathroom floor. He lay there, thinking of how he criticized Mooseface Tyler, how he looked down upon Gordie. The shame he felt when he got caught peeping at lithe, supple little Katarina Svensen.

Fred Kramer's chest tightened with grief and remorse, and the tears spilled out of the corners of his eyes and trickled down into his ears. He wished he could turn back the clock. He wished he could take it all back. He wished, he wished, he wished. . . .

Fred Kramer tied his brother's boat up to the little dock and pulled in his basket of panfish. He loved the long days of summer, and especially loved it when his brother and family couldn't make it up north to take advantage of their vacation home. Fred was all too happy to run up north to take a look at the place and make sure it was secure.

He didn't recognize the boat he tied up next to, but he recognized the man in the fish-cleaning shack. Mooseface Tyler.

The shack had two cutting boards and two basins, and Fred hoisted his basket to the countertop and began to sharpen his knife on the honing stone that was tethered to the cabinet. "Hey, Moose," he said.

"Hey." Mooseface stopped cutting fish long enough to wipe a bloody, scaly, slimy hand across his forehead, then lift his beer to his fleshy lips. Fred noticed the stringer of fish he was working from, and he noticed the number of fish heads in the basin, and, by quick reckoning, he realized that Moose was about double his limit.

"Nice catch," Fred said.

Mooseface fixed him with an ugly stare, took another swig from his beer without taking his eyes off Fred, and then scowled and went back to work.

Fred spent the next thirty minutes working side by side with the man in silence, and eventually, Moose picked up his empty stringer and his bucket of cleaned fish, left all the fish guts in the sink, and walked away.

And then, because Fred was never one to hold a grudge and liked to think of himself as filled to the brim with Christian charity, he promptly forgave Mooseface and his transgressions, finished his work, threw a few fish scraps to the cats that circled the shack like sharks, wrapped all his mess along with Moose's mess in newspapers and threw it into the garbage can. He threw buckets of lake water onto the counters, cleaned up the shack, took his fillets and headed back to the house. He carefully bagged them and tucked them in the freezer. No telling when he was going to get back up here; he might as well take a little bit of heaven home with him.

Fred felt amazingly fortunate to have a place like this cabin to visit whenever he could. It had a great kitchen, and Fred liked to cook.

Right now—he checked his watch—he needed to pack up and get back to the city. And he needed to do it before the sun went down.

It was a month before he again got back up to the lake. Fred stopped at Doc's to find out where the fish were biting and found out three important things. First, that the crappies were biting on orange cheese balls; second, that Babs Van Rank had died; and third, that Mooseface Tyler had turned over a new leaf, come to Jesus, perhaps, and had taken it upon himself to start picking up litter around town.

Fred bought a jar of the cheese balls, made a mental note to say a few kinds words to both Mooseface and Gordie Van Rank, and went fishing.

Fred sat for the rest of the day with Babs's death worrying him. He felt so bad for Gordie, and hoped that Babs's last minutes were peaceful and not full of fear.

The news he got at dinner was more disturbing than even the fact that Babs had been murdered. Mooseface Tyler had caught the famed albino pike, killed it, and taken it to Gordie to be mounted. That news made Fred kind of sick to his stomach. He'd heard the legend of the albino pike ever since he'd been coming up north. Everybody had, but nobody Fred knew had ever seen one. That made it all the more magical in the imagination. That there actually was one was wonderful; that the only place to see it was dead and hanging on Mooseface's wall was disgusting. He mourned the loss of the magic.

Fred lost his appetite and went on home to his brother's place. Tomorrow he'd try worms. They were almost a sure thing.

Fred sat on his brother's couch and watched the blazing color of the sunset out the picture window. He felt the need for the perversion building in him, and he spent the evening praying for it to go away.

Eventually, it did. He stir-fried tofu and vegetables, then later popped popcorn, watched television for a while, then went to bed, happy to have beat the demon back one more time.

On his way home, Fred stopped at Gordie Van Rank's taxidermy shop to pick up his mounted walleye. A tasteful little bell rang when Fred pushed open the door, and Gordie called out from the back room. "Be right with you," he said.

Fred admired the mounts on the walls as he waited.

"Fred?"

Fred turned, and there was Gordie, looking the same as always.

"Heard about Babs," Fred said, his heart filled with compassion. "Came by to see you."

A soft smile crossed Gordie's face. "Thanks, Fred. That means a lot. They got the folks who killed her, you know. They killed her and Cara Trenton and a bunch of tourists. I did a couple of days in jail before they found the scum who did it, but it's all behind us now."

"I can't imagine what you're feeling," Fred said.

"Still kind of numb, actually. Funeral was just Saturday. Can't believe it. Still expect her to come walking through the door."

"Keeping busy?"

"Got more work than I know what to do with. I'm having to ship some of it out of town. And I'm also trying to deal with The Tickled Bear. That's a lot to keep me occupied." Gordie looked toward the wall. "Speaking of which," he said, and pulled Fred's beautiful walleye down and handed it to him.

"Wow," Fred said. "Nice work, Gordie."

"Came out real nice."

Fred paid him, collected his receipt and made ready to leave. "Well, don't be alone too much. Maybe the next time I come up, we can grab a beer or something."

"Thanks, Fred," Gordie said with sincerity. "I'll look forward to that."

As he left, he saw a dark-haired man escorting a beautiful woman across the street into Margie's diner. They were both dressed nicely, and Fred felt happy for their happiness.

When he got home, he put the frozen fillets directly into the freezer, called his brother to report that the cabin was in good repair and all was well. Then he hung his walleye over the fireplace and admired it.

He felt inordinately tired, so he undressed, brushed his teeth, set the alarm, got into his pajamas and crawled into bed.

A few minutes later, he sat up, his breath coming hard, a cold sweat popping out from his forehead. Exhaustion settled into his left arm to the point where it felt like a dead appendage, and a fiery pain crawled up his jawbone. The pressure on his chest was immense.

He only had one phone, and it hung on the wall in the kitchen. He'd never make it, he knew. A better use of the minutes he had left was to get himself right with God. Then maybe the pain would subside and he'd make it to the phone. If not, he was prepared to meet his maker.

Wasn't he?

It only took the flash of an instant for Fred to review his life. He'd been a good man. He had done everything by the book. He was nice, he paid his bills, paid his taxes, was courteous, looked for the good in people. He never acted on his negative impulses, and he didn't drink, didn't smoke, didn't chase skirts. He'd lived a frugal life, ate low cal, low fat food, and had an enormous savings account that his brother could use to put some of his kids through college. Fred could meet God with a clean slate and an open heart.

What a waste. If he had it to do all over again, he'd live. He'd *live!* He'd smoke and drink and get married seven times. He'd have a dozen children and waste money. He'd tell guys like Mooseface Tyler exactly what he thought of him, and he'd spend those long sultry evenings up north looking through the window at lovely young Katarina Svensen.

Fred Kramer's chest tightened with grief and remorse and the agony of his heart in spasm, and the tears spilled out of the corners of his eyes and trickled down into his ears. He wished he could turn back the clock. He wished he could take it all back. He wished, he wished, he wished. . . .

ONE QUIET EVENING IN THE WAX MUSEUM

Muffy sat down in Mr. Edgar's old creaky wooden desk chair and set her backpack on his desk.

"Study," she said to herself, opened her pack and took out her biology text. His desk was mildly cluttered with invoices, papers and dusty paperweights. She opened her book, set her pack on the floor and tried to concentrate.

"Study," she told herself, but she knew she wouldn't, not until she had explored a little of the place. The delivery she was waiting for could come any minute, and perhaps she'd never have another chance to see behind the scenes, as it were, of the old wax museum.

Muffy, home from school on a whirlwind weekend trip to see to her ailing mother, had been visiting Victoria, an old high school friend who waited tables at the tiny pie shop across the street from the museum. Just as Victoria was turning the sign from "Open" to "Closed" that night, old Mr. Edgar came rushing in, hat in one hand, car keys in the other. He said he had an emergency and had to leave, and would she please go over to the museum office and receive the delivery he'd been waiting for all day? It should come soon. He pressed a worn twenty-dollar bill into her hand.

She looked at Victoria, who looked at the clock and shrugged. "I could use the money," Muffy said.

"It's late and I'm tired," Victoria answered. "Tomorrow's my day off. We'll hang out then."

Muffy turned back to Mr. Edgar and smiled.

He hustled her across the deserted street and through the side door of his office. "Leave the package there on the floor," he said, "and lock the door when you leave. Thank you. Thank you."

"Sure," Muffy said, the twenty equaling a week's allowance on her parents' thin budget. She needed to study anyway. Next week were finals. What quieter place than a wax museum?

Too quiet.

Maybe there's a radio.

Feeling naughty, like she did when she snooped in other people's medicine cabinets, she opened Mr. Edgar's desk drawer. The wood was sticky, and she tugged hard. It lurched out of the desk and all Muffy saw were a hundred creatures looking up at her. Looking at each other. Looking mystified. Looking crazy. She stifled a squeal, then, heart pounding, realized that it was a drawerful of glass eyes. Of course. Wax people needed glass eyes.

She closed the drawer and moved a little bit away from it.

No more exploring. Now study.

But it was too quiet. Way too quiet. No dorm noise, with people giggling and eating, no campus sporting event, no loud music next door, no hair dryers, no humming machinery, or smell of freshly delivered pizza. Just a drawerful of eyeballs.

Wonder what else?

Vargas County used to be home to the northwoods' only amusement park, Enchanted Pines. Muffy remembered going on the Ferris wheel when she was a little girl—it all seemed like brightly lit magic to her. Then she heard the words bankrupt, and default, and there was resentment among the locals, and soon the Ferris wheel disappeared, leaving only the two giant triangles and an axle between them to rust. The midway booths blew down and were vandalized, the driving range was reclaimed by the swamp until only the 150-yard marker could be seen at the edge of the woods. The skeleton of the old roller coaster shone whitely in the moonlight and attracted kids of all ages to mischief of all types. In fact it was a hand-in-hand walk on the overgrown narrow-gauge train tracks that led to the loss of Muffy's virginity one night, over by the petting zoo. The animals were all long gone, except for Jimmy Miller, who finessed her out of her panties so fast she barely knew what was happening until it was over. Jimmy Miller. Ha. Wonder whatever happened to him?

The truth was, it had been five years since she'd been back to White Pines Junction. She'd moved out of state the summer before her senior year to live with her aunt, and from there she went to the local community college, and now she was in her last year at the state university on student loans, grants and scholarships. When she got the word that she needed to come home to see her mother, she hopped the plane, looking forward to seeing Victoria and hoping to run into Jimmy Miller. It had been over five years since that night in the Enchanted Pines, over five years that she had been away, dating guys that somehow never measured up to him in her memory. Maybe only because he had been her first. That's what her girlfriends told her. She'd like to run into him again just to see. Just to make sure. Just because.

Anyway, Horace Edgar bought the wax museum from the bankruptcy court and kept it going. Muffy thought he probably owned the pie shop, too.

She wondered what was being delivered so late. It couldn't be coming UPS, could it? Maybe. White Pines Junction probably wasn't on the regular UPS route.

Study, she told herself, and looked again at the text.

Ting. Ting. Ting.

Something metallic was making a little noise on the other

side of the other door—the door that led to the exhibits. Goose bumps ran up her arms. Ought she investigate?

No, she decided. I'm not the bloody caretaker, I'm just waiting for a delivery.

Ting. Ting. Ting.

Louder.

She jumped out of her chair, sending it skating across the floor behind her, wheels screeching, and her heart pounded so loudly and so hard she couldn't catch her breath. Someone was in here. Maybe someone wanting to get out. What if someone was locked inside?

She edged toward the door and listened. Nothing. "Hello?" She hoped her voice would sound full of female authority, but she sounded like a cartoon mouse instead. She took a step back toward the desk, toward the safe circle of desk light, and the tinging started up again.

"Okay," she said, bravely strode to the door, pulled back the deadbolt, slowly turned the knob and opened the door.

The cold breath of the exhibition hall flooded the small office with its overly perfumed smell of wax along with something scorched.

The small desk light shed precious little of itself into the cavernous hall. Muffy felt the walls for a light switch, but found none.

Ting. Ting. Ting.

Way back in the darkest, furtherest. . . .

No way. "Stop it," she yelled. "I'm trying to study." She backed out and closed the door, wheeled the old chair back to the desk and sat down. "Now, do it!" she commanded herself.

Fat chance.

She wouldn't mind going in there if she could turn the lights on. She hadn't seen the wax exhibit in years. Maybe the light switch was inside the office.

There was a circuit breaker. Just as she opened the gray metal door, a real knock came to the outside door. The delivery. Thank god.

She whipped open the outside door and opened her mouth to say, "It's about time," when a greasy, smelly glove grabbed her around the mouth and a toothless, horrifying specter grinned down on her.

"Pretty," it said.

Chainlink Charlie, the village idiot. Everybody thought he was harmless, mumbling to himself, directing traffic that wasn't there, dancing in the parks to music in his head. He had a tarp with coat hangers fastened to it with duct tape and anywhere he could find himself a chain-link fence, Charlie could make himself a home. His portable hovel moved on a daily basis— and he survived on the goodwill handouts of others.

Just tonight, in fact, Victoria had given him an expired pie.

And now he had Muffy, both hands around her head, and she was scared to bloody death. She tried to move away, tried to yell, tried to bite him, but was immobilized.

"Very pretty," he said and smiled, and she would have gagged at his foul breath if she had any air in her lungs to gag with.

He smashed her head into his bony, smelly chest and she could feel him singing as he fumbled in his pants. Muffy had regained her composure enough to know that she didn't want to have anything to do with what Chainlink Charlie had in his pants, so she brought her knee up forcefully and connected just right.

With a grunt, his grip eased. She slipped from his hands and ran to the other door, threw the bolt, pulled it open and walked quickly but carefully through the pitch black hall, arms out in front of her. She tried to be quiet, but kept hearing little sounds coming from deep inside her own throat.

Ting. Ting. Ting.

She altered her course toward the sound. Please, god, was someone in here?

"Gurl? Pretty gurl?" Charlie was closer behind than she thought, and she couldn't stop with the moaning thing, although she knew that her own noises pinpointed her location.

Ting. Ting. Ting.

"Gurl?"

He was right behind her. She ran toward the tinging, and bumped into somebody. She screamed as they tumbled together to the floor, and screamed again as Charlie tripped and landed on top of them.

He lay on her with such a weight and a stench that she desperately tried to wiggle out from underneath him. "No, no, no," she heard herself say in breathless little shrieks.

"Hey!" someone else said, and then the exhibition hall was filled with light. "Hey, what's going on in here?" She heard footsteps and then the FedEx guy pulled Charlie off her and said, "Jesus god!"

Muffy saw that she was covered in blood. Charlie's blood.

"You okay?" the delivery man asked, but Muffy couldn't stop staring at Charlie, who had fallen on a butcher knife held in the hand of the wax figure she had knocked over.

Butcher knife?

She blinked and looked around. Where once were wax figures of presidents and queens, poets and composers, sports heroes, astronauts and movie stars, now stood famous murderers—John Wayne Gacy, Lizzie Borden, Jack the Ripper, Jeffrey Dahmer, Lawrence Pursley, Ted Bundy, The Boston Strangler, Charles Manson, Susan Smith . . . Old Mr. Edgar had turned the museum into a shrine for the criminally insane.

She heard the FedEx guy's comforting monologue, though she couldn't understand it. She let him get her a chair, and when he went to call the police, she wiped the tears from her face with bloody hands and looked again down at Charlie. In his hand was a butcher knife exactly like the one that was stuck in his chest. The wax hand that had held that knife belonged to someone . . . someone strangely familiar.

Not able to help herself, Muffy slowly got up from her chair and walked around the gruesome display to read the card:

Vargas County's only convicted mass murderer, Jimmy Miller, is thought to have gutted twelve young women in two years before being apprehended. While all the evidence against him was circumstantial and he always maintained his innocence, he relished his notoriety and enjoyed his fame. He was killed in prison while awaiting trial.

Mr. Edgar had captured that adorable smirk, she noticed. Before she had run into Jimmy's likeness in wax, he had been standing by the old weathered metal sign from Enchanted Pines. The sign read "The Enchanted Pines Choo-Choo. You must be this tall to ride." With unsteady legs, she bent down, picked up the knife from Charlie's hand and touched the sign.

Ting.

First Date

Mitch Kardashian was the only person in town who knew that he had a secret in his past, and he intended to keep it that way.

When Emmiline had left him no choice but to give her a little extra dose of what she had come to depend upon him and his prescription-writing privileges for, she went to sleep calmly, peacefully, innocently, and never awakened. Accidental overdose, of course, the medical examiner told the grieving widower.

Mitch sold the house, donated the furniture, said good-bye to his pitying friends, and took his dental practice, specializing in the bright white smile, up north where he would likely minister to loggers and fishermen, hunters and outdoorsmen. No more women. Women were trouble for Mitch; always had been, always would be. None of the other men he knew seemed to have the problems he had with them, but Mitch never seemed to get the recipe right. Women were either too good-looking, and therefore more expensive than he wanted to maintain, or else they were too demanding of his attentions, when he required so much time alone, or else they were too bitchy, and he needed a certain amount of adoration if he was going to put up with a woman at all. The perfect woman was probably out there, but he wasn't looking for her, didn't want to find her, and hoped that she wouldn't be in White Pines Junction.

He bought a little office building with Emmiline's life insurance proceeds, and hung out his shingle. Mitch Kardashian, DDS. The Smile Specialist. He had to import a hygienist from the city, but he picked one with small boobs who would defer to him in all ways, and it was easy to find a receptionist who was too old to remember romance, so he figured he was safe, at work, anyway.

Until Tamara Crafts walked through the newly painted office door and eventually sat in his electric-blue dentist's chair.

Usually, the rubber pad under the chair took away the static electricity that was such a problem in the north during the winter, but when he touched her for the first time, the spark arced between his finger and the corner of her mouth with a blue flash. She jerked her head and he jerked his hand back, banging it into his instrument tray, sending bright steel tools flying across the room and clattering to the floor.

"Ow," she said.

"Good lord," he said. "I'm so sorry."

She held a fingertip to the corner of her still-lipsticked mouth.

He, flustered beyond anything he could remember feeling, apologized, then saw to her lip while the hygienist picked up the tools and brought out a freshly sterilized tray. His first reaction was to dismiss this patient and refer her to another dentist. Surely she would never view him the way he required his patients to see and respect him. He needed to be the authority, the one with the expensive advice that they would follow without question.

Then she smiled at him. "It wasn't your fault," she said.

Well, maybe he could salvage her as a patient. Her teeth were natural and straight and strong, and her hair black and luxurious. Her eyes were the lightest of blue, an intriguing contrast with the black hair and brows. He was attracted. He was more than attracted. She had come for a simple checkup, and he gave her mouth one, and then he gave the rest of her one, and before he could stop himself, before he could corral his renegade tongue, he had asked her to dinner.

She regarded him with a coy, wary eye, then accepted with a smile, and he marveled that he was not immune to the power of an incredible smile even though they were his stock in trade.

He floated through the rest of the day with a grin on his face and a bad feeling in the pit of his stomach.

He was an addict. He was addicted to women. He was walking into certain disaster, and he was powerless to help himself. He needed a twelve-step program. But first, he needed to wine and dine and perhaps bed the flawless Tamara Crafts.

That night when he picked her up, she wore a slinky black dress that showed off her mature, voluptuous assets in a mesmerizing way. He was dressed in a polo shirt and slacks, since the only place for dinner was Margie's Diner. "We're just going to the diner," he said.

"Looking nice makes my heart sing," she said. "I'll take any excuse."

That phrase was hauntingly familiar, but he didn't dwell on it. He helped her into his BMW roadster and they went to the diner in style.

Margie seated them in a corner, where Mitch toyed with Tamara's hand and pretended to be fascinated by the boring world of investment brokerage. Tamara was the only stockbroker in town, which meant she had a lot of money—he found that very attractive—and lots of real estate. The heat grew between them as dinner wore on, and she pretended to be on the edge of her seat as he discussed the future of dental bonding polymers.

At one point, during the inevitable first date history revelations, he asked her if she had ever married. "Long ago," she said. "Divorced many years ago."

"Kids?"

"My son is grown. What about you? Married?"

"No," he said. "No, no no no no no. No, no. No."

She fixed him with a queer look. He made a mental note for

the future that one "no" was sufficient.

When they'd finished their coffee, Tamara offered to show him a piece of property she was thinking about buying. He accepted. First, she said, she had to stop at her place and change into jeans.

Going to her place was good. Changing into jeans was good. Things were progressing, and as they sped down the county road in the late summer daylight, Mitch thought that maybe women weren't all bad after all. This one had intriguing possibilities.

Her house was small but perfectly appointed. Mitch wandered around the living room, looking at her art, handling her knick-knacks, touching her lamps, while she was upstairs changing. He went into the kitchen to find a cross-stitched phrase mounted in a heart-shaped frame. *As ye sow, so shall ye reap.* The kitchen was beautiful, in a rustic, northwoods way, with shelves of canned fruit in front of a lighted panel, so the light, through the fruit, cast a warm glow throughout the kitchen.

"Here you are," she said. "Ready to go?"

She was a vision in a light blue sweater over jeans. Her slim hips and long legs were just the right flavors of eye candy. "You look fabulous. Your heart must be singing up a storm."

She smiled. "Thanks." She pointed to the cross-stitch. "Did you see this?"

He nodded, then did a double take. It said, *No smoking. Curfew ten p.m.*

"I stole that from the women's dorm at Kansas State."

"Bad girl," he said, and put his arm around her. "I like bad girls."

She laughed, a tinkling, flirty laugh that tickled his innards, and as they walked from the kitchen, he looked back again at the little sign. Sure enough, it said no smoking.

She opened the garage and rummaged until she found a big

yellow flashlight that she handed to him. "Let's take my car," she said, and opened the car door. He got into her Mercedes SUV and let her take control of the date. He was comfortable letting her lead. A less confident man might not be, he reassured himself.

She pulled out of the driveway and after a few turns, they were on a county road that went straight through the north-woods for what seemed like a dozen miles. She had a nice soft classical piano CD in the player, and they zoomed through the fading daylight as if in a dream. Neither spoke.

Then she slowed, and the bleached white bones of an old roller coaster came into view. It was off in the weeds a ways. Further on were the two triangles of a Ferris wheel structure that had been partially dismantled, and he could see the remnants of little buildings and what was at one time probably an amusement park midway.

"What is this place?" he asked.

"This is it," she said, pulled into a weedy spot, killed the engine and opened her door. "Bring the flashlight. It'll get dark soon."

As she said that, her face turned in just the right shadow and she looked exactly like Emmiline. The sight gave him a start, but when he looked again, it was Tamara. Of course it was Tamara. The waning light was playing tricks on him, he thought. Besides, it hadn't been that long since he lost his wife. It was a normal thing, he knew, to continue to see a loved one out of habit after death. He jumped out of the car and ran around to join her, shaking Emmiline out of his system.

"Enchanted Pines," Tamara said. "An old amusement park that went bankrupt a dozen years or more ago. It's been for sale for just that long, but nobody has wanted to buy it. It's a great piece of property, twenty-four acres, including a narrow-gauge railroad track that runs clear around. I'm thinking of developing it."

"Developing it into what?"

Mitch followed her through the weeds, knowing he was getting burrs in his socks, and not very happy about that. Clearly this wasn't the woman for him. He liked women in jeans, but jeans with high heels were much better than jeans with hiking boots.

She shrugged. "Lots of options. Could grow ginseng, could do a resort, maybe some housing . . . cemeteries are high-return properties if the taxes stay low."

"A cemetery?" Mitch shivered and looked around at the growing shadows. He wanted to go back to her house where it was cozy. He wanted to see how she'd decorated her bedroom, and if she had a wine cellar.

"C'mon," she said and grabbed his hand.

He'd feel better about all of this if she had brought along a blanket and pillow. He followed her lead, stumbling behind her as she crossed through the weeds and the occasional overgrown path to a little railroad track. "See? Isn't this cute?"

Mitch especially didn't want to be here. Emmiline's father was in the railroad business. All her money—now his money—came from inheriting his stock. Mitch always considered spending the evenings with his in-laws the dues he had to pay for marrying their heir. The old man was boring in the extreme and his nagging wife the worst the gender had to offer. Mitch had history with railroads, and this miniature one was making him think about things he'd rather not.

"It's getting dark," he said.

"There aren't any boogies out here," she said, and laughed. Then she let go of his hand and ran off down the train tracks into the gloom of pine trees and dusk. It was clearly a "come and get me" move. He fumbled with the big, heavy flashlight, his heart pounding a little loudly in his ears, but as he hurried, trying to figure out how to turn on the light, he tripped over the small metal rail and fell face down.

The big glass lens shattered.

The night closed in.

"C'mon, scaredy cat," he heard her taunt from the distance.

"Emmiline!" he shouted. Oops. He was here with . . . what was her name? "Tamara, I mean," he called. "Tamara, I broke the light."

No answer except the wind in the trees. He could see their tops silhouetted in the rapidly fading light and they swayed back and forth, the sound amazingly loud. He stood up, then threw the remnants of the worthless light off into the distance. He brushed off his clothes, felt around for torn places where he could be bleeding, but found none. "Tamara! Come on."

No answer. He started off down the tracks, carefully picking his way, hating her more and more every step.

And then he realized what this was. This was a setup. Emmiline was behind this. Shivers arced up his body like the blue spark that had introduced Mitch to this woman. This *demon*. Emmiline had returned from the grave to exact her vengeance, and what better way than on railroad tracks in the dark.

He remembered his two much-older brothers locking him in the cellar at their house whenever the parents went out. They'd just throw him down the basement stairs, lock the door, and then turn out the light. He'd crawl up the stairs and whine at the door, and, now and then, whenever one of them got up to go to the fridge for a fresh beer, they'd say, "Did they getcha yet, you little sissy? Did the basement monsters taste your toes yet?" and he'd pull his feet up under him and start to cry.

Just before the parents came home, his brothers would let him out and threaten to kill him if he told. He lived his life in abject terror until they all left home. When Mitch went away to dental school, he left for good. He didn't need terrorism at the hands of his brothers now that he was an adult, and he was sure they'd continue to hand it out.

Emmiline knew about his fear of the dark.

He heard an owl, and the creepy sound of bats flying too close to his head. Mitch was out of his element. He was a city boy. He needed to be in his office, in his home, with a hefty Scotch and ESPN. What the hell was he doing out in the woods—with another woman? Hadn't he sworn off women, just this morning?

But this wasn't another woman, he realized. It was *Emmiline*. It had to be Emmiline. The railroad business. The cemetery referral. The needlepoint in her kitchen. Emmiline used to do needlepoint. And she graduated from Kansas State. And what was it she said when he picked her up for this wretched date? "Looking nice makes my heart sing." Those were the exact words Emmiline said to him the night he picked her up for their first date. *The. Exact. Words.*

Darkness oozed from the thick stand of trees and surrounded him. He couldn't see his feet. He was afraid of stepping off the train tracks and tripping again. He didn't know the lay of the land. He didn't know what was beyond the tracks. He didn't know if it was bog or lake or highway or what. The darkness was complete. He'd never seen such darkness. It was never this dark in the city. He couldn't even see his hand in front of his face. He tried. Couldn't.

"Okay, Emmiline," he said. "I got it. I *get* it. Come on, now. Let's go back and talk this over with a glass of wine."

No answer.

"Emmiline."

No answer.

He stumbled on something but managed not to fall. He bent over to retrieve it. A short, stocky piece of tree branch. He felt the ties and rail and knew he was still traveling within the track. If it was intact all the way, all he had to do was keep walking and he would end up where he started. Surely he'd see car lights as he neared the highway, wouldn't he? He hefted the branch in his hand. It would be a good weapon in case a bat wanted to bite him or nest in his hair, or wolves came around sniffing the scent of his fear.

"Emmiline! Do you want me to apologize? Okay. I'm sorry, all right? I'm sorry."

He was beginning to hear noises in the woods that he didn't understand. His heart pounded so loudly in his ears that he was afraid he wouldn't hear something if it sneaked up on him. He was beginning to see pulsing red globes in the periphery of his vision, but it was so dark, that was all he could see.

And now this.

He was so afraid he thought it might be best if he just sat down on the train tracks, tucked his feet up underneath him and waited for morning. Except that she was out there. She'd come back, find him and call him a sissy. Emmiline.

"I'm no sissy, Emmiline," he said. "I'm not falling for it this time. Come out. Come out wherever you are." He hefted the tree branch and tried to feel brave.

But he didn't, and when something swooped right next to his ear, he jumped, stumbled and almost fell again. He was totally unequipped for this.

He sat down. And waited, fear closing in.

Then he heard her, Emmiline, that traitorous bitch. She was walking down the train tracks. He could hear her shoes swishing through the weeds. She couldn't see him, he knew. He stood, crouched, and stepped off the tracks. Goddamn her. He thought he'd done the job right the first time, but apparently not. He wouldn't fail a second time.

Just as she came up next to him, he swung the branch with

all his strength.

"Mitch?" she said just before he connected.

That wasn't Emmiline's voice. But it was too late. She went down hard, and he didn't need a medical degree to know what was running out of her skull as it lay crushed on the rail.

For a moment he felt a little disoriented. A little confused. He sat down on the rail next to her body, and put the tree branch down. Funny how he wasn't afraid anymore. He had other things to think about.

He sat there a while, feeling a little bit hung over, until the night turned cold. He felt sorry about the woman. Jeez, it wasn't her fault. He wondered who her money would go to, but then he put that thought right out of his head. He sat up and started making his way slowly in the darkness back to her car. He'd take it back to her place, walk home and chalk this whole distasteful adventure up to a bad date. Women were trouble, and one of these days he was going to have to learn that.

Computing Fate

Kevin Leppens woke up to the sound of an engine idling. A car was waiting outside on the street in front of his house. He heard it because his bedroom window was wide open; it was July and the night was still to breathless. He checked the clock, it was two-thirteen in the morning.

Normally, it was silent as a tomb out there. Coyotes yipping at each other were about the only sounds that came this far north in the night. In the winter, the night itself made crackling noises as the thermometer plunged, and everything expanded as it froze. Sometimes he imagined he could hear the aurora borealis as it shimmered overhead, but never had there been a car idling in front of his house at two-thirteen a.m.

Maybe someone was going to the airport.

He punched his pillow and turned over.

The car continued to idle. And then it quit.

Kevin waited to hear car doors, quiet whispered conversation, as whoever it was did whatever they did. But nothing. The car engine stopped and nothing else happened.

Kids. Making out. Having sex in the backseat.

But he knew that wasn't right.

First thing, there weren't any kids in this area of town. Secondly, he knew it was for him. He'd been expecting it.

He'd outwait them. He didn't need to go out there, and he couldn't believe they'd come in here.

He pulled the covers up against his neck and tried to relax. It

219

was comforting, in a way, knowing that they were finally here for him. He didn't have to look over his shoulder all the time anymore. The endgame was in sight; and the next move was up to him.

He hoped.

They couldn't take him the way they took the others; he was too old. But he was on to their game, and they'd finally come to get him.

Well, he'd see about that. He'd resist. He'd resist all the way.

Kevin spent the rest of the night listening, heart pounding. When he got up at dawn, the car was gone. He hadn't heard it leave. Perhaps he'd dozed off. Perhaps he'd dreamed it. Regardless, he got up with a mental list of a dozen things to do; another set of dead bolts on every door, window locks; he'd even check with Julia, his landlord, about ordering some wrought-iron bars for his windows.

As he trundled down the front walk, headed to Margie's for coffee and breakfast, he noticed the tire prints in the dust outside his house. They looked entirely too ordinary. He hadn't dreamed it. There wasn't much traffic on this little spud of a road on the east side of White Pines Junction where he rented a little bungalow cottage.

He chose White Pines Junction because it was remote, and quiet, and he could do whatever he wanted. In the summer, people took their kids to the park across the street, and Kevin worked on his computer at the little table in the dining room where he could hear them laughing. He liked hearing little kids laugh. But most of town was centered around the lake, and he didn't have any use for that.

He'd won the Pepsi sweepstakes merely by being at the right place at the right time, and by the time he had collected his enormous check, his bags were already packed. He got out of Boston and came to this little place, way up in the cold, remote northwoods. His parents had followed him here from Boston, or at least they'd tried, but his dad had gone back and left his mom here by herself. Kevin didn't really want her around, but she had proved herself to be self-sufficient and no bother. He just felt uneasy, as if he had been the cause of their broken marriage, and as if she were now his responsibility, both financially and emotionally. He couldn't imagine a woman living alone all year around up here, it was such a harsh place. Yet she did it. And so did other women.

Anyway, the tire marks in the dirt looked pretty ordinary, but he knew that they were made by a car full of not-so-ordinary.

Kevin got to the diner, grabbed a morning newspaper from the counter, and sat down. Margie floated over with the coffee pot, righted a mug, and gave him a nice morning smile.

"The usual for you?"

He nodded, and smiled, and within five minutes he had a bowl of steaming oatmeal with raisins and almonds and brown sugar. And an orange slice. Perfect.

He had just poured fresh cream around the edges of his oatmeal when the bells on the door jangled. He gave a shiver, and then took up a spoonful of steaming oatmeal.

A big presence in plaid cotton sat down across from him, filling the red vinyl booth with fresh air.

Lloyd Bunnington wiped off his ever-present ball cap and set it on the seat next to him. He drilled Kevin with pale blue eyes.

Kevin's spoon stopped halfway to his mouth. Then it continued its trip, but Kevin had no time to savor it. "Hey, Bun," he said.

"Kevin." Bun turned to Margie, who hustled up with the coffee pot. "Two eggs poached, dry toast, please. Mmmm, that coffee sure smells good."

"Good morning, Bun," Margie said as she splashed fresh coffee into both cups.

"Miss Margie," he said, but his eyes were fixed solely upon Kevin.

As soon as she left, Bun said, "Boot up that computer lately?"

"Every day," Kevin said, but he knew what Bun meant. Bun wanted to know when the next child disappearance was going to be, and Kevin didn't know. Kevin didn't want to know. In fact, after Margie and Jimbo's boy, Micah, had been taken, Kevin had predicted the next disappearance, and Pastor Porter's baby had been taken, right on time, right on target, right on the precise goddamned dot. When Kevin heard about the disappearance, he erased the program, removed its entire existence. He hadn't even kept a backup copy. Then Julia Morganstern's grandson went, and Kevin didn't know if he was glad he'd erased it or not. And now—

"It's coming soon, isn't it?"

"Couldn't tell you, Bun," Kevin said. "Don't have that program anymore. There are some things we're not meant to know."

Bun eyed him over the rim of his coffee cup. He sipped, then set it down, his big old, working-man's hands moving restlessly on the tabletop. "I can feel it, Kevin. I felt it, I saw it, *I was in it* when, you know, when it took"—Bun looked around to make sure Margie wasn't listening—"Micah Benson. I know what it feels like, and I'm feeling it again. The feeling started yesterday and it's growing. Some kid's going to go in the next day or so, isn't that true?"

Kevin looked down at his oatmeal.

"Isn't it?"

Kevin nodded, then he looked up at Bun. "But you don't have to worry, because it's coming for me."

Bun sat back and regarded Kevin with squinty suspicion. "You? Why you?"

"Because I know about them. I figured out their game once,

I could do it again. But I won't. I don't want to."

They stared at each other as Margie approached the table and lay Bun's breakfast down. "Everything all right here?" she asked.

"Just fine, ma'am," Kevin said, and smiled up at her.

Bun waited until Margie left, then moved his breakfast out of the way. "Who are they? What are they doing? What do they want? Where do they take the kids?"

"I don't know any of that. I don't want to know."

"Well I do, by god. And I want my kin back. My baby sister and my little boy, to come back and grow up like regular children. And Micah. And the pastor's baby, and every one of those lost children who have been disappearing out of here in the last hundred years or so."

"Well, maybe when I get there, I can try to send them back." Kevin's spoon vibrated against the oatmeal bowl. His hand was trembling. He put the spoon down.

Bun squinted at him again. "You really think you're going, don't you?"

Kevin nodded.

"But what if it ain't you? What if, while you're packing your bags to go, some other kid gets snatched?"

"Nothing I can do about that. It's not my fault. I'm not the one taking them."

Bun pulled his plate back in front of himself and began to eat, but Kevin had lost his appetite. It was real, now, he could feel it, too. It was a growing pinprick feeling on his skin in addition to the dread in his heart when he thought about that idling car.

He pulled a wad of money from his pocket and peeled off bills for the tab. "I've got to go see my mom," he said.

Bun smiled, held out his hand. Kevin shook it, but when he

tried to let it go, Bun held on. "Send me those three babies back."

Kevin nodded, the lump that had formed in his throat keeping him from talking.

"Send 'em all back," Bun said. "I'll take 'em all."

Kevin kept walking, out the door and into the bright sunshine.

"Mom?" Kevin turned the knob and opened the door, after knocking a couple of times. He shouted into the over-heated interior of her little house, not a whole lot different from his little cottage. "Mom? You home?"

Nobody locked their doors in White Pines Junction, it was one of the little perks of living in a small town. Kevin went in, where he heard her footsteps upstairs.

"Hi, honey. I'll be right down. Coffee pot's on."

The new kitchen was a beauty, Kevin had to admit. Apparently, the remodel had struck the death knell for his parents' marriage, but Kevin had seen that coming from many years away. He was just sorry that his dad had to go back to Boston and into obscurity. Kevin hadn't heard from him since.

He poured himself a cup of coffee, added cream and sugar, and wandered into the little living room to sit in the big chair and wait for his mom. He didn't know what he was going to say to her, didn't know how to break the news, or even if he was going to break any news, or if he'd just sit a while and spend some nice time with her before he left. Maybe he'd write her a note.

A few minutes later, she came down the stairs looking younger and prettier than Kevin had ever seen her.

"There's something more than wonderful about living up here," Louise Leppens said. "Aren't we the lucky ones?"

Kevin raised his eyebrows.

"I won a trip to Rome! I leave on Sunday!"

"Mom, that's great."

She was all abuzz with travel arrangements and tour books and pamphlets and itineraries, and Kevin listened, but sorrow hung increasingly heavy in his soul and he had a hard time rising up to her level of enthusiasm. As she talked on and on, he realized he had some final arrangements to make about his money, and he better do it soon, because the blanket of dread that accompanied the electrical charge he could feel increased exponentially with the passing minutes.

He gave his mother a long, slow hug and stroked her hair and told her how much he loved her. When she pulled back from him to question her son's unusual display of affection, he found that he couldn't meet her eyes. He pecked her on her soft cheek and left, headed to the bank.

Like a dying man, he thought. He ought to be relishing every moment, every sparkle on the lake, every flutter of bird wings. Instead, all he could think about was how unfair it all was. Here he was: young, rich, single and smart, and he had to be ripped out of his comfortable world into something mysterious and unforgiving.

But to deny it would be stupid, so he went ahead and made his list. He jettisoned the idea of bars on the windows and decided to take a more practical approach of putting his affairs in order. Bars on the windows would mean nothing. In fact the idling car engine meant nothing. It was probably just there to serve notice. Give him time to kiss his mother good-bye. Back up his hard disk. By the time he was finished with Anthony Brumbach the banker, Kevin's hair was beginning to stand on end at the nape of his neck. He was beginning to hear and smell the crackle of electricity as well as feel it, and the air began to feel thin and eerie.

He felt panic rising. He wrapped up his business at the bank, secure in the knowledge that not only his mother, but a couple of local charities would be much better off financially in the event of his death or disappearance. He made it clear to the banker and his notary that if he disappeared, they only needed to wait one full year before they disbursed his estate.

Then he got out of the bank and into the fresh air, but the air didn't have that freshness for him anymore. Nobody else on the street seemed to notice that anything was different, but Kevin felt as though he were becoming less dense.

He wondered if he could bargain with them. He wondered if he could bribe them. He didn't know what they had in store for him, but he was pretty sure he didn't want it. He liked his life. He didn't want it to change.

He went home to his cottage, not to barricade himself in, but to negotiate from as much a power point as he knew how to attain. Perspiration was beginning to dampen his clothes, and he felt a headache coming on.

Once inside, he put on the teakettle, booted up his computer, and sat at his kitchen table and stared at it. He felt breathless as the room began to feel lightly blue, and he got a sinking, nauseated feeling.

He realized there was nobody to call. Nobody to save him, nobody for him to say good-bye to, save his mother, and he'd already done that. He had no girlfriend, no pet. His father had written him off in a cruel and abrupt way.

He typed in a quick note saying that he was gone and would never return and left it sitting on the screen in his computer. He brewed a cup of Earl Gray and turned the stove off.

Then he sat back to wait.

Maybe they were coming for him for reasons other than his computer skills. He hadn't done anything with the knowledge that he had, little that it was. Maybe there was another reason he was needed.

Needed. He liked the sound of that.

He'd always been a computer geek, thin and not so good-looking, and while not anti-social, not pro-social, either. He was a misfit, which is why the cottage on the edge of White Pines Junction way up in the northwoods was so appealing. Everybody up here was a misfit of sorts. And the fact that it was such a queer place with such queer goings on appealed to the macabre side of him. That people would actually raise families up here, knowing the risk. Well, it was just exactly the place for weird Kevin Leppens.

And now, for the first time in his life, he was needed somewhere.

That was kind of a nice feeling.

From somewhere, but not across the street, he heard children laughing.

He ought to call Bun, to let him know. He ought to call his mother, so she wouldn't worry.

Bun would know. His mother would worry anyway.

Daylight failed as the sun lowered behind the trees, and the air grew thinner and bluer. He heard the music, wanted to follow it, follow the laughing children. He wanted to be one of the laughing children—had he ever laughed when he was a child? He needed to be needed, he wanted to do things that had meaning, not just sit in solitude in front of a computer screen all day long, spending found money.

This isn't a bad thing, not a bad thing at all, he thought, what they have to offer. Laughing children is a good thing. They must need me, need my help. Who am I to deny children my help? It could be everything I've been trained to do, whatever they want of me.

When he heard the car pull up outside and idle there, he stood up like a man, grabbed a jacket and went out to meet his destiny.

It was a black limo, its exhaust pluming out in the blue air.

The back door opened as he neared, but he couldn't see inside. It was so black, so dark, it seemed fathomless. He wanted the promise, he ached to have the fulfillment they offered, so he got inside, but when he stepped through and the door slammed behind him, he had a sudden, very bad feeling.

SULTRY NIGHTS

Margie woke up, her vagina pulsing, the heat of another sex-centered dream flooding her with inconceivable lust. Her side of the bed was perspiration-soaked; even her hair was damp. Jimbo snored the sleep of the innocent and unaware next to her.

This wasn't sinning. She had no control over her dreams.

She slipped out of bed, put on her robe and slippers, and went to the kitchen for a drink of something cool. It was August, and hot as hell. The streetlight shone on parched trees, parched and withered grass. Snow had shown up in every single month some time in Vargas County, and if there were snow outside now, she'd run and jump into it naked. She could use a little ice on her body at the moment. It was three-forty-six a.m. She'd have to get up soon to start the morning shift.

She poured a glass of water and sipped it, standing in the darkened kitchen, in front of the window. These dreams were beginning to interfere with her work, with her life. They were coming almost every night now, and every night she lost another hour or two of sleep. Her concentration was flagging; her energy waning. She had too much to do every day; she couldn't keep losing energy.

Yet she found herself going to bed early. She liked the sensations, the feelings, the incredible sexiness of them. They had nothing to do with Jimbo; their sex life was satisfactory. He was the only partner Margie had ever had, so she had nothing to compare, but they were happy together, and she really enjoyed the closeness of their intimacy.

But these dreams. They were raw, uninhibited, lose-your-mind kind of lusty things. She was afraid she was being seduced by a demon—what else could introduce her to something so deliciously evil?—and it scared her. She was afraid for herself, her eternal soul, and her family. Because she liked it. God help her, she liked it.

As always, she wanted to snuggle up to Jimbo and have him make the kind of love to her that happened in her dreams, but it wasn't the same. He was too real, too heavy, his breath too harsh, and while she always enjoyed the closeness of sex with Jimbo, it never sent her into the heights like these dreams.

And it made her feel guilty. Like her secret lover had aroused her and she was just using Jimbo for gratification. She knew he wouldn't mind being used, but Margie couldn't shake the feeling that whatever this was, it was evil, and she was playing into its hands, and including her sweet, innocent husband.

She wiped her face with a dampened dishtowel, finished drinking the water, and then went back to bed. Jimbo snored softly on his side facing away from her. He had no idea of her secret dream life. She never wanted him to find out.

She lay awake for a long time before sleep reclaimed her, but when it did, it was deep, dreamless, and satisfying.

Pamela McCann passed the two-mile mark and smiled to herself. She felt good. Her gait was smooth and easy, the track soft under her Nikes, and the morning fresh and delicious, though it was already warming up to be a hot day. She wore only her running shorts and a sports bra. Her short, naturally red hair flopped with every step.

Everything was good in her life. Everything except two things: Love and money.

She snorted her appreciation of the irony. At least her body was strong and lithe. She felt good, she looked good, and she'd have life knocked if she could only get a handle on her finances and the romance part of it.

Running was a good opportunity for her to clear her mind of all the garbage that accumulated during the day, and it was currently accumulating a lot. When she bought the hundred acres up north with her inheritance, she thought that she had a good investment for her future, as well as enough left over in the bank to work on developing parts of it. She had plans to put about twenty acres into farming ginseng, another twenty into upscale home lots, another twenty into a forested park and the rest she'd leave vacant and wild for the moment. The farming and the homes would keep her busy for a good long while.

But as soon as she signed on the dotted line and put the deed into the safe-deposit box, the stock market took a dive in what appeared to be, for all intents and purposes, a generation-long bear market. That left the rest of her money unavailable, as she was unwilling to sell her blue chips for a fraction of what she had paid for them mere months earlier. So she was land-rich and cash poor. And that kind of land required capital to develop as well as maintain. Taxes never went down.

At least she'd had the running track built before the crash. It was gratifying to see everybody use it—running, walking, biking, playing with their dogs. All winter long, while the rest of the countryside was ten feet deep in snow, the track could be seen, as people either packed it down by using it or brought their snow blowers out to keep it visible. It was even busier in the summer, of course. So she'd contributed to the community and that endeared her, as much as possible, considering that she was an outsider.

She rounded the corner, noted the marker and clicked off mile three in her mind. Still feeling good.

Somehow, the money situation would rectify itself, she knew. Money was just one of those fluid things that came and went. She'd had a hand-to-mouth job before her dad died, and now she had money. If she suddenly didn't have money again, she'd survive. But boy, she sure liked having money, even as briefly as she'd had it. And her soul was already attached to this land. She didn't even want to develop the home sites because she didn't want to part with twenty acres, even if she did parcel it out two acres at a time. But, of course she would have to do that, and do it sooner rather than later. Chances are, she'd have to rid herself of the whole twenty in one whack to some other developer, one who wouldn't take as much care with the development. She hated the thought, but understood the realities of life.

Money. Money was a temporary problem.

The other problem was more permanent—as permanent as a child can be. Pamela had been up to visit Wolver and hadn't had a period since.

Wolver, who had taken his name from the ferocious wolverine, lived in a cabin deep in the woods with no modern conveniences at all. He had a wood stove that heated his cabin, and an outhouse behind. He used kerosene lamps on the rare occasion when he wanted light at night, and bartered for staples with the animal furs he got from his traps and the meat he hunted. He hunted and fished and lived a solitary life. He'd like it if she came up to live with him; he'd be thrilled to know that they were expecting, but Wolver's lifestyle was not the life for Pamela, and she knew she couldn't ask him to come to Vargas County and live respectable. It wasn't in him. It wasn't in her to boil diapers on a wood stove, either.

She had decided to pay him another visit as soon as she passed the three-month mark. So many fetuses didn't make it to that point, and she didn't see a need to throw two lives into turmoil unless there was reason for it.

Three months was tomorrow, by the gestation calendar she had found on the Internet. But she hadn't needed the calendar. She'd known immediately when she was pregnant, because the dreams had stopped. She'd had the most incredibly sexy, delicious, slurpy dreams, starring nobody in particular. She'd wake up panting, shaking, vibrating, she was so hotly aroused. Perhaps that's why she went to see Wolver in the first place. And got herself knocked up.

She had a little morning sickness to confirm her suspicions. Now, it might be her imagination, but she was pretty sure she could see a bulge in her normally athletically taut tummy. It was time to go see Wolver again. Tomorrow.

Mile four.

Pamela slowed to a walk, pulled off her headband and shook out her hair. She walked the next quarter mile to her car, cooling off and rehearsing how the reunion would go.

She knew how it would start. He would be delighted to see her. He would give her a big bear hug, put on a pot of coffee, and somehow they'd be shed of their clothes, the coffee forgotten, within ten minutes. She and Wolver had incredible chemistry.

And then after, as they lay together sated and smiley, cozy and snuggly in his soft warm bed, she'd tell him. He'd grin big and say, "Really?" And then he'd hug her and it would all be so magical, right then, right there. It would, for a moment, seem possible to be a family. But that's how Wolver lived. In magic land. Outside of any normal reality. So Pamela would brighten his day and then she would ruin it. Because she and the baby couldn't live in the woods with Wolver, and Wolver couldn't live in town with her and the baby. They needed to talk about what to do.

She got into the SUV, started it and turned off the radio just as the first raindrops hit the windshield. Good timing. Then she headed home, making a mental checklist of things to pack for her trip up to Wolver's. She wouldn't need the condoms.

She got home, took off her wet clothes and looked at her poochy tummy in the mirror. "Ready to meet your daddy?" she asked it. Then she smiled, shook her head at herself for talking to a piece of tissue that was maybe a half inch long, and jumped into the shower. She'd make an appointment to see a doctor first thing next week. She'd ask Julia to recommend one.

Lexy pushed open the diner door and saw Amanda, her sister, sitting in a corner booth. Lexy waved, then took off her raincoat and hung it on the coat rack. "Okay, okay," she said as she walked up to Amanda. "What's the emergency?" She slid into the booth seat opposite, and checked her watch. "I've got a shampoo and cut at nine."

"I'm going back to Ricky," Amanda said.

"Don't be silly." Lexy signaled Margie and turned her coffee mug right side up. When she looked back at Amanda, she saw tears in her sister's eyes. "Amanda. What's going on?"

"I can't stand it anymore," Amanda said. "I'm just so lonely."

"Join the club. That doesn't mean you should go back to that goon."

"He could change."

Lexy looked up at the ceiling. "Good god, Mandy. You know he isn't going to change. One of these days he'll kill you, not just blacken your eye or break your wrist."

Amanda fingered the wrist that Lexy knew still bothered her and probably would never again work right. She sighed. "You're right. I know you're right. That's why I need you, Lex."

"You haven't called him or anything stupid?"

Amanda shook her head. "I called you instead."

"Smart girl. So tell me what's really going on."

"It's these dreams, I think. I can't stop these dreams. They're so erotic, and they make me so horny. And that makes me lonely."

Lexy laughed. "Jeez, must be something in the water here. I've been having some pretty wild dreams myself."

Margie came by with the coffee pot in one hand and a stack of dirty dishes in the other. She seemed to be unaware of herself. "Dreams?" she asked Amanda.

Amanda blushed and looked down at her hands.

Margie sat down at the booth and set the coffee pot and dirty dishes on the table.

"Yuck, Margie," Lexy said, and pushed somebody's half-eaten eggs away from her, but Margie ignored her.

"Tell me about the dreams," Margie said.

"Are you having them too?" Amanda asked.

Margie nodded. "Sex dreams," she whispered. "Sinful."

"They're too good to be sinful," Lexy said, but only got dirty looks in reply from the two women across from her. "Hey. You prudes can be mad about them, but I like it. I always wake up at the crucial moment, but I have my toys that finish the job."

"Hush," Amanda scolded.

Lexy dumped sugar and cream into her coffee and stirred it.

"Then we can't be the only ones," Margie said.

Lexy looked at Margie's face and saw a drowning woman needing a life raft. "I'm sure we're not the only ones, Margie," Lexy said. "Maybe it's the northern lights. Or the change in seasons. I don't know. They're pretty powerful, I must admit."

"Horrible," Margie said. "Wretched."

"Well . . . ," Lexy said.

"Who else, do you think?" Amanda asked.

Lexy looked around the diner. Julia was having breakfast with Dr. Mitch the gorgeous dentist. The concept of having breakfast out with a man wasn't lost on Lexy. So Julia and

Mitch had finally broken the ice and slept together. Julia probably hadn't been sleeping at all, not with that good-looking guy to keep her entertained.

She looked back at Amanda. Maybe Julia's dreams had led her to the bed of Dr. Mitch Kardashian. Wouldn't that just be like a man to figure out how to give women the hots? "Julia," she said.

Margie stood up, leaving the dishes and coffee pot on the table.

"Hey," Lexy said.

Margie turned around. Lexy gestured at the mess. Margie swept it all up, and made for the kitchen double time. She came right back out and approached Julia. A moment later, the ladies excused themselves from the good doctor's company and headed toward the coat rack.

The two women put their heads together and whispered, but Lexy saw Julia nod. Confirmed. How very odd.

She brought her coffee cup up to her lips for a sip, then thought better of it. Four women who all ate at Margie's diner, all having the same weird dreams. Maybe it was the coffee.

"See?" she said to Amanda.

Julia turned and smiled tentatively at them, then went back to her seat. Margie nodded at Lexy, and a chill ran through her bones.

Wolver was chopping wood when Pamela pulled up. He was bare chested and wore raggedy jeans. The black T-shirt she bought him last Christmas hung from a nearby tree branch. He smiled at her as she parked, then finished splitting the piece of pine and threw it on top of the sizeable pile he'd been making.

"Shouldda called," he said. "I'd have dressed."

"You look dressed," she said as she walked over and put her hands on his pecs. He was gorgeous, no question.

He kissed her cheek, and wrapped his big, wood-chopping, steamy arms around her. He made her feel small. "I'd have shaved," he whispered.

"You don't have a phone," she said, "or I'd have made a reservation."

He smelled her hair, and ran his hands around her back. Then he pulled back, and she watched his eyes as they searched her eyes, her face, her clothes. Wolver's place was where Pamela came to feel appreciated. He put his hands inside her jacket, pulled her to him and locked his lips onto hers in a wonderful welcome-home.

"C'mon in," he said, taking her hand and pulling her toward the front door. "I'll put the coffee on."

She giggled like a little girl. She couldn't help it.

Pamela and Wolver had made magic the first time they met when he was working for the Department of Natural Resources and she was teaching an environmental politics class at the local community college. She took the students on a field trip to a lake up in the northwoods, and Wolver—his name had been Daniel Wickam then—had drawn the short straw and had to escort them around and answer all their questions.

The minute they laid eyes on each other, the students disappeared and they spent all their time maneuvering to get alone. Finally, he slipped her his phone number, and that started a love affair that kept them each satisfied in their own way.

Wolver found that cabin on a piece of property in the middle of nowhere, and Pamela inherited a fortune, and despite the lifestyle changes, they had found a way to get together usually at least once or twice a month. Occasionally their separations were longer, when things got busy, but the unconventional relationship suited them.

And the sex was fantastic. Pamela had never known someone like him. He delighted in every inch of her. He pinched, probed, licked, sucked, kissed and named each body part, with a playful, worshipful ease. She fell for him, all the way.

This time, it was hard for her to keep from telling him that there was a new body part for him to name. Not yet. Soon. And when it was over, she felt soft and sweet and feminine and loved. As always.

She snuggled down into his side, smelling the warmth of the cabin and its little woodstove, smelling the warmth of Wolver and his bed and she was as contented as a woman could ever be.

"You can't stay the night," he said, and that broke the spell. He always wanted her to spend the night. He usually tried to get her to move in and never leave.

"Why?"

"There's something in the woods," he said, idly toying with her hair. "I can't get a fix on it, and probably won't unless we have a first snow and I can see tracks. But it's out there, and I don't know what it is."

"You don't know what it is? What could it be?" She turned and looked at him, but his eyes were fixed firmly on the ceiling. "Is it a person?"

"It's big. I hear it snuffling."

"Bear," she said.

He shook his head. "Like no bear I've ever seen. Or heard. Or smelled."

Pamela had to believe him. Wolver was smarter about independent, survival living than anybody. "Are we in danger?"

"I don't think I am. But I don't know about you. If this thing is staking out territory, you're an invader."

"You're scaring me."

"That's why I need you to leave before dark."

"Are you hunting it?"

"Not yet. I'm hoping it will move on. I brought all my traps in. I don't want—I don't want it in my traps."

She whined a little sound deep in her throat to let him know how disappointed she was. He turned toward her and gave her a big hug. "I know, sweetie. Me, too. I'd just feel better if I got a fix on this thing."

"Okay." She looked out the window and saw long shadows. "That's soon," she said. "I never even got the stuff out of my car."

"Come up again next week. Between now and then, I'll try to get a handle on it, so you can stay over and we can make juicy-juice all night long."

"Mmmm," she said. "That's what I want to hear."

"I love you, baby," he said, kissed her forehead, and then leaped out of bed.

Her moment to tell him about Wolver, Jr., had come and gone. She'd come back to tell him next week.

When Regina Porter woke from her nap on the sofa, she woke with her hands in her crotch. Head still full of the thrumming, syrupy pounding of her dream, she leaped up and smoothed her dress over her legs. Pearce was at the church, preparing for Sunday. He didn't know about her dreams. There was no need for him to know. She'd spent the morning making cookies and bundt cakes—all the ladies of the church were contributing baked goods, and Margie was selling them in her diner, so the church could buy new choir robes. Regina loved to bake, but it became exhausting work.

Especially since she hadn't been sleeping well.

She went to the kitchen and washed her hands, then lost herself in wonderment of the feelings that these dreams had brought out in her. Obnoxiously enough, she didn't think of Pearce when she woke, she thought of Doc. She'd like to have Doc, big, sweet, open-faced, calm, kind Doc put his hands on her and tease her passions until she flew away like she was doing in these dreams.

He didn't feature in her dreams, though. She couldn't quite visualize who or what it was that ignited her imagination so. There was an impression of big, of round, of kind of humpy, but there were no facial features. It wasn't like her adolescent dreams of movie stars, or Pearce, when he'd been courting. She felt too old, too proper, too clergy-wife to be having lusts like this, and it stole her appetite and made her feel guilty in front of her husband.

No, if Pearce—god forbid—should die, Regina would have no reason to move away from White Pines Junction. She'd make a home for herself here, and as soon as she bought a little cottage for herself with Pearce's life insurance, she'd march right on over to the tackle shop and gift that precious Doc with one of her best lemon poppyseed bundt cakes.

But in real life, Pearce was expecting his call to a new parish any day, and he sometimes came home early just to check the mail. Pity. He'd just got used to this community. Regina was growing to love this place. She didn't want to leave it.

She didn't want to move away from Doc.

Regina blinked him away from her mind, dried her hands on a fresh dishcloth and felt the top of the two bundts she'd taken out of the oven just before her nap. They were cool and ready for a dusting of powdered sugar.

By the time another week had rolled around, Pamela found herself full of anxiety. She felt as though the father of her unborn child, Wolver, the love of her life, was in danger, and she was powerless to do anything about it. Pamela liked having a little control over the things in her life. Her body, for instance, her finances, her destiny. That thought gave her a little chuckle as she rounded the three-mile mark on her run. Her reproductive system had taken over her body, world conditions had taken over her finances, and her destiny was up to the whims of the gods. She had no power, not really, and she was kidding herself if she thought she did.

Still, she'd like it better if Wolver had a phone.

When she got home from her run, she was surprised to see his Jeep in her driveway. He came into town occasionally, but she usually knew when to expect him. And he never stayed long. He only lived two hours north, but when he gave up town life, he really gave it up. He must be out of something important.

She pulled into the driveway behind him, got out and went into the house. He was at her kitchen table with a small glass of bourbon in front of him.

"Hey," she said. She eyed the bourbon.

"Hey." He smelled rangy and looked like it had been a while since he'd slept. His eyes were red-rimmed and bloodshot. This was not like Wolver.

"You all right?"

"Better now," he said, and drank down the bourbon. "I needed that."

"You need a bath," she said. "Get out of those clothes and I'll wash them."

He nodded, and started unbuttoning his shirt. Pamela knew that when he was ready, he'd say what he came to say. He stood up and shucked his clothes, right there in the kitchen, and walked naked into the bathroom. She scooped them up from the floor, and put them in the washing machine. She'd wait until they'd both showered before turning it on.

But her insides jangled. He hadn't hugged her or kissed her. He hadn't seemed particularly happy to see her. Something was troubling him. Something big, and in Pamela's pregnant female mind, it could only be a problem between them.

"Whatever it is," she whispered to herself, "I'll survive it."

She put her hand on her tummy. "We'll survive it." She sat on her bed and waited for him to finish in the bathroom. Generally, she'd rip off her clothes and join him for a good giggly, sudsy mutual scrub, but not this time. He needed his space, and she had a feeling she was going to need hers.

He came out of the bathroom with a towel around his waist, and climbed immediately into her bed.

Maybe he's sick, she thought, as she wrangled her way out of her spandex. She took a fast shower, powdered, perfumed, blew her hair dry, but by the time she got back to the bedroom, Wolver was snoring.

She slipped in next to him, waking him slowly with gentle caresses.

"Mmm," he said. "Feels good."

"Tell me," she said.

He turned onto his back, put his arms behind his head and stared at the ceiling. "I just needed to come to town. I needed to get out of there."

This wasn't like Wolver. Pamela just kept rubbing his scalp with the tips of her fingers.

"There's something out there. There's either something there or I'm losing my mind. Either way, it ain't right, it ain't human, it's like nothing I've ever . . . known before." He paused. Rubbed his face.

"You saw it?" She tried hard to keep her voice soft, quiet, intimate. He was like a skittish wild animal, and she didn't want to spook him.

"Sorta. Maybe. I don't know. God, I don't know."

"You're safe here, babe," she said. "Take a nap."

"Yeah . . . ," he said, and drifted off to sleep.

"Okay," Margie said to the women collected in her living room. "We need to make this fast before Jimbo comes home."

"Jimbo doesn't know?" Lexy asked.

"No, I told him this was a meeting of the high school booster club."

She ignored the few snorts and muffled laughs that passed through the assembled.

"I'm at my wits' end," she said. "There's something going on here, and we need to find out what it is, because it isn't normal, and if it's wickedness or evil, then we need to take steps to be rid of it."

"The dreams are harmless," Natasha said. "They're good for our sex lives."

"But we shouldn't *all* be having them," Julia said. "That's just plain creepy."

"This isn't the only creepy thing that goes on here," Margie said, and, for a moment, everyone thought of Margie's missing little boy, Micah.

Louise Leppens broke the silence. "Anybody here ever do any dream analysis?"

"Not since the Northern Aire burned down," Amanda said.

"Are we being poisoned?" Lexy asked. "Are these hallucinations?"

"Are the men having the same dreams?" Louise asked.

Everybody laughed. "If they did," Lexy said, "we'd all be pregnant."

"Settle down," Margie said, clearly disapproving of all the women being pregnant at once. "That was a good question about dream analysis."

"I think dream analysis," Kimberly said, "is a view into one's personal psyche. This seems to be a shared dream. Are we all having the same dream?"

"Good question," Margie said. "Are any of you dreaming about anybody in particular? Anybody you know?"

"No!" Regina Porter said, a little too quickly, and then she blushed.

"It makes me think a lot about Paulie Timmins," Lexy said, "but I don't see his face while I'm dreaming. But there is something. Kind of big and round. Humpy, sort of. It's not like I'm having sex with it, but I want to. Or something. It's standing just out of my line of sight."

There were nods in the audience, and Margie, standing by the kitchen door, leaned against the doorjamb. There *was* something, kind of big, kind of humpy, sort of.

"What else?" she asked.

"Sometimes I think I wake up just in the nick of time," Julia said. "When I wake up, I'm afraid that if I slept a moment longer, if I was in that dream for just a second more, that I'd die."

More nods.

Margie remembered that, too. "Think it's safe to say all the women in town are having these dreams? What about in the county?"

Nods amid shrugs.

"Sister Ruth?" Lexy asked, and the women tittered with nervous laughter.

"Yes," Margie said, looking pointedly at Lexy. "I spoke with her today. She's having them as well."

"Jeez," Lexy said. "Now there's a mental image."

"Don't be cruel," Margie said. "She's a woman, just like the rest of us."

"I don't think there's anything we can do about this," Julia said. "Just like there's nothing we seem to be able to do about the other things."

Margie watched the women in her living room debate the situation. She found comfort in knowing she wasn't alone, but, by the same token, she worried about the evil of it all. This was something taking control of the dreams of every woman in the county. That was some powerful magic.

It made her want to move away. Take her remaining son and husband and get the hell out of this place. Just walk away from the diner. Just walk away from Sister Ruth. Just walk away from Doc and the sheriff and all these women, and the memories, and the nightmares—

But she knew she never would. She had knowingly put her family at risk before, and not run away from it. The price had been one son. The price of this nocturnal pleasure would be heavy too, she knew, but it had yet to reveal itself.

No, she'd never leave Vargas County. She'd never leave White Pines Junction. She'd never leave the diner, Sister Ruth, her friends . . . she'd never give up those dreams voluntarily. That thought felt like sin. So she was a sinner. Who wasn't?

"So let's say it is a force of evil," Kimberly was saying. "What's the point?"

Margie didn't want to listen to what Lexy and the rest had to say about that, so she backed into the kitchen and arranged cookies on a plate. This meeting was a good idea in that it opened the doors to communication, but nothing was going to be decided.

She brought the cookies out and set them on the coffee table.

"It's progressing," Natasha said. "It started slow, but now it's every night, and it's more intense, and now there's that . . . that creature on the sidelines. One of these nights it will show its face."

"Yeah," Kimberly said. "And I'm afraid that whoever it is, whatever it is, I'm going to recognize it."

Margie shuddered.

In the morning, Wolver looked a hundred percent better. Pamela made orange juice, pancakes and bacon, and he ate everything that came off the griddle and drank a whole pot of coffee. "Going to hang around for a while?" she asked from across the table, holding her coffee cup in both hands.

"C'mere," he said, and scooted his chair back from the table. She went to him and he pulled her down onto his lap and nuzzled his face in her breasts.

"I've got to go back up. It's like a disturbance in the force." They both smiled.

"I've got to fix it."

"Stay a couple of days. There's nothing that important up there." She didn't like the whiny quality of her voice.

"It's important," he said.

She nodded and wrapped her arms around his neck. *Tell him now,* she thought.

He pushed her up off his lap just as she was ready to open her mouth. She scooted around to the chair next to him.

"The thing is," he started, then rubbed his face. "The thing is, I think I recognize this thing. I've seen it out of the corner of my eye, or in my dreams, or my childhood nightmares or on some movie sometime, or something."

"Tell me," she said, affection pouring out for him in a volume she never knew she contained.

He looked her straight in the eyes. "I think it's me," he said.

"I don't mean to be crude," Dr. Sanborn said, "but it's like all the womenfolk have gone into heat. I'm dispensing birth control like crazy. Even Audrey has been a little uncharacteristically amorous these days."

"There's definitely something strange going on with them," Doc said. "Even I've noticed it. Regina Porter, who hasn't been in the shop all summer, has been in every day in the past week. Flirting."

"None of the pills seem to be working, though. I've got more pregnancies than I know what to do with. Margie Benson is expecting. Even Kimberly, who swears she hasn't had sex with a man since they put Cousins in prison. Nine months from now we're going to have a boom. Good thing Audrey's past that stage."

"Jeez," Doc said. "It's not like this place needs more kids. What's the county doing, repopulating itself?"

Hutch Sanborn set his empty beer glass on the table and wiped his mustache with the cocktail napkin. "Speaking of Audrey," he said.

"Yeah," Doc said. "Better get on home while it lasts."

"My thoughts exactly. Good night."

Doc saw Hutch to the door, and turned on the porch light for him. When the doctor drove away, Doc turned off the light, closed and locked the door, then went back into the kitchen. It was a cold, lonely house. He wondered if there was a way he could capitalize on this breeding energy that was going on in town, but he wasn't exactly the attractive type, the only place he knew he could go would be the bar, and he didn't go there, and Regina Porter was the only one attracted to him anyway.

He slumped into the old couch and turned on the television. There was only one channel, and it was fuzzy, but it was better than dwelling on his solitude. Maybe John would be home sometime soon. Someone to talk to on this very lonely night.

He grabbed the bucket of terminal tackle and tools that always sat in his living room next to the coffee table, and his hands started the endless job of making leaders while his eyes tried to make sense of the snowy TV and his mind wandered to soft skin and how nice it used to be when Sadie Katherine was there.

Pamela fretted over Wolver for a week, and then she decided that worry and stress wasn't doing the baby any good. She needed to go check on him to make sure he was all right. Besides. It was time he knew about the baby. She didn't want him to think she was hiding the information from him. When a week had passed, she thought that was sufficient time, it wouldn't give him the impression that she was too pushy, too needy, too aggressive, so she threw an overnight bag into the car and headed north.

What she found when she got there was alarming. Pamela always knew that there must be something a little bit odd about a man who only wanted to live by himself in a cabin in the woods with no modern conveniences, no neighbors, no social contact, but until she was considering making a family with Wolver, she never really saw him.

He was sitting on his woodchopping stump when she pulled up. He was just sitting there, not drinking coffee, not resting, just sitting, staring into space. Pamela had never seen him motionless before.

"Hey," she said.

He gave her a wan smile.

"You okay?"

He shook his head no.

"What's the matter?" She knelt in the wood chips next to him and put a hand on his thigh.

He shook his head. "I feel like I've accomplished my purpose."

"What's your purpose?"

He shrugged. "No clue."

"Honey," she said. "Come inside. I'll make you some tea."

It was as if he hadn't heard her. "I dream all the time about all these women. Having sex with a dozen women a night. Only I'm not myself, I'm some kind of a creature. The creature I see sometimes—" he swept the woods with a hand, and then it fell back into his lap like it weighed a hundred pounds.

"Wolver, you're starting to scare me."

"I can't sleep. When I sleep, I can't rest. I can't remember my childhood. My earliest memories are about a year ago, just before I met you." He looked at her, his face drawn, his eyes haunted. "Why is that, Pamela?"

"I don't know, babe. I think you ought to come home with me. Maybe too much solitude is catching up with you."

"I can't believe that will help. I feel like I'm finished, and I don't know why."

"Come home with me. Just leave your stuff. We'll come back and get it later."

He didn't move.

"Wolver? We're going to have a baby."

A crease furrowed his brow. He looked down at her kneeling at his feet. "So that's it," he said. He nodded.

"Honey?"

He nodded again, then stood up and walked off into the woods.

When two days had come and gone and he still wasn't back, Pamela tidied up the cabin, took the black T-shirt that still smelled like him, and went home. She worried about her baby, who it was, what it would become, but then she decided that worry wasn't good for it. She tried not to think about what it might be.

"It's gone," Margie said out loud. She hadn't realized the nighttime sexual presence was that palpable all day, all the time, until just this second when it quit. The demon had released her.

She took her hands out of the big bowl of salad that she had been tossing, wiped her hands on a clean cloth, threw it over her shoulder, and walked out into the diner.

All the women were looking up, as if the thing that had weighed them all down for months had finally vanished, leaving their heads light, and they automatically looked up. Like vixens sniffing the air.

Soon they all turned and looked at each other, and at her.

She knew if she started laughing, they'd all join in. But strangely enough, she didn't feel like it.

SISTER RUTH

When the phone rang, Margie looked at the clock before she answered. Two-forty-seven a.m.

Jimbo was in bed next to her, and Jason was asleep upstairs, so if it wasn't one of their relatives in trouble out of state, it could only be Sister Ruth.

Margie picked up the receiver, held it to her ear and listened.

Raspy breathing.

"Hello?" she whispered.

"Margie?"

"Sister?" Margie tried to keep her voice low, but heard a snort of disgust from Jimbo and knew he was awake.

"They were here again tonight," Sister Ruth said in a small voice.

"Are they gone?"

"Yes."

"Good. Then you can go to sleep."

"No, I couldn't possibly sleep. I'm so afraid. Could you come?"

"There's nothing to be afraid of," Margie said. "They're gone."

"They'll come back."

Margie sighed. "Not tonight."

"Micah was here this time," Sister Ruth said in her little girl voice.

Margie sighed, resigned. Sister Ruth knew how to play her.

251

"Okay," she said. "I'll come."

Jimbo gave another snort. "That's the second time this week," he said.

"Hush," she said hanging up the phone. "It's my ministry."

"You're killing her."

"She's killing herself," Margie said and swung her legs out of bed. "She just needs a little company while she does it."

Jimbo turned on his side away from her.

"I'm taking your truck," she said as she pulled a sweater over her nightgown and stuck her feet into her sneakers.

Sister Ruth waited in her nightgown on the sidewalk in front of her small house. Margie pulled up in front, set the brake, and, engine running, got out and put down the tailgate.

"Bless you," Sister Ruth said.

Margie watched, helpless, as Ruth maneuvered her bulk, using two canes, down off the curb. She backed up to the tailgate and sat down, one massive haunch at a time. The truck bed sank and Margie wondered how long it would be before Sister Ruth's weight broke the tailgate or lifted the front wheels right off the ground. When settled, Ruth wiped the perspiration from her face with the dingy hanky she always carried and nodded, breathlessly.

"You hold on tight," Margie said.

Ruth nodded, and took a tentative grip on the vinyl-covered tailgate chain with one impossibly small hand. The other held her two canes.

Margie put the truck in gear and let it idle down the street. The diner was only three blocks away. She pulled around back, parked and let Sister Ruth heave herself to the ground on tiny, tortured feet while Margie opened the delivery door to the kitchen.

She propped the door open, turned on the lights and brought the big bench around to the baking table.

Sister Ruth, leaning heavily on both canes, came through the door, enormous breasts, like two small children, swinging inside her tent of a nightgown. She sat on the bench, wheezing, and mopped her red face, whispering, "Thank you, thank you, God bless you," all the while.

"This can't go on," Margie said as she fired up the gas stove, grill, and started emptying the contents of the big stainless steel refrigerator onto the table.

"I know, I know," Sister Ruth said, her tiny eyes critically surveying the food in front of her.

"I'm not a twenty-four-hour food service," Margie said.

"I know. Bless you."

Margie saw the greed in Sister Ruth's face as the bounty of food appeared, and it sickened her. "Jimbo's getting tired of it, too."

"They frighten me."

"You know they're not going to hurt you," Margie said as she opened a pound of butter and put it on a plate.

Sister Ruth licked her lips. "It's stressful," she said.

"Eggs?" Margie asked.

Sister Ruth nodded.

Margie had never seen Sister Ruth eat. This night, as in past nights, she prepared a meal suitable for at least six and put it before the six-hundred-pound woman who looked at her with apology in her eyes and made no move toward her fork until Margie left the room. She left twenty-four scrambled eggs on a platter, a pound of cooked bacon, a leftover pot roast, a dozen bagels, strawberry jam, a gallon of milk, the leftover fried chicken, a cherry pie and a half gallon of rocky road ice cream, all within reach, and went into the diner to refill salt shakers and dust window sills while Sister Ruth quelled her stress.

No one Margie knew had ever seen Sister Ruth eat, and

Jimbo was the only one who knew about these late night trips to the diner.

A half hour later, Margie, bleary-eyed and out of patience, went back into the kitchen to find all the food gone, every bite, chicken bones picked clean and piled neatly, and dishes stacked.

Ruth's tiny little eyes were glazed over and her thin reddish hair bounced as she jerked herself awake over and over again.

Margie piled the dishes in the big sink for Babcock to do in the morning, wiped down the table, wiped Sister Ruth's chin, made out the bill, then sat down for a heart to heart.

"Ruth."

Ruth's eyes snapped open and blinked as she tried to focus.

"Tell me about Micah."

Ruth gasped with either the memory or the lie, Margie couldn't tell which. "He was with them this time," she said. "They were singing as they moved through the house."

"They walked through the house?"

"No, not walked. I feel them first, then I hear them, then I smell something like hot electrical wires, then I see them. It's like moving a projector. The picture of them moves through the house and they don't seem to know it. They don't see me."

"Then why does it scare you so much?"

Sister Ruth's little piggy eyes filled with tears and her face scrunched up into a horrible mask of itself. "You try living with it," she choked out, then started to hiccup.

Margie put a hand on the woman's arm, felt its dampness, thought she could feel the bacon grease oozing from her pores.

"You can't keep calling me like this," Margie said. Sister Ruth began to wail. Margie moved her chair closer and tried to put her arm around the woman, but her back and shoulders were so massive that Margie's hand only reached to the back of her neck. Sister Ruth hadn't bathed in a while. Margie quelled her repulsion and stuck to her message. "You're eating yourself to death, Ruth," Margie said, "and I can't continue to be a party to it."

"You have a diner," Ruth said, then blew her nose into her napkin. She wiped her eyes. "I pay you for what I eat."

"You need to come during business hours and eat in the dining room," Margie said.

Sister Ruth started to cry all over again.

"Now tell me about Micah," Margie insisted.

Sister Ruth's eyes widened and the tear tracks on her greasy face were left forgotten as was the moisture in the corner of her nostril. "He was singing," she said. "They were all singing, like at camp, only—only it wasn't very happy."

"Was he okay? Was he hurt?" Margie felt as if she was selling out her belief in Jesus by asking another person, almost as if she were asking a gypsy psychic, about the fate of her lost son.

"He looked the same, Margie. Not a day older. All the children were there, ghosting through my living room. *Right through the walls in my house.*" She gasped again with a memory. "That nice boy Kevin was there."

"Kevin Leppens?"

Sister Ruth nodded, then hid a massive belch inside her hanky.

Margie took a long moment and looked at this gigantic caricature of a woman and her heart was flooded with compassion. "Maybe they pick your house, Ruth, because you've always loved them."

Sister Ruth looked up at Margie with a faint hope in her face. "I always have. I always have, you know. I taught kindergarten all those years."

"I know," Margie said. "They come to you now because they feel safe around you."

"Think so?"

Margie thought this might be a transformational moment.

Sister Ruth clung to this shred of hope with a terrible desperation. "Absolutely. Don't be afraid of them. Welcome them."

"Oh, Margie, you could be right. Of course you're right. Bless you. Bless you."

Margie stood up. "C'mon. I can still get an hour's sleep before I have to come back here for the breakfast shift."

While Sister Ruth unloaded herself from Jimbo's pickup, Margie made bold. "You need some help, Ruth. You need to see someone about your eating disorder and your weight. One of these days you won't be able to go out at all anymore. You're not young."

Margie slammed the tailgate as the enormously obese woman negotiated the curb. "Don't call me anymore at night."

"I won't," Ruth said, gasping for air.

Margie wondered all the way home if she'd spoken too harshly. Just before she stepped into her house, she paused for a moment to smell the predawn summer air in the northwoods. Home. Son and husband sleeping inside. She looked at her pudgy thighs and considered a diet, but then maybe not. Pudgy was as far as she'd ever get.

Then she heard them, like someone gently turning up the speakers, and she smelled it, just like Sister Ruth had said, and the air thinned out, turned a little blue, and a laughing bunch of children appeared in midair and moved down the street.

"Micah?" Margie asked, breathlessly, and stepped off the porch to follow.

She saw her son, laughing, happy, clapping his little hands with the others, a hundred or more kids, singing, joyfully singing.

A tear squeezed out of Margie and she looked for the familiar grief that had been her constant companion since Micah had gone, but it wasn't there anymore. He was still gone, of course, and he wasn't coming back, but now that she'd seen him, she was settled in her soul.

After the strange apparition disappeared, Margie, contemplating the strangeness of life, climbed into bed with Jimbo and snuggled up to his warmth. As she listened to him snore, thinking about waking him, another tear squeezed out with gratitude, because in that weird place Micah and the other kids had been taken, they were strangely safe. They had a new nanny. In the middle of the joyous, laughing, singing children, Sister Ruth, weightless and eternal, was clapping and laughing along with them.

Margie felt honored to have served Sister Ruth her last meal.

She placed her hand over her belly that was just beginning to swell with new life.

It was time for hope to thrive.

ABOUT THE AUTHOR

Elizabeth Engstrom is a sought-after teacher and keynote speaker at writing conferences, conventions, and seminars around the world. She has written ten books and edited four anthologies, and she has over two hundred short stories, articles and essays in print. With her fisherman husband and her dog, she lives in the Pacific Northwest, where she teaches the occasional writing class and is always working on her next book.

www.elizabethengstrom.com